D1602874

IOWA

Patrick Moore

Iowa

First HARD CANDY Edition 1996
First Printing July 1996

ISBN 1-56333-423-2

Manufactured in the United States of America
Published by Masquerade Books, Inc.
801 Second Avenue
New York, N.Y. 10017

For Dino, as always.

And for my family with great love.

Special thanks to David Groff, Sarah Schulman,
Charles Hovland, Karen Finley, and my loyal friends.

Gone

I.

Quiet, quiet house. As always, Ann roused herself without the alarm clock because the day begins whether you want it to or not. The cat was lying on her chest, in ecstasy, nursing on the fuzzy blanket while its claws flexed in and out with the purrs. Ann was sometimes revolted by this little display of affection from the usually uppity cat, but, today, rubbed its head, petted around the ears and chin, before pushing it over on Glen, who was still snoring away. "Need to put on some coffee," she thought her automatic morning thought and pulled on her velour robe. Today was Wayne's birthday, and everything had to be perfect, everything needed to work out for a change. "Got to get to work," she thought the other automatic morning thought and moved out to the kitchen. This was Ann's territory, bordered by the stove, the refrigerator, and the table, with the sink as operations central. All day long she would stand at this sink washing, rinsing, and then scouring the stainless steel. The world was narrowed to these few square feet and, if that little area stayed perfectly ordered, Ann fervently believed that everything would turn out right.

She hit the switch on the Mr. Coffee that was always set the night before and, almost immediately, the hiss of hot water began in the machine. Ann stood for a moment, blankly watching the coffee dribble out. She and Glen drank their coffee black. Used to drink it with Cremora, but now black. They could go through nearly ten pots of coffee during the day, drinking it as a beverage for all occasions—morning, meals, relaxation, company. They drank so much coffee, in fact, that she needed to regularly clean the Mr. Coffee of the sediment that built up in its plastic bowels. Today, though, she decided not to clean the machine because Wayne hated the smell of the vinegar solution breaking down the coffee stains and billowing up out of the vent on top. She stood watching the pot fill up to the four-cup level now, needing a fix, until the automatic words came again: "Got to get to work." So she began, convinced that time was too short even to take a morning pee before filling the sink up with suds and starting in on the few plates left from late-night snacks.

Glen was a living Folger's commercial, with the waves of coffee smell drifting into the bedroom like a magic carpet to carry him into the kitchen. His nostrils moved just a bit, wrinkling his thick mustache. The long nose wriggled a bit more, and he became aware of the cat nursing on top of him. The cat, named Kitty, was actually his pet to start with, but had taken on Ann as its main object of affection. He found the cat in a bar in Canada. There he was, sitting, drinking a rum and Coke, when he heard this hissing from the far end of the bar. "Goddamn worthless Indian. What a worthless people," were his first thoughts as he looked down. Glen had no time for the sob stories of the Indians. "Those people get a check from the government every month. No wonder they never work! Every month they get that check and go straight to the liquor store." No, Glen had no time for those people, especially when they were abusing animals. "Goddamn Indians are supposed to respect animals," he muttered under his breath as he watched an older Indian man holding a cat to the bar. Furry little white kitten. Covered in cat puke and blood dripping off the Indian's hairless arm and down onto the white fur. Blood and cat puke and what a mess. The Indian was chuckling low in his throat and every few minutes would explode with laughter, "This cat's a booze hound," and pour some whiskey into the cat's panting mouth. Glen couldn't take it, but wasn't up for a fight. In his best wheeler-dealer manner, he leaned down the bar and said, "Hey, buddy, give ya ten bucks for that cat."

"No way, man, this cat's got a pedigree," the Indian slurred back.

"Oh, I didn't realize." Glen decided he was going to have to use all of his considerable cunning in this case. "Well, seein' how that's a valuable animal, how about ten bucks and I throw in a bottle of Canadian Club?"

He remembered the Indian's face bobbing around slowly, mulling over the offer, and then sliding the cat down the bar like a drink in a movie. He rubbed Kitty, calling her "Kitter," remembering her blue eyes looking up at him, exhausted, that night. Glen rolled off the bed and put the cat back down on his pillow where it curled up contented. He moved stiffly into the hallway without putting on his robe. Too sleepy. Just by the door, though, he was confronted by a full-length mirror reflecting his body. Big, fat stomach looking like it was grafted on the rest of his lean, muscular body. The arms still powerful, the legs still trim. A grunt, and he moved on to the kitchen for the coffee. He and Ann didn't kiss, didn't bother with that stuff first thing in the morning.

"Today's our son's birthday," she said even before he drank his first cup of coffee. Her voice, when discussing something that made her nervous, had begun to get sing-songy and it bugged the shit out of Glen. He didn't even want to talk this time of morning, and then every sentence had to be one of these little ditties. He grunted, saying he knew what day it was. Christmas Eve.

Like the laggard soldier of a small army, the final member of the family woke in his bedroom. Wayne tried to fight off waking, wanting the small headache from last night's drinks to continue. Wanted to keep rerunning the morning dream of sex. Wayne's erotic dreams always occurred in the morning. He found this morning's fantasy so strange as to be almost sickening. In the dream, Wayne was some strange sort of creature that lay floating in the water. The primary part of his body was his dick, which was so long that it resembled the neck of a flamingo. In fact, the entire fantasy was set in the Florida Everglades, which he had seen on a TV nature special. Wayne lay in the warm water with his giant flamingo cock waving in the tropical air as a boat slowly drew up beside him. There were two brawny men in the boat dressed like fishermen, wearing high rubber boots and rain slickers. Yet, Wayne, or whatever creature he had become, knew that under those outfits the men were sweating, the wiry black hair of their chests coursing with sweat. They hauled him up into the boat by grasping his huge cock. Wayne, in the dream, was some mutated water lily lying limp on the bottom of the boat watching their calloused, stubby hands work up and down on his heaving organ.

But Wayne knew that waking and throwing off the fantasy were inevitable because of what day it was. The day of guilt. Loved, doted on, and squirming like a lobster in boiling water. The clock said 11:30 when his eyes opened to the white room with blond wood furniture and psychedelic-red shag carpet. He could hear the scurry-scurry sound of his mother in the kitchen, expectant. Waiting for love, he thought vaguely. And he did love her, so much that she pissed him off. It made Wayne angry to be lying with his hard cock pressing up against the sheets and to be loved. He knew he could never be what was expected. Love didn't mean that his mother could share his life. He tried to make the image of sex come back to his mind even as his morning hard-on yielded to the unsexy thoughts of the day.

Spooky the dog came in wagging his half-sure tail at Wayne. Spooky the dog loved unconditionally—the great gift of animals in this world, to love the misfits. "Get up here, come on," he said softly with a few pats to the bed, and the mangy dog bounded up with licks and wags and much rolling on his back. "What a little mess you are," he told the dog with its Labrador head, black terrier body, and a tail that curled up from yet another unknown species. Spooky's joy subsided as quickly as it had begun and he fell asleep with his head poked under the cover. "Third dog I've had in my life. First Snuffy, then Moose, and now Spooky. Dogs get some stupid name, run through their lives and leave. Nicer than people." The fluffy white cat sat in the doorway watching but not deigning to come in, giving him a cool blue-eyed stare before marching out. "Hate that fuckin' cat," he thought. "Can't even have a Christmas tree because of that cat."

"Have to get up. No way around it because I can even hear Dad up shuffling around. Dad can usually outsleep me." Glen was famous for being able to fall asleep in any setting, including at the dinner table, where he often nodded off in mid-mouthful and woke to finish chewing ten or fifteen minutes later. Of course, that was in the old days when he worked long days and nights in a meatpacking plant. Glen slept to keep the horror of that job away from him, the refrigerated rooms full of bleeding animals being taken apart. Now, he and Ann left every year to spend eight months in Canada helping the same meatpackers come to the wilderness and kill a bear or catch a fish. COME EXPERIENCE A WILDERNESS VACATION! The hours were even longer there, but Glen was happy in his wilderness setting. That Ann hated it was of no concern to Glen, and in Iowa, in the winter, he slept.

Wayne's brown polyester velour bathrobe waited at the bottom of the bed for him, half on the ground. Spooky the dog wriggled to life and wagged out the door as soon as Wayne moved. His mother heard him coming and was waiting for him in the kitchen as soon as he emerged from his morning pee. "Happy Birthday," shrieked her desperate voice as she hugged him. Her regression into this shrill baby voice in the past few years depressed him. It was as if all of her armor had been stripped away and there she stood, waiting to be hurt, waiting to suffer. He hugged her soft vulnerable body encased in a green polyester bathrobe and felt her smooth lips on his cheek. "Her face is the same," he thought, looking at her, "the skin still beautiful." Ann's skin was the color that is often called peach, unwrinkled, her slight overbite outlined with a bit of orangish lipstick and her watery blue-gray eyes peering out from behind large glasses.

Glen had already settled into his recliner in the living room and was engrossed in *Family Feud*—"Glen, turn that damn thing down!"—but Wayne went in to hug him. Even a full hug had become somewhat forbidden, and they simply grabbed one another's arms in a handshake. While their hands were joined together, Wayne looked at his father's face and compared it to his mother's. He had once thought of his father as the most handsome man on earth, beautiful black hair swept back from brown eyes and a Roman nose, dashing in a white T-shirt that revealed his athletic form. Now all he could see was the permed hair on his father's head. The Perm was all the rage in Iowa and Ann sported a similar style. The Perm gave everyone the same tightly frizzed old-lady hair—"SO EASY TO TAKE CARE OF"—and Wayne had to admit that several years before he succumbed also. "God, am I glad I got rid of that perm," he thought because it looked so perverse to him now. It almost made him angry to look at the glob of hair that seemed scooped out of a bucket and plopped on top of the head. "What this place does to people. Look at my father's beautiful movie-star hair. God forbid anybody would enjoy themselves, have a little luxury." Wayne used Jerry the Fat Barber, urging Jerry to cut his hair shorter and shorter until Wayne looked like a criminal.

On the brown plastic kitchen table lay an envelope that Ann had been hovering around, anxious for the few seconds of ritualized love that were bought by the usual card/cash present. Wayne's parents long ago gave up on clothing and other presents that were grimly returned the next day after tense hours of staring at the unwanted gift. Now a thin envelope waited on December 24, with another similar one waiting on December 25. Each contained what this one did. He sat at the table, slowly ripping the cream-colored paper open—an oddly moving Hallmark card and a $100 bill. This called for another round of the hugs, and then it was mercifully over. Unsure of the next step, Wayne and Ann stood awkwardly by the kitchen table until she sighed, "Well, better get back to these dishes."

The rest of the day would blur into a time specific to Iowa. In this limbo, everything is so strikingly slow that the day disappears, blending and mixing into the boredom until one looks up and realizes hours or days or years have passed. Television makes this possible by relieving the need for talk and focusing attention away from any one person. Even the commercials were so fascinating that no one talked during them. The few times the television had broken in their house, the three of them almost panicked. Without the focus of the little screen, they drifted, and conversation seemed dangerously near. But the set was in working order and for the long stretch of the day, Glen and Wayne lay silent in the burnt-orange-carpeted living room watching the screen intently, begging it to blot out the rest. Ann was crazed with activity in the kitchen, washing and rewashing the dishes. "Mom, why don't you relax for a while?" Wayne asked her every so often, but then remembered she was brainwashed early by his stinking grandfather ("That's Woman's Work") to know herself as waitress, cook, maid, and secretary. To sit for a moment would be an admission of guilt for her, of ultimately failing. So Wayne saw her now and then throughout the day as he went into the kitchen to eat or she filled orders from the living room and, though Wayne felt slightly guilty, he didn't care so much as to help, and he thoroughly enjoyed being tended to. "It is my birthday," he thought and went back to sleep on the living-room floor.

"Rams are playing this afternoon," Glen announced with gusto.

"Oh, great!" Wayne moaned. "I was really hoping to watch a couple of good football games."

The TV lineup was tense this time of year because Glen wanted to watch football and Wayne wanted to watch anything else. Wayne stormed into the kitchen where his mother was looking nervous, having heard the prelude to the fight. "Honey, Dad thinks that you should be more interested in sports. He thinks you should maybe at least watch football on TV."

"What? Did he give you that message for me?" Wayne asked too loudly. "You know, I'm right here. He could talk to me instead of telling you." And Wayne hated his father for this, for making his mother take the pain. This is what Wayne really hated his father for—the silence. Glen was defined by his stubbornness, famous for it. Glen refused to take Novocain at the dentist. Glen refused to take an aspirin for a headache. Glen would drive them around, lost for hours, rather than ask for directions. What Wayne didn't realize was that Glen couldn't stand a confrontation and, more than stubborn, he was lazy. If he could make Ann relay a message, Glen didn't have to get into a fight with the kid, didn't have to get into a long conversation about things. There were things he cared about and things he didn't. Take it or leave it. Glen could feel a real passion when he imagined fishing or fixing up the house. But all this tongue wagging about your feelings made him sick, made him feel like an old woman. "Plenty of time to talk when you're sitting in the nursing home," he would say. All the same, his tongue was free enough out of the house. He would spend hours shooting the shit down at Norm's Tackle Shop over a cribbage tournament. But there was a difference. A difference between telling stories and talking, because a story is always about somebody else. Even if you're talking about something you did, in a story you become a character—somebody else. So Glen just lay back and waited it out.

"Glen, it's Wayne's birthday. Let him choose." Glen didn't care to actually negotiate a settlement but left the living room for long enough so that Wayne could put on HBO with its endless barrage of action thrillers. "The city," Wayne thought and the words were magic, happy with the promise of mindless violence and available sex. The film that afternoon was a buddy movie set in Los Angeles and when one of the cop heroes was shot, his partner ripped off his shirt to bind the wound. Whenever male flesh was on screen, the living room would fill with tension, tension greater than the limp narrative of the movie could have supplied. Wayne's eyes photographed and stored every bared white curve of the man's body, his arms and the hair under them etched like acid into his brain, taking over his body, offering what he feared he might never find. On screen the man's skin was streaked with sweat and dirt as the gold-orange skyline of LA loomed behind him. The cop leaned over his dying partner, leaned down to whisper sweetly to him, and Wayne could imagine the chiseled faces shifting slightly, lips meeting, tongues moving into mouths, into wet crotches.

"SPECIAL REPORT," said the television. "SPECIAL REPORT," and the words scrolled down the screen. Over the men, over the image of man touching man, the words typed out a private message: "You are in immediate danger. A low-pressure system has created a vacuum around you. Vacuums of this variety are particular to the Midwest and have resulted in explosions of little faggots throughout the region. Little queers have been sighted throughout Iowa screaming for help and begging for mercy or escape. The Mental Health Advisory Panel has advised that all queers, cocksuckers, and buttfuckers take special precautions during this storm season by avoiding contact with images of naked men, all thoughts about sex and, especially, by not touching their genital areas. While binding the genital area with cloth or other material is recommended to prohibit pleasure, excessive tightness can also cause an unintended pleasurable sensation. The Advisory Panel, in emergency situations, recommends leaving the Midwest and reminds that fatalities and shattered nerves have occurred due to this natural phenomenon. This has been a test of the Emergency Broadcast System. In the case of an actual emergency, you would receive instruction about where to go for safety. We repeat, this has only been a test."

This was the geography of pain—the television in the corner, Wayne on the floor straining toward the television, and Glen behind him boring holes through his head, watching for the telltale sign. Tick, tick, tick went the clock, and another movie rolled on with blood and muscles and bombed-out streets. After a few hours, Wayne stretched, oh so casual, and slinked off to the bathroom. The bathroom is the center of a secret universe in any young man's life. In the bathroom, mirrors reflect greasy hands and pumping groins and objects going where not intended. In this bathroom, Wayne removed his robe, removed his underwear, and gazed into the mirror. His eyes squinted so as to make everything blur, not real, and his hands moved slowly, and someone else's hands felt his chest with some hair but not much yet, and their hands felt his legs still smooth and their hands tugged at the fine hair lying under his arms. Slow starts the dance, hips moving slowly as the images flow quickly past closed eyelids. The images of a body sitting on the sink, leaning back on arms now massive, showing a chest that draws him down, draws him toward smells that are the smells of his own body as Wayne leans his head down to his own chest. All the while, it was the roar of TV, the clatter of the kitchen, that made the act obscene. It was the juxtaposition of the mysterious and the deadening life just beyond the thin door that perverted these lovely rites. After it was all done, the evidence could just be washed down the drain or disappear under the shower stream, flushing out of the house and back into darkness.

There was an empty space far underneath the bathroom counter where Wayne stored jerk-off magazines, and he reached under, groping for the tattered pages. Wayne had sent away for this particular magazine even knowing the great danger of discovery that lay in the plain brown-paper wrapper. He looked at the crude drawing of a hairy man on the cover and turned immediately to his favorite story.

DAD'S BACK

Dad left five years ago today. I was doing the same thing that day when I heard the door thud firmly shut. That day, too, I was lying here in the bathtub with the water sloshing up on my white skin. Everything looks about the same five years later; my body's marbled with a sleek layer of muscle now, but is still mostly smooth except for the wet black patch of hair washing around my fat cock. I run my hand over the arch of my smooth tits and pull at the big nipples, watch them stretch and harden. A thin line of black hair starts just above my navel and spreads gradually as it moves to my legs. The stomach is still rockhard, but more chiseled than it had been, more like sculpture in a museum. I wonder if our bodies still look alike. His was the same, smooth, but much bigger, with bulging biceps with a tuft of black hair swallowed in the deep pits. His cock was different, though, I remember as I feel underneath myself, feel the hairless, clean ass and push at the hole that grabs eagerly at my finger, that licks and sucks the finger. Two of the fingers are wandering around inside me now, feeling the slick tunnel up there while I look at my jerking cock, comparing it to Dad's. Mine is light pink at the thick base and graduates to a sunburned color around the swollen head. His was better, more mysterious, with its dark brown color a shock against the clear white of his thigh where it hung down when soft. My cockhead blooms up every time my heart beats, and I stroke it wishing it was another cock, a better cock.

The water's leaking up me as I pull my sticky asslips apart, filling me up like an enema, warm and strange.

Now the thought of a dark cock comes to me, the thought of it pushing its way past the slack barrier and into my ass with the water being shoved further and further up. My ass aches with the thought of water and cock and the man I want over me, fucking me deep and slow in this steamed-up bath. His face would look down at me with deep, blank eyes staring into my face, the thick black hair wet and pushed back over his forehead. Screwing my body that looks like his, but smaller. Screwing my body that he owns because he made it and now he does what he wants with it. I think of that long brown cock sloshing around, mixing precome with assjuice, think of the big man with a body that looks like molten marble raising his arm and planting his sweating pit on my face, think of its strong odor, it makes me gasp for air and swirl my tongue around the bowl of it and think of it and think of it and I shoot pearly strands all over, letting the water rush out of my ass. Dad's been gone too long.

Grandma Selma had now, at 6:00, called three times to say that she would be expecting everyone at 6:30. Each time Ann assured her that the family would be there, even though they had been late every year. The worst year was the previous one when, in a fit of father/son camaraderie, Glen took Wayne to the VFW for the special one-hour-of-all-you-can-drink-for-free-on-Christmas-Eve afternoon special. Arriving two hours late, Glen promptly fell asleep, Wayne threw up on some of the presents and Selma cried. This year neither Glen nor Wayne had discussed going to the VFW, having been chastened throughout the year by Selma on a regular basis. Now, at 6:25 everyone had showered and dressed, with Ann checking and rechecking the plastic laundry basket that contained the presents for Selma and her current husband, Jim. The presents included two bottles of whiskey for each of them (taken only at the last minute because they all remember the year Grandma got thirsty in the afternoon) and a sweater set for Selma. The fat jugs of booze sat smugly in the laundry basket, rattling up against each other while Wayne looked at them. Ann and Wayne had their coats on and were prepared to go through what they called "the leaving fight," where they would beg Glen for between five and ten minutes to leave the house while he drank coffee. Even Spooky had his collar and leash on and was sitting at the door expectantly. Each time someone would make a tentative movement to leave, Spooky would jump up and claw at the door in excitement. A few minutes later, he would calm himself and prepare for the next round. The cat was not invited; it was too haughty and unpredictable outside. Nothing could shove Glen out the door before he was ready. It was hard to say what would finally make him feel ready. Most likely it was when the boredom of being nagged outweighed the promise of boredom in the trip before him. The only thing that shortened the wait by the door this night was the phone ringing again. "Glen, you know who that is! Don't answer it! Let's go!"

The weight of the day lifted as they felt the cold night envelop them. The blackest of skies, almost too black for the stars, rested heavy overhead. "Like a movie," Wayne thought. They stood there still for a moment while the wind died down and the neighbor's dog stopped barking and the towering silence of Iowa crashed down. The picture window of the house next door revealed a vibrant scene of three little kids ripping through wrapping, bows flying in the air, and the parents laughing and drinking in the background. No squeals escaped the thick glass. There was a very certain set of rituals prescribed on these special nights, and people adhered to them religiously, afraid that in breaking them they would destroy the few minutes of joy mixed in with the hours of tedium.

"Okay, let's go," said Glen, pleased with himself, pleased with the night as he opened the door of the pickup. Each year they piled into the pickup to go to East Locust Street on Christmas Eve, as the night was known to people who didn't know it as Wayne's birthday. Always the cold, an intense cold, biting so sharp that they laughed and complained as Glen insisted on the motor warming up before turning on the heater and backing the pickup out onto the icy asphalt street. The three were packed tightly, with the laundry basket on Ann's lap and Spooky on Wayne, wiggling and wagging. The route through town dampened the festivity a bit, and suddenly they went quiet, searching for some sign in the dark houses and empty streets. Three or maybe four cars were pulled up outside some of the houses revealing the gatherings inside that would be centered around the television set and Christmas tree. Ann had a great disdain for such pretentious displays as flocked trees or formal dinners or anyone but family invited or, God forbid, eating in a restaurant. "What do they want all that for?" They could feel assured in their lonely journey through the poor section of town that no one here would break the peace or peer out the window on a night like tonight.

Selma's house was on East Locust Street in the section of town described as low-class because it often flooded with the spring rains that overfilled the Sioux

River. It may seem strange to divide a little cow town into class sections, but the people in Cherokee surely did. "Why, I wouldn't be caught dead living down by the river. Those people still eat catfish!" On this street, where Wayne had lived in a house next to Selma for the first five years of his life, resided a collection of characters who wheeled through the memories of his early childhood. In the first house lived the family of "Soup" Cates, who ran a junk store in an old stable. To the dismay of his neighbors, who called his wife "that dirty Indian," some of his wares were stored on his front lawn. Next to the Cates mansion was the trailer, long abandoned by this time, of Ethyl (pronounced "ee-thil"—like "evil" with a lisp) who at one time had held daylong canasta tournaments for the local old bags. The next house was one where Wayne had spent many, many hours. This rather grand old house was where Donnabell Cummins and her husband, Bud, raised their family and, occasionally, Wayne as Donnabell was his baby-sitter through much of his life. Donnabell held many, many different jobs due to her legendary temper, her raven hair, and the loudest voice in three counties, which you could often hear bellowing about the DAR. Donnabell's favorite description of almost anyone was "sonofabitch" and she was likely to use it on anybody foolish enough to denigrate her, her family, or the United States of America. The rest of the houses on the block were transitory in their occupants and were often rented rather than owned, which was the ultimate sign of worthlessness in Cherokee.

Selma Leary Cooper Brauer Moon lived at 225 East Locust; she had outlived two husbands and was at work on her third. Grandma Leary had been a constant companion to Wayne over the years in different parts of this rickety white house with dark green trim. On the front porch, she had read excerpts of *Alice in Wonderland* to him over and over from her encyclopedia set, neither one of them seeming to realize that the full book existed somewhere. In that old house stuffed with junk, one could almost imagine Wonderland while climbing up the rickety stairs to the attic where Selma's canvases were propped against the wall. There were the closets filled with old wrapping paper and picture albums. There were mysterious little rooms stacked to the ceiling with boxes. In the dirty kitchen, they would make pottery or stitch ragged pictures onto scraps of pillowcases. On the back porch, they would glaze pottery and build birdhouses. In the fenced-in backyard, where Wayne would fall and sprain an ankle on one snowy afternoon, they played Fox and Geese during the winter. As they pulled into the driveway, Selma's old turkey neck poked her head onto the porch and turned on the outside light.

Spooky lead the way in, followed by Wayne and a set of warm memories when his grandma surrounded him with her arms, smelling of powder, cheap perfume, and old oil paint. "Happy birthday!" boomed her voice, a close second to Donnabell's in loudness. He looked in amazement at her for the millionth time. Selma was well over six feet tall, with *I Love Lucy* red hair and dressed in the polyester slacks she also painted in; for Selma was an artist. In the town of Cherokee, Selma wrote poetry for *Ideals* magazine describing the countryside, painted endless desert or mountain vistas, and had dabbled in every known art and craft (many of them learned during an extended stay in the Nut Hut after her second husband's death). Selma was an innovator, too. A regular Marcel Duchamp of the prairies.

Who else in Cherokee would have thought of covering a canvas with dried leaves, spray-painting it, and then removing the leaves for a ready-made artwork? Who else here would have written a poem about an outhouse called "The Little Old Gray Biffy," paste it onto boards, Decoupage them, and then sell them over the radio until they were a fixture in every local bathroom? Many mornings on KCHE's *Swap Shop* show you could hear Selma holding forth like it was a private conversation, "Well, Betty, what do you think of Mr. McLaughlin in the hospital? He drinks like a fish, you know. I just called to say I made up fifty more Biffy plaques, if anybody's looking for Christmas presents."

They moved immediately to the kitchen table after removing coats and gloves and the dialogue, seemingly repeated verbatim each year, began. "Jim! Jiiiim! Turn off that TV and get in here. The kids are here. Oh, he never stops watching that damn thing. Let me get you kids some slippers—the floors are cold in here."

"I'm fine, Grandma," Wayne said at the mention of pom-pom slippers. "I don't need any slippers. I have thick socks on."

In addition to all her other projects, Selma knitted slippers fanatically. "Oh, I have been so busy making slippers." Ann had received more than twenty of these pairs of knitted slippers in poly yarn that made the feet infernally hot as they closed up around the ankles with a giant pom-pom bobbing about on the instep. In moments, they were all de-shoed and slippered. Invariably, there was also the search for seating around the table. Selma had never mastered collecting the right number of chairs, which left guests sitting on furniture from sewing stools to small stepladders. Above all, though, the eclectic seats needed to be durable, as Selma would crash against them, bang the oven door into them and set scalding-hot pans directly on their surfaces.

"Now, what will you kids have to drink?" Selma leered, the thought of whiskey giving her a good taste in her mouth. "I'm having a Seven-Seven. How about some eggnog or a beer, or some Cold Duck champagne?"

Everyone agreed quickly on Cold Duck, knowing that Selma also produced her own wine and could offer it up at any moment. This extraordinary brew involved nothing so old-fashioned as harvesting grapes and stomping them. No, this fine vintage was created from Welch's grape juice, sugar, and yeast poured into a big glass jug with a balloon secured over the top. As the grape juice fermented and fermented, the balloon grew threateningly. The initially innocuous jug would sit in a corner of the kitchen for months. After a few weeks, the balloon would begin to rise like a halfhearted erection. In about a month's time, the balloon would have swollen tautly and, from that point on, would stretch visibly each day. If you put your ear close to the bottle, you could hear a symphony of hisses, creaks, and little farts coming from the jug. Wayne had been scared as a child when he had stayed over at Selma's. He had thought all night of that flatulent jar brewing in the kitchen. Then, nearly two months into the process, almost as an anticlimax, the balloon would blow off, squirting a small amount of wine onto the ceiling that Selma had no time to be concerned over. Because the drinking had begun.

Jim, Selma's husband, hobbled to his position at the table when he heard the pop of the Cold Duck cork. Jim sat exactly at the point where Selma would have to make him move every few minutes to get into the oven.

These were Selma's and Jim's usual positions, as they would normally have their feet in the oven on winter nights. Come in and there they would sit, the oven door open and baking at 350 degrees with their feet jammed inside. The house was like one giant oven with the furnace turned full blast, space heaters purring, the oven door open, and even a burner on the stove turned on to provide one last flickering heat source. It was easy to understand Jim's being cold, as he was a little worm of a man that everyone hated, with a few wisps of hair on a greasy bald head and a shriveled body that couldn't possibly have weighed more than one hundred pounds. Jim's conversation tended to be extremely limited, even by Iowa standards, and could be summed up by four quotes, used individually or in any combination:

"Ain't the way it used to be."

"Something's gonna happen."

"Gonna get worse before it gets better."

Grumble, tobacco spit, grumble, "Goddamn it."

Miserable little Jim gathered himself up to the table while Selma finished preparations for the Birthday Meal. Jim waited with his whiskey and 7UP on one side and his champagne in a juice glass on the other, using a toothpick to scrape the grime out of the crack down the middle of the table. Inside, his scrawny heart beat hard with excitement for this the most festive day of the year. Selma, too, nearly swirled around the kitchen, feeling as if she were wearing a hoopskirt. Joy. Selma reminded herself to slow down on the hootch. "No crying this year," she vowed silently while looking at the dinner she had lovingly prepared. "To make a feast and have the family around you—what could be better," she asked herself as she hummed a few bars of "Waltzing Matilda."

"Say, Ann, that's a cute top you have on," Selma shot out coquettishly. "You've got a good-lookin' girl there, Glen."

Wayne told himself repeatedly that there was no reason to hate this, no reason to feel such rage. Each year he begged them to go out to a restaurant or to cook the food themselves, but each year Selma threatened to throw a real fit and he relented, agreeing to sit through this meal. Selma had evolved the menu over the past five years or so, along with the table settings that included paper plates she decorated with Magic Marker drawings of holly berries. "Aren't those plates cute? Did 'em myself." No one found that too hard to believe. This year's innovation was plastic cutlery. "You know me, I hate dishes," Selma said, eyeing their half-empty glasses and offering more Cold Duck.

Waiting for the frozen pizzas to finish cooking, Selma served her special Jell-O salad that nightmarishly combined lime Jell-O, carrots, and green olives. No one was quite sure where this recipe originated, but it probably had mutated out of an actual recipe on the back of a Jell-O box after a day of drinking. Selma was what is often termed "a two-fisted drinker," starting the day with a beer, moving on to apricot schnapps, vodka in the afternoon, and whiskey in the evening until she passed out during Johnny Carson. Ancillary drinks included Kahlua, Drambuie, peppermint schnapps, fine wines, and rum.

"Selma, I just love this salad," Ann said bravely as Wayne kicked her under the table.

Ann was the best at making kind comments about the meal each year but the next course did even her in. Out of the oven emerged a large ceramic bowl weighted down with several heavy plates. After removing the plates, Selma flipped the bowl over onto a platter with a greasy thud. For reasons known only to her, Selma had created an enormous shrimp ball out of Mrs. Paul's frozen shrimp. This ball was then sliced like a deep-fried basketball, with the onetime shrimp barely revealing their original forms, like fossils. Indeed, the entire dish seemed prehistoric. Complementing the shrimp was Selma's Christmas Eve specialty: frozen pizzas enhanced by her topping of fried hamburger and Velveeta cheese. All this and side dishes of radishes and celery. This was the Birthday Dinner each year. Wayne poked at a slice of shrimp loaf and thought, "Couldn't they do what I want on one night of the year?"

Selma had a new topic of conversation that had dominated for months, "Oh, Wayne, I don't think you should go so far away for college. I hate to think of you in that big city. I worry so much. I worry about your dad hunting those damn bears in Canada, and now I worry about you in that big city."

"Pittsburgh isn't a very big city, Grandma."

"But all those drugs they have there. You wouldn't ever try those, would you?"

"No, Grandma," Wayne assured her, having already used LSD, coke, and pot on a regular basis, even in Iowa. But Selma had begun to wind up for the real attack.

"Now, when you get there, Wayne, do you think you'll find a girlfriend from the school? I don't want you to be lonely, and you know how I worry."

"I won't be lonely, Grandma," he said, while thinking, "Just like you weren't lonely when you got married three times, drank like a fish, slept around, and abandoned your kids. And now you come at me with this bullshit clean-living tirade?" Selma knew how to make people hate her love. The guilt and hate and love lay like little puddles of gravy on Wayne's plate, where he dipped into each. He looked at this woman. "Once there was girl named Alice." His constant companion. His best friend. "Oh, I'm late. I'm terribly, terribly late." This most-beloved old woman. "Eat me, said the cookie." And he couldn't quite believe the hate mounting inside him.

Dinner had taken a brooding turn and was mostly silent, except for Selma's occasional tirade that erupted at irregular intervals, often after a slug of her whiskey had kicked in. The light in the kitchen was bright, bright, and the air was hot and close. Sweat ran down Wayne's back, and he felt his mother suffering next to him, saying silently, "I'm sorry it has to be this way but I don't know how to fix it." And he felt his father withdrawing, farther and farther, until only his sleepy face and permed hair remained. Selma used to sport a sort of bouffant, swept up in back, but she had also succumbed to the perm craze and after taking a gulp out of Jim's Cold Duck glass, looked up with wild eyes to ask, "So how do you kids like my hair? I decided to get this short curly do at the Jet Set. I told Diane that I wanted to get rid of all that hair, I couldn't mess with it anymore."

"I like it, Selma, and I bet it's so easy to take care of," Ann said, her voice singing its miserable song. Selma nodded in hearty agreement. In the back of her head, Selma had positioned her big barrette with the things that looked like chopsticks holding it in place, forgetting that there were only a few short strands of the gaudy red hair left to hold. Wayne looked across the dirty table the way he had looked so many times at his grandma. This was a table where magic had occurred, where the most extraordinary objects had been created from toothpicks and clay and thread and colored markers. Wayne wondered how many hours had been spent with him at this exact position, looking over to Selma for another of her endless stories or one more prize from her bag of tricks. It shouldn't have worked out this way, he thought, that the woman he so cherished had been reduced to this. Her big red blouse with the floppy neck had a nasty grease spot on it and stretched tightly over her belly to meet the green poly bell-bottoms covered here and there with some paint that had missed the desert landscape, escaping from the canvas to the real world. Wayne saw in those little specks of paint a person who used to be, who had disappeared from the Iowa landscape, sucked up like a drop of water by the parched earth.

"Do you kids want birthday cake now or do you want to wait for a while?" Selma asked, like every year and, like every year, they wanted to wait, hopefully avoiding it altogether. "Well, should we go into the Christmas tree, then? Do you need help, Jim?" In the past year, Jim had developed a disgusting condition that could only be described as gangrene of the left foot. In fact, his little toe had fallen off the week before in a very matter-of-fact way and was thrown in the garbage with no more than a "gonna get worse before it gets better." It's not that people didn't go to doctors in Iowa, they went religiously. But there were so many old people that the doctors eventually lost interest, thinking that the old coot was going to drop in a few months anyway, so why bother with major surgery? So Jim's condition worsened and he hobbled in, grumbling and drooling a bit of tobacco juice out of the corner of his mouth, "Time for Johnny, yet? He come on, yet?"

"Jim, if you turn on that goddamn boob tube, I'll kill you!" Selma shrieked from the kitchen.

"Ain't the way it used to be," grumbled Jim with a surreptitious brown spit into the corner.

Everyone took their designated places in the stuffy living room adorned with knickknacks and Selma's artwork. Glen dissolved into Selma's recliner, Jim in the other recliner with his rotting foot propped up, Ann sat on an uncomfortable-looking footstool ("Don't worry about me, I like it."), and Selma perched with Wayne on the couch. Spooky lay wherever he wanted, full after the steady stream of scraps he was treated to during dinner. Selma usually liked to feed Spooky candy, too, and never quite grasped why the dog would throw up after an hour's worth of chocolate-covered cherries. The Christmas tree was a shock for Wayne each year. It stopped him in his tracks this year, and he thought that Selma really had cooked up about the most disgusting tree he'd ever seen. The tree, which sat crookedly on top of the television, was no more than a foot and a half tall, made of brutal wire sticks covered with festive aluminum foil. On the tree were a sparse assortment of Christmas balls in red and green that Selma had bought at the Day After Christmas Sale at Alco. Presents radiated out from the base of the television rather than the tree, which could accommodate only a few small ones propped up next to its tiny white plastic base. Selma had wiscly refilled her glass before coming in and, after taking a shot, let out her whoop of "Wayne, are you going to play Santy Claus again this year?"

In Wayne's estimation, this was the most unendurable

part of the night. One year his father had gotten too sleepy to hand out the presents and the task had fallen to Wayne, who had been trapped in the job ever since. Wayne read the tacky gift card on each present out loud and then sat it in front of the lucky recipient. There they sat, mouths slightly agape, waiting for the plastic belts and underwear and gag gifts and scratchy sweaters. Selma always got the most presents and, dispensing with formalities, tore into them with fury immediately, not waiting for the others. Wayne made the rounds for what seemed like hours, hearing Selma hooting, "Oh, look at this driftwood sculpture Marion sent me from California. Oh, I love it, I just love it!" She shook the jugs of booze with big laughs each time they gurgled, "This'll keep me happy a few days!" Ann unwrapped each item carefully, holding it up and cooing. Jim opened each and complained that he didn't want it. Glen had to be coaxed to open his presents at all before falling asleep. "Hey, droopy eyes, get with it or I'll steal those presents for myself," Selma warned, and could have meant it with one more drink.

Finally, Wayne's deliveries were over, and he was confronted with his own treasure trove. Unfortunately, the timing meant that Selma had already finished and was unoccupied, allowing her to scrutinize his face as he unwrapped each gift. The first stopped him dead in his tracks—a big pink Miss Piggy doll. "That is so cute!" Selma shrieked in a voice loud as a jackhammer. "I couldn't resist. I thought you could have her in your college room." Why, he wondered, would this woman think he wanted a Miss Piggy doll? What could she possibly see in his face that would bring her to the conclusion that he would cherish this thing that she had spent several dollars of her measly Social Security check on? He carefully sat Miss Piggy on the floor, hoping that Spooky would chew on it.

Wayne then continued on through several packages of underwear and socks ("Wayne, I know better than to try to buy you clothes") and two sweaters of maroon and gray velour. The last package was small, though, and Selma became unnaturally quiet when he picked it up. Her mouth pursed and she leaned back from him slightly. The sleigh-ride scene paper came off hard, having been taped to the sides of the watch box inside. It was a Timex watch box, and he thought, "Oh God, she's gotten me an ugly watch, something else to put away and never look at again." He thought that this was killing something inside of him, shutting down more and more just to survive. One door after another shut in his mind. He was farther and farther away from these people. Wayne decided that he didn't even know who they were anymore. He started to open the last box, straining to keep his face completely blank. Wayne could see that the watch box was filled with tissue paper, as if someone had blown their nose twenty times and hidden the evidence here. It was unlike the other packages, unnerving in the casual way it was assembled. He began to feel more and more uncomfortable sorting through it as Selma watched him soberly. Wayne was about to ask what this was all about when he saw the most extraordinary object wrapped in one of the wads of paper.

"This must be a mistake," he said weakly. Lying carelessly in the paper was the ring that for years had ridden above the arthritic knuckle of his grandmother's hand: her wedding ring that was not a common wedding ring but an ornate circle made of three types of gold. Black Hills gold, bought in the fifties or sixties, that wrapped impure strands of metal about itself in the form of leaves and vines. How many times had his grandmother's hands kneaded clay or threaded a needle or turned a page, and his child's eyes would watch the flicker of gold on her finger. In a child's eyes, that flickering gold was magic. In the way that an object can represent someone, this ring had been Selma. He was surprised that he hadn't noticed it missing from her finger earlier at the table. His eyes were unexpectedly, unaccountably wet as he looked up to her and saw her staring back and wrapping her old granny soft arms around him and it was no longer the same place, not bad now, but long ago, when he couldn't see all the bad, didn't know, still cared. For a moment, a wall collapsed, and all the pain, all the years solidified into a band of gold. And he thought, "this a very strange place, indeed."

From this distance, the town of six thousand people could have been a metropolis, its lights shivering in the cold of an Iowa December. The lips of the valley puckered around the pitiful edges of the town that had always looked more than it was. The great desolation of empty fields stretched limitless under the light cover of a moonlit snow, such a thin blanket that the brown earth raised itself often, destroying the smooth white. Only the groaning joints of the car broke the constant silence of the night here, and even that low noise was enough to cause the farmers and their wives and their daughters and their sons to grumble in their sleep—"Past ten! Who's makin' that goddamn racket?"—before returning to dreams best not remembered. This was the silence that hummed at a high pitch deep in one's ear, desperate to be heard, insistent on muffling any noise.

Even though the inadequate heater in the car barely removed the frost from the windshield, Wayne found sweat beading up on his forehead and back and the underwear clinging around his crotch. Driving here was such a fight against the geography, so intense must be one's concentration, that it breaks you down after a while. When the fields stretch so far and the sky arches and arches away, it seems that no amount of driving could cover the miles. Wayne pulled off onto a country road that still retained a hard-packed gravel surface, crunching and slipping under the wheels. And he sat. The engine rattled, and when he took the light pressure of his foot off the accelerator, it gave a final shiver before dying. How quickly the cold returned and what an ultimate cold, a cold that never leaves a body, a cold that caused the muscles along the back of his legs to contract away from the crinkly vinyl seat. Wayne's legs were fitted into tight jeans that caused a slight chafing along his inner thighs and, like all his clothes, were uncomfortable, the fabric pulling in on the body, accusing that extra pound's existence.

In the still coldness, Wayne thought of his grandfather who gave him this red car. Used, of course. Wayne still didn't know the make and model of it. Everyone else knew the make and model of their cars in Iowa. There's even the *Blue Book,* that says how much a car is worth with each passing year. Everyone loved to talk about the *Blue Book* in Cherokee—"Hey, Glen, you gonna trade in that Impala while it's still worth somethin'?"—but Wayne couldn't seem to figure it out or even see why it was so interesting. Wayne had always felt the obligation to love his grandfather, for this car if nothing else. He definitely felt he should at least like him a little. "I did when he gave it, even hugged him," he thought. "Hadn't done that in years." Wayne hadn't touched his grandfather in years because, unlike Selma, he never felt anything for the old man, for no particular reason he had never liked the guy. Wayne had hugged him the day they picked up the car even though his grandfather stank under the denim-look shirt he wore for weeks at a time. His body had a real stink to it: rotten, smelled like old meat.

Wayne switched on the radio to waves of static up and down the dial. Of course, KCHE in Cherokee would have been playing Christmas carols had it not already signed off. Sometimes on these cold, clear nights an Omaha station would come in playing music that seemed like some kind of magic. He yearned for those Top Twenty hits that he knew others were listening to, maybe even dancing to, maybe even touching each other to in the faraway cities that he would strain his eyes to see on these crystal black nights, praying to see a glow like the northern lights from Chicago or, beyond hope, New York City. But only the local towns with strange names of Aurelia, Alta, Paulina, Correctionville, Larrabee, and Moville gave some orange glow to the sky here and there.

Wayne pulled out a bottle of cheap vodka from under the seat and, grimacing, took a swig of it. "Got my good taste in liquor from Selma," he thought, looking at the Georgi Vodka label, $3.49 a fifth. Looking up at the sky, Wayne thought of calling the telephone number for Studio 54 in New York City very late at night, hoping that someone would be passing by the phone and pick it up to let the roar of the crowd dribble through the wires those thousands of miles. For Wayne, New York had become something more than an actual city with the mundane problems of everyday life. For Wayne,

New York was a movie set, a stage play, an arena where everything was possible. Never having been far outside the borders of this state, his images of city life were drawn greedily from the media, etching each television scene in his mind and cutting out photos from magazines. *People* magazine was a particularly rich source of raw material with endless stories on the celebrities who would never live anywhere else other than in front of terrifying subway stations and gray skyscrapers and Central Park and Studio 54. His most prized clipping was, in fact, a feature on that very nightclub, that one building that seemed to be the center of the universe. Unfortunately, the story had only two photos: one with Liza Minnelli whirling on a glittery dance floor and the other of the imposing entrance. The photograph of the entrance showed a stern-looking man surveying the desperate crowd pushing to be admitted, their hands waving crazily. Wayne had studied the faces of that chic tumble of people and could see that there were women in white mink jackets and sequined gowns but he could also see men in white T-shirts and one particular man who stood there, defiant, in a black leather jacket with a great drooping mustache. As Wayne had carefully pasted that story into the notebook where he kept all his New York clippings, he ran his finger over the face of that man and felt that something was there, waiting for his arrival.

Nothing but static from the radio, no word from the cities tonight. And so there was nothing left but the crashing silence around the car, nothing to betray the people scattered in rickety little shacks all over the state. It's a sin, everyone knows, to be awake and moving around in this stillness that judges you and asks—what could you want at this hour of night, what are looking for, what is your excuse, where are you going, what decent act can happen at this hour, why are you wandering and what could you possibly find now?

Iowa, the Buckeye State. December 24, 1980. An eighteen-year-old sat next to a snowy cornfield. So quiet that if you closed your eyes, you could discern life stirring in the form of rustling animal sounds from the ditches and field. Animals don't sleep, but move through the night exploring the terrain, looking for food or just wandering. If you didn't breathe, you might have heard the thud of the cow's hoof as it kicked the clods of dirt searching for straw, the little rushes of pheasant feet alongside the road, the rubbing of a threadbare deer against a tree, and the liquid waves of a fox flowing along the ground toward a scent. The fox smelled the rancid meat left for him, the pieces of fat scattered around the gleaming jaws of steel. He—for the fox was a he—pushed himself along on his belly toward the trap and thought it beautiful with its industrial glow against the white of the ground, thought it to be like a jewel or a necklace about to close around his neck. You might have heard the fine fur around his mouth rustle as he turned black eyes up to the moon, never blinking, and nodded his head twice. Nodded that narrow fox face and lowered his lips to the waiting meat, decaying and stinking and leading him down. And the clang, snap, ring, ring of metal against metal against flesh was almost unbearable in the dark car alongside the cornfield, as midnight came to a young adult in Iowa.

Wayne recalled walking these ditches many times with his father, their shotguns at the ready in the dim winter afternoons as they stalked pheasants, waiting for them to whir up from underfoot. His father would wait for Wayne to take the first shot, and nobody ever said the boy wasn't a good shot. All one can eat on a pheasant is the breast. The rest of the bird has stringy, boney meat so you need to shoot ten or fifteen of the birds and toss their tiny guts onto the snow. And then down they go into boiling water to take away that particular gamey bird smell. And that was the point where Wayne always had to stop because the wet turquoise feathers around the neck looked so sporty, so dignified, that he could never rip them out. Yet he enjoyed it later when they would be chewing their way through the white meat, avoiding the buckshot. "Careful you don't get a piece of shot. Remember when it broke Dad's tooth after he bit down on it?" He and his father could think of something to say to one another back on those winter days, and the conversation and laughs would roll along effortlessly while they trudged through the snowy fields. Then one day the conversation stopped without warning. At the same time Wayne realized he was no longer supposed to kiss his father. Suddenly there was a wall of restraint and new rules.

Feeling he must have the sound of the motor at least to stop the ringing, rushing silence, Wayne slowly turned the ignition key while thinking of a man's body; not a particular man's body, but a chest that sort of summed it up. With the click of the motor catching, he saw an arm. Pulling the gearshift, he imagined the flesh around the arm and the way that dark hair looks like a nest in the pit. It was strange to think of bare flesh in this cold, but he did think of it, and the thoughts took over. He barely felt the cold as he slipped out of his coat, thinking now of a very particular body, a body that was poised on the line between boy and young man and man. Wayne pulled off his black sweater and unbuttoned his white shirt and pants. With each piece of clothing that Wayne shed, the body of the boy/young man/man became clearer. The slapping of the cold air seemed an appropriate reprimand to forbidden thoughts of the male body that now had a face and a name, and its name was Carl. The name, face, body, smell, and voice of Carl rushed around Wayne's mind throughout each day, intensifying at night until Carl's presence was almost palpable. Wayne ran his hand over a bared hairless chest that shivered and wrinkled in the icy air. Their chests were both smooth, not yet darkening into the hairy excess of age, but Carl's burned with a whiteness Wayne yearned to touch. He had never touched this boy he loved. Wayne sharpened his thoughts, resolved to think so intensely about Carl's chest that he would be able to possess it. And in his mind, the chest, reconstructed from precious few memories, drew nearer until the white heaviness of the boy's breasts closed around his face. Wayne thought of his mouth encasing the hollow there, letting his tongue wander out not to taste, not to explore, but simply to give pleasure. Wayne knew that nothing could ever be more satisfying than to give complete attention to those few inches of heaving, wanting skin. But then a mistake. Wayne glanced inadvertently to the rearview mirror, and the obscene sight of his tongue poking out to lap at empty cold air broke the image beyond repair. Roughly pulling his clothes back into place, Wayne knew that whatever direction he pointed his car, there was only one possible destination tonight. This clear intent lead him to steer back around onto Highway 71.

One drives without thought in Iowa, hypnotized by

the broken white or solid yellow of the median. The car pulled itself onto the highway, pointing to the valley, and accelerated with a mind of its own. Wayne saw one light then, only one light teetering on the horizon and glanced to it, then stared. And there was only one light over the valley, which pulled him on and pulled him in as the car rushed faster. The red car moved of its own accord, drifting slowly to center and then, floating on the black road, veering to the shoulder. The seat moved beneath Wayne, and his body followed it as he stared at that one light, shining and guttering as if ready to pitch itself into the gully. Floating, as the first tire explored beyond the pavement and then the second. Eyes still locked on that distant beacon, speaking, urging—"What is the time and where have they gone?"—urging over the scream of the rubber tires clutching to the road surface, to any surface that might hold. Again the whisper—"What is the time and where have they gone?"—demanding an answer. The light flickered, taunted, and flickered one last time before it was gone. A cool stroke on his cheek passed before Wayne's face, taking away the pain. The car lurched back into control as he steered calmly onto the Highway 71 Bypass, not that there is much to bypass in Cherokee, Iowa.

Wayne thought: Christmas is the dumbest. Everybody makes stupid remarks about being a Christmas baby—"I betch ya get less presents!"—but the truth is that Christmas babies have a hard time of it, weird feelings jump on you every year, all twined up like one of Granny's yarn balls, all these feelings and memories mixed together like a Coke commercial—Joy and Birth, but then despair and death all making you nervous, waiting for something to happen. But it never quite comes. For example, even when Wayne's mother proudly told the story of the night he was born for the zillionth time, it just seemed sad that she said there was never a snow like that before, not one that she could remember. The snow flakes began just as she was coming out of the house with Wayne's father on the way to the hospital. "Huge snowflakes," she would say with her eyes opening wider, "like white hankies made out of snow." The thing that struck her, though, was their lightness and, as she bent over the window of the car that night and blew lightly, they flew into the air, swirling up and then drifting down again. Wayne thought, "I'll never be happy like that at Christmas. I've never seen snow like that."

When he was little, at this time of year Wayne's parents would drive him through the streets of the town to look at the lights. Almost everybody would decorate, really do up their houses for the Christmas season. The big houses out here in the hills usually had the best lights. They must have spent thousands of dollars to coat the houses in lights, but people said it was worth it and it was. Some were mixed with bulbs of all colors sprinkled along the wires, others all blue or red or green. Some were constant, but others blinked on and off. Those were the big shots' houses—the doctors, lawyers, construction-company owners: McLaughlin, Miller, McMillen, Ament. "Catholics," Wayne thought, "always looking down their noses even though all their daughters had to get married quick." But houses all over town were decorated, even the little shacks near the river. Sometimes it was just a strand of lights around a door or window frame but with a whole block done up, a whole town done up, it was incredible. Wayne's house, too, had pale blue lights on the big fir tree standing proudly out front. Inside, he remembered sticking the limbs in the tall plastic Christmas tree, wrapping the strands of light around it, draping it with asbestos angel hair and, finally, carefully placing the angel on top. Over the years, the decorations disappeared; starting with the outside lights ("too much mess"), then the Christmas tree ("the cat'll knock it over") and then every last tiny note of festivity in that house, except for a Santa Claus candle on the kitchen table.

People lost their interest in decorating. Only a few brightly lit houses remained, and they had the same lights year after year, as if the bulbs were never taken down. The *Cherokee Daily Times* discontinued its decorating contest, and the steady stream of cars stopped parading slowly along colorful streets during the Christmas season. All that remained were the dirty tinsel angels hanging from the street lights on Main Street. The little town was so quiet, deserted, as Wayne moved down the first street off the bypass, meandering and putting off the thoughts of a boy on the other side of town. Here was the first of five nursing homes stuck along the outskirts so that one only occasionally had to look at their guilty facades, especially this time of year when maybe the family came to collect the bed-wetting, drooling, babbling old fool for the one day it seemed absolutely unconscionable not to. Or maybe not. Maybe there was just that Swanson's TV turkey dinner with dry stuffing and sweet cranberries and sweet potatoes and sweet beets and watery, watery corn. The Christmas cookies on plastic platters waited for old veiny hands that no longer even wanted dessert, or to look at the Bing Crosby Christmas special on TV. "Get those goddamn carolers out of here so I can get some sleep!" But they didn't sleep and their outlines were at the windows, straining to see every car that went past, their faces pressed hard against the window glass, not thinking, only looking for some sight that might bring it all back. People don't realize what goes on in old folks' homes, they don't realize that it is a mixture of the most mundane and the most extreme of horrors. Do you know, for example, that old people don't sleep? Didn't think so. Do you know that they are absolutely sex-crazed? Didn't think so. But look in some of those shoe boxes the old ladies love to stuff with tissue paper. The Whopper. The Big One. The Double-Headed Gut Buster. Take a look in some of those cigar boxes supposedly full to the brink with war medals. Alligator Clamps. Peppermint Love Lube. And The Works Enlarging System. That's the problem with these towns; there's always some horror behind the walls.

"Whistler's House," Wayne thought. "This is the nursing home where they finally put old Whistler. God, what a sight!" Whistler on Main Street, walking back and forth between the Sunrise Bakery, Hawley Allison Dress Shop, MacIntire Novelties, J. C. Penney, and the savings and loan. She wore a path in that sidewalk shuffling along. She looked like some horror movie with her boney wrist and hand slapped up over her mouth as if she was so petrified that she couldn't look. But the real scare was under that hand. Cancer. They'd taken out her jaw; her face was cut in half. Everybody hated Whistler—from the people in the stores that took her money, to the kids that screamed and laughed, to every sneaky, whispering old coot that lived in town. When they laughed or whispered or dropped the change in her hand without touching her, she would start the squealing, whistling noise that was really just her telling you off; but the madder she got, the louder she got and the noise would take over the store or street, piercing and shrill and that really got her worked up. Finally, they put her here in the old folks' home. They doped her up, like all of them, but she still wandered the halls. Wayne imagined her at one of the rest home windows, breathing onto it, making that low whistle sound and wiping her finger through the mist, spelling out a little SOS message, "Too long." It faded and she breathed out her writing pad again, "Too long."

They always put schools next to the nursing homes, probably so that the old codgers can hear the hoots of the kiddies to cheer them up. "Lincoln Elementary. Fucking bastards. Tortured me for five years. I can hardly look at it now." Here Wayne hit the two hundred pound mark in the fifth grade, a fact that was well reported to the kids behind him in line during the yearly weigh-in. That prudish bitch of a nurse let out a shrill little scream telling everybody's weight. "Two hundred and two pounds, five ounces." Oh, she must have loved it, loooved it! People don't know; people forget how much it hurts. How much it still hurt. Beaten and sworn at and tortured by the cute little kids so that later in life it doesn't go away even if you're not really fat anymore or don't stutter or aren't so retarded as you were. There was a little group of fat kids who used to hang out, but their faces looked different now that they were seniors in high school. "What about Kim," Wayne thought, "so starved that she looks dead, the skin hanging from her arms and her face? Her jeans are so tight that I'm afraid they'll get ripped by those hipbones of hers and her eyes bulge out even more all outlined in blue. I don't get skinny, though, even with the days of Dexatrim jitters and all the Ex-Lax."

Driving past the VFW, Wayne looked for his friend Pussy's big boat of a car. She was called Pussy or Pussy Galore for her loose reputation and voluptuous figure. He would hook up with Pussy here when she wasn't in the midst of an intrigue with one of the town cops. She loved cops. "Veterans of Foreign Wars," he rolled the phrase through his mind, wondering if he had ever seen a veteran there at the VF. If so, veterans were indistinguishable from the drunks and the good old boys and Pussy standing by the bar in her cheap parka trying to hit on old men. The bronze statue out front of the man crouched with a bayonet ready to strike never seemed appropriate for a sleazy bar. Each time he walked into this place, Wayne expected to see a dignified group of men in solemn uniforms quietly discussing world events. A dusting of snow had covered the statue on Christmas Eve, giving it an ashy, fragile surface and the soldier looked scared, cold.

Wayne decided that this driving around had become a waste of time, a sick game where he put off getting to his destination as long as possible. "Afraid," came the answer in his mind when he wondered why he didn't just go right to Carl's house. The fear came stronger when he tried to imagine the smell of Carl. He thought Carl had no smell at all, either bad or good. For some reason, that would be the most sexy—if he had no smell, if he didn't smell real. Wayne decided to just run into the VFW for a second to see if Pussy was there. He pulled into the almost-empty lot, still looking for Pussy's car. "Not here," he thought, not sure whether he was relieved or disappointed. But when he opened the front door of the bar, Wayne knew immediately that Pussy was indeed in attendance as the sound of her singing blasted out. Loud, very loud. Going up the three steps into the bar area, all that one could hear was Pussy singing along with the jukebox to the current hit from Elton John/Kiki Dee, "Don't Go Breakin' My Heart." She stood at the almost-deserted bar next to one of the two old men who were the only other patrons desperate for a drink on Christmas Eve. Pussy performed both parts of the song, using her screwdriver glass as a microphone. In a low voice, she sang Elton's part to the old man—"Don't go breakin' my heart"—and then swung around, throwing herself onto a bar stool to wail Kiki's response—"I won't go breakin' your heart, babe." The old man leered at her big tits, embarrassed but turned on.

Wayne tapped Pussy on the shoulder, and she swiveled around with a shriek, "Ooooh, you big hunk!" pulling his head between her boobs. " 'Scuse me," she said to the disappointed old man as she pulled Wayne over by the jukebox. "Happy birthday," she whispered. "What are you doing here?" Continuing on without giving Wayne a chance to answer she confided, "This place is deadsville tonight. But! But! That old guy is buying me so many drinks. He's a salesman staying out at the Western Inn. Do you think I should do it with him?"

"He's not what you'd call gorgeous," Wayne said reluctantly.

"Any port in a storm, baby. Shit. My dad dropped me off and is drinking up at the Twilight. He's gonna pick me up on his way home and if I'm not here, he'll have a shit fit." Pussy wrinkled up her face in frustration and Wayne got the mild shock her appearance always produced. No Dexatrim for Pussy. At least, not for weight-loss purposes. Pussy was a big woman, and that's how she liked it. Her face was round as a moon under the wispy bleached-white hair, eyes glaring out from under layers of bright blue shadow. Pussy was wedged into her favorite jeans tonight, and her purple T-shirt could hardly survive the pressure of her chest. "Guess I'll just hang out here and get loaded," Pussy moaned dejectedly until she heard the refrain of the song again and started wiggling around, giving a little wave to her date at the bar.

"Well, I've gotta get home. I just stopped for a minute," Wayne lied, feeling impatient.

"No, stay. He'll buy you drinks, too. He's really loaded," Pussy said, freshening up her strawberry-scented lip gloss.

"I don't feel like drinking tonight," Wayne said, with Georgi vodka on his breath. "I've spent all day with my family."

"All the more reason to get ripped tonight, then," Pussy yelled. "Well, all right, then. Happy birthday, and I'll see you after this Christmas bullshit. Bye-bye, baby," she said, trotting back to the eager man at the bar.

Wayne knew intimately every street, alley, highway, parking lot, and driveway of Cherokee. There was great mystery in the tiny roads that led behind houses to a place where nothing stood, so many roads leading away from his destination, but he steered the car down them anyway, just to see how they looked late at night. These roads were built during the heyday of Cherokee, when the railroad brought a great bustle of activity and turned a cowtrail into a port in the Midwest fields. Those glory days brought a resort to town where bathers floated in the waters of a magical spring that brought health and serenity. A great resort hotel where the wealthy swept along the cobblestone paths in silk gowns and proper jackets, and yet few know exactly where it was, how it left, why there is absolutely no trace of its existence except in Selma's drunken stories. A town of faded glories. Now shacks lined the street, close by one another, huddling for some warmth. How fragile they looked, these cardboard-and-aluminum houses, when stuck next to the occasional surviving grand old house with whirling cupolas and wraparound porches and attics full of secrets.

Wayne thought, "You fat freak!" as he drove past one of the huge old houses owned by his teacher. This teacher, Mr. A, just barely held together the persona of a high-school teacher until at night the careful facade began to crumble in private. People wondered and speculated about the goings-on in the rooms of this house. Wayne also wondered but could only guess. The reality of Mr. A's existence was mundane but exceedingly fragile. Rambling through the halls of the old house, one word came into Mr. A's mind continually—"dead." "Dead!" a voice screamed in his head constantly and sometimes the voice also screamed, "Empty." One day, Mr. A would probably take up Whistler's position after the vibrating, deserted halls of his old house finally drove him out. Let me just tell you a secret. Mr. A had found the Lord, and the Lord resided in a secret compartment of his brain, wanting to get out, and the Lord called Mr. A a sinner. The Lord said, "You must not think of it." Those were the moments when Mr. A could just barely hold it together, the moments when he reached out for his little black book to write, to scribble the messages from the Lord into the diary, because if he committed them to writing they would seem somehow more bearable, less resonant in his head. These infuriating missives from the Lord were accusations of guilt, divine rambling designed to block out sinful thoughts.

The Lord Says:
Little Miss Mary Muffett Bo Peep has lost her sheep. That spider scared away the sheep, the rams, and the ewes.

Oh, Mary. If I could get my hands on you, I swear I'd throttle your neck. Those sheep, you've lost those sheep. You hairless little cunt. I can't really blame you but... Oh, Mary, you little peep.

Now the sheep are gone. You have to realize that a sheep doesn't just come from nowhere. Spiders, yes, you can get a spider at most finer department stores, but sheep are in demand.

I don't want to talk about it anymore, Mary. I'm just sad, sad for you. Because now you're alone. No sheep. No company. Just spiders who aren't very good talkers. Mary.

Strange messages from the Lord came to Mr. A even as Wayne silently drove past. Mr. A transcribed these messages quickly into the book and tried not to think of the sins that the Lord accused him of. Mr. A refused to look down at his body, at what it had become. He just concentrated on the belief that one can have two lives and prayed that he could adhere the shuddering parts of his vision while at school. Because in Iowa, Mr. A knew, we have our freaks, we have our untouchables, and we know how to deal with them. One day Mr. A could even be imprisoned in Cherokee's most imposing landmark, the Mental Health Institute, or the MHI, or the Nut Hut as the kids call it.

Wayne passed Mr. A's house, passed through the grand old streets of the country club set and drove listlessly down the curving MHI road, half expecting to see Mr. A sitting on the fortresslike porch, waiting to be taken in and hooked to the table that might stop the scream. "I can imagine seeing Mr. A here at the Nut Hut," Wayne thought. He could imagine him strolling toward that great gothic tower of red brick surrounded by idyllic lawns landscaped to calm and repress. Wayne recalled a horror movie in which a doctor was driving through a torrential rainstorm toward an insane asylum, through grounds much like this, and suddenly a flash of lightning showed the inmates to be in the fields, in white gowns, standing still. He shuddered and locked the door. This is where we finally deal with our freaks. So desperate are people to stop the ridicule, the otherness, that they look forward to the electric bolt that rips through their brains, destroying the hurt, making the world fade away finally. We deal with those who are different, the freaks, we deal with them decisively.

"I can't imagine Eric having a dad who runs the Nut Hut and talks about something stupid over dinner after spending the day ripping out people's brains. This place looks like a country club, but just think what his dad knows. Eric just goes on with his guitar and Simon and Garfunkel collection and his acting while his dad tears out brains." The car swooped past Eric's large house, and Wayne took note of the glow in the upstairs window. "I know you're watching a movie on HBO or humming in the dark or talking to Mr. A on the phone.

Fuck you, Eric. Mr. A doesn't know it yet, but we've both lost you—lost you to that girlfriend you spend all your time with."

Eric didn't know that people often stirred outside his window, walking the grounds or driving and thinking of him. Eric was an unsophisticated boy who didn't know anything even as Mr. A called for the fifth time that night, desperate to hear a voice other than the ones in his head. Mr. A possessed only one photograph of Eric, but oh, what a photograph! The shot was taken at Eric's family's cabin, where Mr. A was once invited in easier times. The cabin sat picturesquely on a little lake in Minnesota. In the hot, confused afternoons, Eric would swim in the lake while Mr. A would sit on the porch with a glass of iced tea. "What an exquisite torture, this!" Mr. A would think as Eric ran back up to the porch, unaware of his body's power. Eric's body always seemed inappropriate to his Norwegian ancestry: a thick meaty chest that was lightly coated in hair that grew thicker and glossier as it flowed down across his stomach and into the tangle around his cock. A sleek, wet otter. Yet Eric's arms and legs were nearly bare, graceful, and made one want to pinch, to slap, to give them some experience. Just one photograph, though. One concrete item for Mr. A to center his desire around and dream about the dark cock that must lie heavily under that swimsuit. The smell of it and the thrust of it would overcome him until the older man would pick up the phone and angrily punch in those seven numbers once again.

The teen's phone rang, and Eric picked it up immediately, "Hi," went the voice of the teacher straining to see through the phone wire, straining to see the boy's body.

"Hi," went Eric because he didn't know anything, and jerked off thinking about his girlfriend while talking to a fat fifty-year-old man. "I'm watching *Apocalypse Now.* It's great. Can I call you when it's over?"

"That will be fine," Mr. A said peevishly, angry not to be invited over. Tonight he thought he might show Eric some of his writings, finally just hand them over to see if Eric would see the brilliance of them. "I just wanted to talk to you about a part I think you should do in the spring play. Actually, don't bother calling tonight. I'll be going to bed soon. We'll speak tomorrow."

"Okay," Eric said in the sweet way of boys who don't know anything. Eric was too vague even to fully realize that his cock was lying hard in his hand. Eric hung up without a thought about the fat pain of a man across town, yearning for a boy, yearning for a boy.

It was a dreamy, swirling path Wayne drove most nights, etched on the snow, but the route that Wayne chose through town was hardly accidental because he followed it almost nightly, putting off the ache of his final destination. Carl was the fleshy magnet that drew him along his route. Carl...just another young man unaware of pain. Carl lived near the Nut Hut grounds and while Eric was truly ignorant of desire, Carl may have known something, but one couldn't be sure; because a haze always drifted over Carl's thoughts, revealing nothing and looking ominous. Halfway down the steep road that led to the swimming pool was Carl's house, looking exactly like the one before it and the one after it and all the others that lined the street. What a strange name. Carl. Carl Gunderson. An exotic name that had hints of Vikings or stoic Germans. Strange names filled these small towns peopled with immigrants and their children. Carl would be awake, Wayne knew. Carl rarely slept before the early hours of the morning and rarely awoke in time to attend the first class at school, which was only down the hill. Carl's room, like the rooms of many teenage boys, was in the basement of the little crackerboard house, like a bunker or a locker room. Carl's house had the ubiquitous picture window with a Christmas tree standing dark and bereft, watching over the home as a red car pulled up quietly.

The drama, the speeches, the scenarios so often rehearsed in Wayne's mind re-ran feverishly as he sat frozen in the car, sipping out of the bottle of vodka and mouthing the words, just once, just once, not daring to do it more, "I love you." Wayne crept across the lawn. "I know you're in there, Carl," he thought, seeing the boy in his mind. The body and the hair and the face and the messy room. "You have to know why I'm creeping across the yard of your Crackerbox Palace, and you have to know why I knock on your window this late at night. You have to. Nobody's that stupid." Carl's face appeared at the window and he jerked toward the basement door after Wayne knocked softly at the small window.

When Carl opened the door, Wayne held up the bottle of Georgi vodka and said quietly, "Want to have a birthday drink with me?"

"Whose birthday?" Carl asked in his most dazed voice. His dark blond hair straggled down over his face, and the white and gold of his skin was revealed under the tank top and shorts.

"Mine, asshole," Wayne said as he pushed past Carl as casually as he could and went down the hall to his room. Carl's room looked like a teenage prison cell with the cement-block walls covered with stupid posters for The Cars and girlie calendars. The small television in Carl's room was tuned to the *Star Trek* reruns that he watched religiously each night.

"I just drove by Eric's. Did he call you tonight?"

"No. His phone's always busy," Carl muttered as he turned the volume up a little to hide their voices, not that there was much to hide. The bottle of vodka was passed back and forth with little swigs. "I don't really give a shit. All he does is hang out with Mr. A and talk about acting." Eric's new position as an intellectual, coddled by the teachers, did not sit well with Carl. Carl and Eric used both to be bad boys, naughty, sexy boys who knew they could get away with it because they were beautiful. They were the boys who had fights with their fathers in the early morning hours after wrecking the car and getting arrested and insulting their sisters and drinking too much and, finally, were thrown out to huddle together on a friend's couch with their strong arms carelessly linked together.

"I know. He's gotten really boring ever since they're best friends," Wayne said, taking the bottle back from Carl and enjoying the taste of the wet bottle top. "Captain Kirk's lookin' a little fat in this one. Looks like he's gonna have a heart attack from holding his gut in." Carl must have liked *Star Trek* because it had so many heroes. Wayne thought that Carl would like to have been one of those easy heroes who never had to slave away in a school for years or work.

Carl watched Captain Kirk and Mr. Spock intently while Wayne pretended to watch but was actually watching Carl. Wayne sat in a lemon-yellow bean-bag chair while Carl sprawled on the single bed. What components are wrapped up into a package to make a person so unbearably sexy? Nearly everything about Carl added another notch of desire, and Wayne's hands itched and burned wanting to reach out those few inches to touch what one certainly wanted and one certainly did not. If Wayne had reached out, time would have slowed to a searing thump...thump...thump of the heart, not unlike someone killing himself when the knife slides so slowly or the ground rushes imperceptibly closer or the pills work their way like worms down the throat or the click never quite comes from the shiny black barrel.

Wayne thought nervously, "Now I have a hard-on, so I can't even move my arms." He beamed out a thought message toward Carl that said, "I want you, I want you, I want you." His eyes were slashing along Carl's form, dissecting this desire. "It's his arms I want the most," he decided, because they were so powerful but completely natural. Wayne followed the arc of the biceps, building to the forceful shoulders. And covered with gold hair so soft along the hard white skin and thickening to brown, tufting out from the armpits. Wayne had seen Carl's stomach only a couple of times, but its ridges stuck in his memory. The legs were sturdy, proud, and hairy in gym shorts. Most vivid, though, was the face, framed by shaggy yellow-brown hair, the nose straight and long over the thin lips and focused by beautiful gray eyes.

There were many beautiful boys in town, but Carl was special because of something other than his body. In all his trim, muscular package, he was helpless, and Wayne said silently, "I'll help you. I'll take care of you." Wayne would do the algebra and trigonometry that were incomprehensible to Carl. He would cool off the teachers complaining about never listening or showing up in class. Wayne wished he could destroy himself along with Carl through liquor and fast driving and fights. Carl made Wayne want to take care of him by just showing his body in that effortless jock way.

"What's your family doing for the rest of Christmas?" Wayne said, breaking the silence between them during a commercial.

"Going to Iowa City to see Granny," Carl said, smiling his trusting blank smile.

"Lucky you. I went to Selma's for a delightful frozen pizza. You know how artists are."

"Tell Selmoid hi for me."

Wayne's mind rushed on, analyzing, making silent accusations. "But what about your brother?" he wanted to say. "Will your brother be there? Your brother who was run out of town for we both-know-what? Will you be seeing your brother, and are you like your brother, and do you think about it late at night or right now? Where your brother was girly, you're macho...where your brother was tall and gangly, you're short and sturdy. But there must have been a reason, something in the mind or the body or not having a father; and this is my hope, my only real reason to think that there might be hope, that I could finally have you. Because I have never even seen you naked, I have never held you, not even your hand. God, why this pain? To torture and hate and I hate and am hated and could very easily be like your brother and forced to leave and would you think of me then or would I be tossed in some basket that says 'Freak.'"

The vodka was creeping over both of them and, as is the way with liquor, sometimes it makes you active, and sometimes it makes you want to sleep. Tonight they were both drifting but Wayne could still see the episode of *Star Trek* where the crew of the *Enterprise* was held hostage on a planet where the aliens had telekinetic powers, could force people to do things with their bodies while their minds shrieked out in protest.

"I've never seen this one," Wayne lied.

"You're kidding! I've seen it about a million times," Carl murmured. His head nodded back and forth a bit while he chewed on his upper lip, watching intently.

Kirk and Lieutenant Uhura were in a sort of small Roman amphitheater, and the aliens were forcing Kirk to bend Uhura over a low bench, about to kiss her. Her eyes were lined in thick black with long, false eyelashes fluttering at the sight of her secret hope.

UHURA: Captain, I'm so ashamed. Please help me.
(Tears run down her face as their lips move closer.)
KIRK: Close your eyes, Lieutenant. Don't give them the pleasure of seeing you suffer. Close your eyes.
(Their lips join in a long, trembling embrace.)

Carl's eyes closed and he snored softly, his body pitched sideways on the bed with his arm reaching out gently in a ravishing gesture. Wayne's eyes licked at the body, desperate, not knowing where to take it, and thinking finally, "I won't let them see me suffer. I won't beg for someone's body like a dog for a scrap. Good night, Carl." Wayne wished he knew what Carl was dreaming about, but Carl wasn't the type to remember his dreams. He left quietly for home, where a solitary bed waited like an accusation.

II.

Washington High School hugged the ground closely in a faux–Frank Lloyd Wright ribbon of red brick and concrete, an auditorium stepping down the low hill at its far end. The remainder of Christmas break had melted wordlessly past through days and nights of television-watching, until even the most hardened could barely stand another *Bewitched* rerun or round of *The $10,000 Pyramid*. Wayne returned to this cold brick building for the home stretch in Iowa, the last months of endurance that promised to end a harsh prison sentence by dangling the excruciating possibility of escape. On the flat January morning, the students rushed back to Washington High, happily admitting relief at being separated from their families for a few hours a day. The winter days in this splayed-out-in-the-middle-of-nowhere state are marked by a sunlight so harsh as to be painful, more unwelcoming than the dark of night. In these coldest of months, the sun was unable to melt the ice that enveloped any object foolish enough to stand still for long. From the windshields, the streets, the tree limbs, light reflected into a constant glare, doubling its terrible intensity with every surface it struck.

The entrance to the school from the parking lot was a huge set of stairs that never seemed to have any traffic, as if everyone had already gone in or was still preparing to leave. No one would talk much in these early-morning hours as the young minds convinced themselves they were still asleep and dreaming. Wayne was terrified in these halls, frightened of possible threats, from humiliation to exposure to pain, all of which had often been a reality during his years in this and other similar buildings. To protect himself, he had learned to walk quickly, purposefully, as if no one could possibly affect him. As he walked, he kept in his mind's eye an image of himself as he would like to have been. This form that floated beside him was compact and cruel and bulldozed its way down the hall spreading fear. Cowards always long to be the bully, and Wayne imagined snatching up weaklings like a toad darting out its tongue to snare and devour flies. But, of course, this was the thinnest of defenses, and one that left him ever more vulnerable as the slightest cruel act, each act building on the last until Wayne stood, fragile, brittle enough to break.

This day, like every day, began with homeroom, where all students were accounted for and registered as present. Homeroom always began Wayne's sleepy day on a strange but exhilarating note as it was presided over by the young Mr. Zelle. Mr. Zelle's presence was erotic in the extreme for Wayne. Zelle was one of Wayne's fantasy types: a jock covered—literally coated—in black hair. He taught geometry but looked like he should have been a coach, virile but soft, outgoing but with a secret. "I know your secret," Wayne said to himself sitting at the plastic desk. "I don't have proof but I can feel it. You'll never admit it but you can't hide." Wayne knew that they could be, both of them, destroyed by one small admission because what is obvious cannot be prosecuted until admitted, the shame comes with confession. This made Mr. Zelle all the more tantalizing as Wayne floated through the endless fantasies that sustained him here. Wayne stared slyly at the obscene bulge in Zelle's hideous black slacks, almost smelling the strong odors that must have been welling up beneath. "Is he wearing underwear?" Wayne wondered, remembering a few months ago when he snuck in early and wrote a message, in ink, directly onto Zelle's desktop. "I want to suck Zelle," it said. Wayne had watched Zelle's face closely that morning as he walked in, took his desk, and sat down. There was no expression from a face utterly frozen and protected from this dangerous compartment, a face that remained blank and handsome as he calmly pushed his pile of papers to cover the unwanted message from beyond.

The morning announcements had started on the PA system, and Zelle smiled out at the students, feeling revved up. "I fucked her pussy," he repeated over and over in his head, trying to tattoo it all over his face. "I wonder if these brats can tell that I had a great piece over the break. I fucked her pussy till she screamed." And suddenly life was good for Zelle. Suddenly life seemed just about right with those dumb fantasies gone and everything seeming possible—wife, a home, kids, married friends over for dinner, and golf on Saturday. "She sucked my big cock, too." He remembered her red lips all over him and could feel his new presence in the room, could smell the aroma from his manly pits and could finally say, with certainty, that he was a respected member of the community. Zelle even found his heart beating a little faster with the announcement of the basketball team's inclusion in the state finals. "For God and For Country and For Fuckin' Her Pussy Good," the words rolled in his mind as he spread his legs a little farther showing all the kids that big piece of Zelle meat.

Wayne felt better now that the day was actually under way, and made his way through the halls with more ease. The strangest aspect of the school was knowing every single one of the five hundred–or-so fellow students, but only ever speaking to a few of them. There were the distinct groups that every school has: the jocks, the hoods, the socialites, the nerds, and the brains. In this school, those who were apart from the pack found the most security hanging with the brains and making the honor roll or showing some sort of talent. However, Wayne felt more comfortable with the hoods, who accepted him for his willingness to smoke and drink and do most anything to erase the day. The transition to Honorary Hood was a strange and satisfying one because it made Wayne feel a part of something. When the teachers cluck-clucked at the good boy ruining his reputation, or his parents looked askance at his new friends, Wayne felt that he had joined an exclusive club. It also helped that this new club included Carl and Pussy and Eric and several more peripheral boys of the most attractive type. Eric and Carl were a part of what, in Cherokee, passed for a gang. They were called the Treds and were tolerated when they did things just as bad as other groups: drinking, shoplifting, wrecking cars. The Treds were tolerated because they were cute and several of them had rich daddies, Eric included. Wayne had never been allowed in the Treds for unspoken reasons. They were a closed group where he functioned as a sometimes mascot, and that "Kick Me" feel could be very erotic. Wayne loved going to get booze for the boys or paying for pizza or defending them to the teachers. Lately, he was less tolerated by everyone in the group but Carl, so he would cruise with Pussy instead and avoid the boys during their wild weekend escapades. Wayne had also distanced himself because he sensed that one reason he was tolerated by the Treds was that they liked freaks; they liked the outlaw status conferred by allowing a freak to service them. And so Wayne was tolerated but not allowed in, not invited to drop by anytime, not taken along on the road trips, not even told what the secret name—Treds—stood for.

He scanned the hallway trying to catch a glimpse of Pussy's yellow hair. He would see her at lunch because they always had lunch together, no matter what. Unless she called in sick. "Carl, sweet Carl," he thought as he watched a couple of guys lounging against their lockers. Wayne had looked for Carl all morning in the halls, by his locker, or having a smoke in the bathroom. But it was part of his general bad luck that their school schedules rarely coincided. Wayne stepped out of the way as a group of shouting jocks rampaged toward their next class. He felt penned in, defending himself not only from the other students but from the raging teachers who daily tried to warp their charges' minds with a full roster of tricks and weapons. Teachers hate kids, hate those who may one day be happier than they and escape, escape the treading of cold halls until forced retirement and the Sioux Valley Rest Home and, finally, the cold box on Cemetery Hill. The teachers had made their choice—no turning back—but they had their revenge every day on the slow, the vulnerable, the different.

Monday, "slooow, dumb day" thought Wayne. More time in study hall than in class, Monday had the best and the worst: Advanced Literature and Phys. Ed. Wayne walked a little more quickly, not wanting to be "off the green." The short time between classes was indicated with green lights beneath the hall clocks. On went the green light for exactly three minutes, and only then were the students allowed out of classrooms without a pass. Catching kids "off the green" was a favorite pastime of Mr. Courtwright, the vice-principal. He rumbled rather than walked with his pink violation pad grasped in one paw, the other one swinging free like a bat, ready to smash any snot-nosed brat who got lippy. Wayne shuddered, seeing him barreling down the mostly-empty hallway toward him. The green light flickered but stayed on as Wayne rushed on to the safety of the next class. Courtwright's eyes narrowed and gleamed as he saw the little faggot running into the room with only seconds to spare, "You walk, not run, in these halls, mister!"

Mr. Paul Anderson was known to all at the school as Mr. A and had gained a certain amount of respect for his devotion to those unlikely to succeed, who just happened to be mostly the beautiful young hood boys. Mr. A was tolerated as an "eccentric" because the school needed good teachers and he was, for an "eccentric," a good teacher, so they kept him on but also kept a close eye on him. Mr. A taught drama, directing the school plays that Wayne was sometimes a part of, but his most-valued class was Advanced Literature. Lit, as it was called, was a rarefied spot in the school, with only ten students and a reading list made up of the great classics of experimental fiction. There were weekly tests, and, in that week, the students read and discussed books that flowed before them from a place so far away as to be unimaginable. Mr. A had poured his corpulent body into a fuzzy brown sweater and too-tight slacks, with his thin wisps of blond hair combed from just over one ear all the way to the other side of his bald head. Wayne wondered why Mr. A stayed here, here in this dangerous place. There was a long résumé of disasters that Mr. A had always kept hidden from the gossiping mouths of Cherokee. His parents' deaths were a central event in changing everything. There was a clear line in Mr. A's memory separating the day they died and everything before. He remembered clearly the day preceding the loss: how it was possible to be happy about the most inane event, how there had been courage that made everything seem possible. However, a light had been switched off when his father's lungs finally gave way and his mother had followed by her own hand. A loss too soon, too unexpected, too cruel to forgive the world for. After that, Mr. A found that he didn't want to fight anymore; he found fight and struggle seemed ridiculous in the face of it all.

Before Christmas, the students had been reading Virginia Woolf and this week were finishing *Orlando,* a book that the school board would have banned if they ever happened to open its innocent-looking cover and read past the first few pages of the formal, beautiful prose. The class sat dutifully, a certain camaraderie holding sway that was unusual for those who were not football players or cheerleaders, and Wayne wondered if they realized what they'd read over the vacation. It seemed spectacularly forbidden to Wayne, but no one, including Mr. A, had commented on Orlando's transformation from a man to a woman and what that could possibly be a symbol for. "Why did we read it if we're not going to talk about it?" Wayne wanted to ask. Eric slouched in the next seat, looking intently at the book as if he hadn't read it yet, which was entirely possible. Eric had been cultivating a sloppy beatnik look for some time now, with his wispy goatee and rumpled black shirt and a smell like he hadn't washed that morning. A vaguely sour odor crept from his greasy hair.

The class's assignment was to write a three-page essay on *Orlando,* and they sat dutifully poised to begin as Mr. A gave his usual instructions, "What I want is not a discussion of plot or theme; we've already covered that. What I want is your subjective experience of this book as it affects you, in whatever form that might take." At the same moment, he thought nervously, "What possessed me to assign this book? What a can of worms." Mr. A looked up to see Wayne staring at him, smiling a small, wicked smile. "Don't start with me, you little creep!" he wanted to shriek at Wayne. He rehearsed the tirade he would unleash on the boy if necessary, "I knew you were a troublemaker from the start, you evil queen. Don't take me on because I know how to deal with your type." Mr. A's head was starting to pound with reverberating voices, and everything was just about ready, could just start unraveling without much more pressure, so instead he asked, "Do you have a question, Wayne?"

"I just wondered if we couldn't write about the theme this time," he asked innocently.

"I've made my instructions very clear," Mr. A said with a victorious finality. His tone of voice seemed to have worked but he was spooked by the gesture—or movement—Wayne made in response. He was not quite sure what to call it. After a moment more of staring, the boy's head had just fallen, sort of tipped over to the paper, and he began to write fiercely, with a complete inattention to the rest of the world. "Just jittery," Mr. A reassured himself and, after the holidays, who could blame him. His plan of holing up to read and ignoring the festivities had turned out to be a complete disaster. With a few weeks of relaxation, Mr. A thought everything would sort itself out, that logic and learning would prevail. He had assumed also that it would be a perfect time for things to take their natural course with Eric. With the name in his mind, he looked at Eric. "Absolutely helpless," he thought tenderly. Yet they saw one another only twice during the break, owing to Eric's dreadful family making things tense. The holidays became torturous. A constant litany in his head and the black book had started to fill its pages. Each morning he would wake and carefully open the book to find page after page of hideous rambling. The days had stretched on and on. Unable to read, unable to sleep. Nothing but eating and hypochondria. He could still feel his lungs today. They felt wet inside of him, filled with some vile liquid impeding the clear flow of air. "What a waste," he thought, recounting the days spent laying flat on his back monitoring the progress of his deterioration. He even devised a home lung test by taking one of those heavy plastic freezer bags and seeing how quickly he could inflate it.

"Something is most definitely wrong," he concluded, thinking of his father, dead while only in his late fifties. "I must rearrange my life. Get it in order, finally." And he visualized a line of neat gray boxes on a blond wood shelf. In his mind, he drew labels on each, making compartments. The first one said "Teaching" in mundane block letters perfectly suited to its purpose. The next said "Art" in three italic letters that brought to mind the contents of the box: several unsubmitted manuscripts, memories of directing Beckett in college, the lovely watercolor he had just begun. The box labeled "Health" he simply turned around on the shelf without looking at it. Another box said "Eric/Escape" in a beautiful flowing hand. The contents of the seemingly empty box were precious dreams, floating, sifted through often in this dreary school setting. He took the most comforting fantasy and held it to his large head like a pillow as it wrapped a scene around him of a spartan artist's apartment in Minneapolis decorated with a few posters, a few of his paintings. On the bed lay Eric, waiting for him to come closer. Waiting for Paul to bring his experienced lips down to explore, to give endless days of pleasure to the soft young body. Eric would take hold of Mr. A's head and guide it to the next delicious spot, making Mr. A lick his dark nipples or his firm balls or drawing his legs back and giving over the deep, deep red of his unexpectedly hairy asshole. Mr. A's eyes turned slightly upward in their sockets. But always there was that final box on the shelf, that final complication, a square black box marked with a gold cross and the slips of paper lying inside of it chattering of guilt and retribution and Hell and death and emptiness and a torture that never ends. Looking at the tousled heads of the class, Mr. A felt inside his pocket, fingering the smooth leather of his book that he had never dared bring into the classroom before and felt his hand caressing the pages, drawing it out, drawing it out of his pocket like a tongue from a mouth.

For Wayne, writing was like a trance, learned intuitively. The world drew back from him as anger bubbled around his hand, tingling all over him as the pen moved without thought. The inanities dribbled out of him without his having to pay attention to them. Wayne refused to do his best, refused to make an effort on something so stupid. Instead, his mind ran back through the book, analyzing it in his head since he was forbidden to on paper. "Weird book," he thought. A man who is a prince or a lord or something like that turns into a woman. Everyone worships the man but can't stand the woman. And it's not like this prince made any decision or said, "Think it's time for me to get rid of this dick." It just happened, late at night.

"What do I care?" Wayne thought. "What difference does some book make to me?" And he knew he was right. Wayne knew that those wrinkled pages wouldn't change anything in Cherokee. Wayne knew that everything beautiful in a book is ugly in real life. In his opinion, the most beautiful scene in the book was the one where Orlando was still a man and had gone to visit the king for some reason. They spent the entire winter in huge, gorgeous tents on the frozen river, drinking and dancing. In the passage, the ice was so deep and clear that Orlando could look down and see eels frozen in place where they had been swimming, caught in suspended animation. Beautiful. But real life was another thing. Wayne remembered going ice fishing with his father in Minnesota. There wasn't anything beautiful about the ice. First of all, it was covered in dirty snow so you couldn't see anything. The whole thing was so depressing and creepy from the outset that Wayne had wanted to cry. There they had sat, shivering and looking down into the murky water through the hole they had drilled. His father had caught a sturgeon, a fish that shouldn't be in a lake, a monster fish that should live in the ocean. That sturgeon, that semi-eel, had wrapped itself around his father's arm, wriggling as he tried to get it off the hook. "It's not beautiful when it's real," Wayne thought. "Eels aren't beautiful, and I bet that turning into a woman all of a sudden in Iowa wouldn't be so beautiful, either."

Wayne turned in his paper early, prompting Mr. A to look up wildly from the writing he was doing and ask, "Are you sure you're done?"

"I'm done," Wayne said numbly. He sat staring out the window at the parking lot, waiting for the bell to ring. Scratch, scratch went the pens and pencils in dog-eared notebooks as these teenagers searched through their easy lives for a pain that related to Orlando's. Perhaps they lost a true love at the prom, perhaps they fought with their families; but Wayne felt, however condescending it might have been, that true pain and isolation had not touched them, did not follow every step, sapping the happiness from their lives. Wayne stared directly at Mr. A's bald spot, hating him for his silence, hating him for it all. Mr. A was scribbling something into a small black book. The fat man's forehead was greasy with perspiration as he scribbled away.

The Lord Says:
Finding your lace hankie along the road,
tells me you were here,
and speaks to me in code.

Yet were I to look once again at your face,
I'd slap it, slap it, slap it
and spray it with Mace.

I'd stop just short of filling you with lead,
'cause you're pretty while suffering
but ugly once dead.

When the green light flickered on, Wayne headed directly to the lunchroom, feeling relief because he would see Pussy for the first time after the long Christmas vacation. Pussy's grandmother lived in Fort Dodge, and her family drug her down there between Christmas and New Year's to see the old gal. The room was still relatively empty, as this was the first lunch period. Wayne immediately saw Pussy at their usual table. She was rooting through her purse, with her hair sticking out from static cling in back. "I'm not doing Dexatrim today. Let's eat two lunches," he said into her ear.

"You sexy thing," she yelled and slapped his ass. "I'm so hungry I had to eat a candy bar this morning in class. Of course, Zelle saw me and ragged on me. What's for lunch today?"

"Hot beef sandwiches with plenty of gristle," Wayne said, rolling his eyes. In grade school they had had the best food. Everything was so good. But now you could hardly eat it. Even so, they got into line facing the women with hair nets dishing up the food. These women were much beloved in the school. They seemed to lack the bitterness of the teachers and would chat a little as they loaded the trays. "How was Christmas, honey?"

Back at the table, Pussy seemed a little quiet. "How was Fort Dodge?" Wayne asked.

"Bummer," Pussy said glumly. "You remember that rich salesman I was with at the VF?"

"You mean the one that looked like Grandpa Munster?"

"Shut up," she continued. "Well, I was supposed to wait for my dad to pick me up, but I was getting kind of loaded on all the drinks he was buying me. He said we should go back to his room, but I told him, 'No way, Jose.' Anyway, he said, 'Just a drink, no funny business,' so I said okay. Shit, man, I could hardly stand up by then, so laying down for a cocktail didn't sound so bad. Of course, when we got there, he started feeling my tits right away, and he looked even more disgusting in that fluorescent light."

"What happened then?" Wayne asked through a mouth of mashed potatoes.

"He tore my shirt, and that was his first mistake, because I gave him a boot in the balls he'll never forget. Then I started crying and walked home with my face all smeared up. My dad was waiting up, and that freak, my mother, was shrieking she'd raised a whore. So I just turned around and threw my ripped shirt at her and said, 'That's right, baby. 'Cause I got the goods, and I'm gonna sell 'em.' Guess what the rest of vacation was like."

"We should kill that Grandpa Munster."

"No," Pussy said, "I guess I deserved it."

"No, you didn't," said Wayne quietly. The rest of

lunch was quiet and kind of tender. Neither one of them wanted to leave the safety of the table. They dreaded the bell that ticked closer and closer.

The day dripped along for Wayne, sitting in study hall bored, but gripped with fear while thinking of the last class of the day. The nervousness had bunched up the muscles of his back, making the chair seem even harder than it was. When the inevitable hour came, Wayne rushed to his locker, racing with the green light to get the hated gym bag that contained the black shorts, yellow T-shirt (meant to be a rich gold), tube socks, and jockstrap that were the mandated outfit for gym. Throughout his school years, this hour had been a constant torture for Wayne, at first because his fatness made it hard to run and jump and pull strongly up to the bar to touch his chin. But later, something more hideous, more lethal, began to bear its teeth in the minds of the young men who surrounded him. An urge began to tick in the back of their necks and in their fists and at the side of their mouths that was hatred, fear of those who may be like what they prayed they were not, and the word "fatso" was replaced by "fag" or "fairy" or "faggot." Worse yet were the words that were clinical descriptions of what it was that Wayne knew he wanted. The words that most accurately described his raging desire were the most devastating. "Cocksucker" could cause Wayne to crumble inside, shrinking back away from his skin to a place lit so dimly that no one could see, no one could reach. And in that dim vacuum resided a fury, spewing fantasies of ripping their smooth flesh with knives and hammers and picks. "I'll kill them someday," he often chanted to himself.

Wayne walked quickly to a corner of the locker room

to change, reminding himself that he must look only at the tiled floors or harsh white walls, but never at anyone else in the room. He must not look at the beautiful young bodies around him because one caught glance could have spelled disaster. Yet he did see the strong body of Chuck, the boy who had acted as his main torturer for years, their roles defined and set. Chuck pulled off his slightly dirty underwear to reveal fields of black hair sprouting around a huge cock that, as always, was slightly hard. "Why can he have a hard-on and everyone is impressed, but if I got hard, they'd kill me?" he wondered, gazing surreptitiously while tying his shoes. Wayne's eyes were fixed on the tangled jockstrap trying to cover the white flesh and red flesh and black hair and the cockhead sticking fiercely out the side of the pouch. Perversely, Chuck attracted him in the never-ending cycle of abuse, respect, and desire, and Wayne often dreamed of Chuck finally taking his body, abusing it inside and out, turning the pain into something else. Chuck snarled loudly at Wayne as he passed to take a piss, "Hey, who thinks the fag's gonna set a world record today?"

The sound of laughter from the boys issued on cue and the terror began. For this day was the culmination of the cruelest test ever conceived: the Presidential Physical Fitness Test. "Sick," thought Wayne. "I don't know which piece-of-shit president it was who thought up this lousy test but I bet it was Kennedy." Wayne could just hear him yammering, "The youth of our country will build their bodies and their minds in tandem," while all the time the only push-ups Kennedy was doing were on top of Angie Dickinson or Marilyn Monroe. Poor old Jackie was stuck at home with her pillbox-hat collection while randy old JFK was humping anything that would stand still. Wayne thought, "JFK had a lousy body and a tiny dick, I bet, and it's his fault I have to go through this every year." Wayne wondered why the hell they cared how many sit-ups he could do, or how fast he could run.

To increase the embarrassment, each student was tested separately, and the figures were recorded dutifully by Mr. Klingborg, the Chief Nazi Sadist Gym Teacher (his unofficial title) whose fat gut and jowly face showed little sign of physical exertion other than stuffing another Pringle's potato chip past his rubbery lips. Were these results actually compiled in the White House, and did the current president say, "Those boys of Cherokee, Iowa! What fine soldiers and statesmen they'll make with those twenty-five pull-ups! The next leader of the free world can be found among those sprinting figures!" Wayne dreamed of college where Phys. Ed. would be strictly optional and he pored over the course catalog putting big black lines through each jock class he would never have to take.

Over the years, there had been innumerable classes where each captain picked his team with the fatsos and the wimps left until the excruciating last. Even in that sorry group there was a pecking order. To be the absolutely last person picked, with groans coming from the other team members, was something dreaded by all who hold in their stomachs and look unconcerned. Along with the fatsos were the one or two mentally retarded kids in every class, and they presented the ultimate smack in the face. One called Chester could barely stand or walk, yet he was once picked before Wayne for a game of kick ball. Chester's wide, blank face had lit up with joy realizing that, for once, he had won, he had been chosen. Those years train the losers to accept being last. Praying to be forgotten in the final moments of class, Wayne had waited until the latest possible moment to walk over to the chin-up bar with Klingborg's face twitching—almost drooling—at the fantastic torture he was about to see. Wayne saw his own arms as frail little twigs next to the bruisers who could haul their carcasses up to the bar twenty and thirty times. This was the hardest exercise anyway, he reminded himself. His fingers wrapped languorously around the cold metal tube, feeling exhausted and soft. Klingborg bellowed, "Come on, be a man for once." The teacher stoked the hate everyone felt for the loser and urged them on to greater violence.

The air in the gym felt moist, sweaty with the emotion directed at Wayne's back as everyone gazed at the part of him they detested the most. Chuck was looking, too, looking hard and wanting to yell, "Look at the arms, those fuckin' toothpick arms and that goddamn flabby middle. I wish I could punch out that girly, swishy face with those pukin' eyelashes fluttering, 'Oh, please don't hurt me. Waah, waah!' Come on, guys, let's put this freak out of his misery. Nobody wants you here, freak. Why don't you go back to your plays and your debate team and your faggy friends? *You're weak!*"

Wayne's body lay utterly limp as he tried to perform the task at hand, swinging back and forth listlessly as sweat ran down his face. "Stare out," he told himself. "Stare straight out into space and look at the lines running to the end of the gym. Just concentrate on those lines and this will be over. This will be over someday. Not so far off," he reassured himself. But instead it seemed endless as he swung slowly in the stale gymnasium air. The boys were laughing so hard they couldn't stand.

Chuck was lying flat on his back, his massive arms splayed over his head, howling with laughter. Klingborg stood directly in Wayne's line of vision, staring into his eyes. There was no hope for this, Wayne thought, and besides the bell had just rung; so he lowered his feet deliberately to the ground and followed his tormentors respectfully into the shower.

This was the arena where they took their pleasure, where they were free to do as they wished. And they wished to do harm, irreparable harm to body and soul. Then it began. Chuck led the way, as usual. Wayne stood mute, naked, not showering. "How did you turn into such a faggy wimp? You fuckin' freak, you make me sick." Wayne turned and looked directly into Chuck's eyes, the wild hate, the sexual excitement, the bulge of neck muscles signaling the horrifying pressure building within. Wayne closed his eyes luxuriously and pursed his lips into a kiss, "Let's see what you can do, big man." Out whipped Chuck's damp towel in a blurred arc as the boys screamed with laughter. Out whipped the rough white cotton, leaving a vicious red welt on the fat-boy stomach, then on the fat-boy leg, then just above the fat-boy elbow. The rhythm of snap, thud, snap, thud echoed in the tiled room as Wayne stood frozen, receiving each increasingly distant blow. Wayne's mind switched off and he no longer felt the blows, he just saw words written on a scrap of paper. "I'm not here now. I'm gone. Gone forever and nothing will ever fix this wrong. The score will never be even. I will hate you forever and I will leave this place and never come back. I will always hate you and hate this town and hate my life here. Hate will be the one constant in my life." Finally the blows lessened out of boredom, and Wayne opened his blurry eyes to see

Chuck's face peering at him like a specimen. Chuck's lids opened and closed lazily with pleasure while he leaned close and said, "You make me sick!"

Wayne was the last out of the locker room after the final bell of the day rang, releasing the boys and girls from the brick-and-concrete bunker of Washington High School. They rushed, strong and refreshed, through the doors while Wayne stood at the exit, staring at the parking lot through stone-dry eyes. He saw the cars maneuver quickly out of the lot. Girls with huge manes of blow-dried hair tossed their heads in the afternoon cold, proud to be a part of this clique or that. Staring through the clear Iowa air, Wayne watched Carl walk sturdily to a car. "He's leaving with boys who hate me," Wayne realized. And Wayne knew that the hateful boys would be young men who would be men who would be old men who would never speak to him and his sort with any respect in this town. No matter what he achieved, because it was a fag who had achieved it. Because a fruit/freak/cocksucking/wimp/blowfly/faggot/buttfucker/asslicker/no-balls fairy had achieved it. Wayne saw Carl's beautiful form pass from hope through the shattering, glittering, Iowa air.

In junior high school, Wayne would walk to Selma's every day after school and wait for his mother to get off work. Those were comforting, regular afternoons, and today Wayne felt the need to repeat the ritual. Walking down to his red car in the nearly-empty parking lot, Wayne thought of the route he would take all those years ago. The fat boy would waddle down past Main Street and then take alleys the rest of the way. The alleys would take him past the back of the dry cleaner's, and he would stop by the steam vent because he liked the clean smell that came out, especially on winter days when the moisture would pour up into the sky. The walk also led past the solemn funeral parlor with its imposing white columns by the entrance. He would make his way to the comfortable destination, winding and winding down to Selma's run-down block through alleys he had ridden his bike through for years.

Today Wayne drove rather than walked and shot through the little town quickly to Locust Street. He parked on the street because Jim had a tendency to back right into a car parked behind his in the driveway. Selma had covered her windows with thick plastic to keep out the drafts, and it seemed that nothing had changed, that the years had trapped her life until it was unchangeable. Going in the porch, Wayne welcomed the sight of the warm kitchen with Selma at her usual place. "Well, my goodness, Wayne," she said, looking up from her little juice glass covered with pictures of sunflowers. It wasn't juice in the glass. Past three and the whiskey hour had arrived. "I'm just trying to finish this dang poem for *Ideals* magazine. Come on in out of the cold. Jim went up to get some Lotto cards at the store."

Wayne felt awkward now that he was here, hauling along the emotion of the day and not feeling the relief of forgetfulness yet. "What's your poem about, Grandma?"

"Well, I'll tell you. It's a newfangled one. Nothing rhymes. Oh, they must think I'm a nut when I send these in. This poem is about you, honey." Selma had set hot water and a bottle of instant coffee on a folded paper napkin for Wayne. "Do you want some sunshine cookies?"

"Yeah, I'd like some," said Wayne, happy that Selma still cooked one good item, the buttery sugar cookies she called "sunshines." "What do you mean the poem's about me?"

"I don't know if you remember," Selma slurred a bit as she wrapped her bony hand back around her drink, "but when you were little you had a pair of bright red overalls. Oh, you were so cute in those pants! You would come over—couldn't have been more than three or four—and sit on my steps and play. You'd go to the driveway and get your little hand full of gravel. You'd tiptoe back over to the steps and pour the pebbles on the porch and laugh and laugh. You thought that was some adventure. I can remember you standing there so clearly. Like I said, the poem's a sad one. The first part is about you as a little boy, and then, before I know it, you're all grown up and ready to go to college in the big city."

Wayne didn't quite know what to say to this, so he just chewed the slightly stale cookie and drank the coffee. It was really the last conversation he wanted to have today. "Everybody grows up, Grandma," he mumbled, wanting to end this.

"But I can remember that like it was yesterday," Selma plowed on. "I can't imagine where all those years went to. Do you really want to leave good old Cherokee?"

"I really do," Wayne said softly as the air seemed to get thicker in the kitchen.

"Now, what does that city have that Cherokee doesn't? You won't know anybody there." Selma would not leave a subject alone once she had started in on it, and now she had taken up a toothpick to clean the crack in the table, a bad sign.

"There's nothing for me here, Grandma. I'll come back and visit. You can come visit me, you know."

"Oh, my goodness, what would they make of an old goose like me in the city? I'd be so busy gawking up at those big buildings, I'd get run over."

Selma's art was strewn everywhere in the kitchen.

Lately she had started making Apple Doll Men and Ladies. “Say Wayne, did I show you this little old Apple Doll Lady I just made? She is so cute. I just love her.” The Apple Doll Lady was made from peeling an apple and then putting it into a low heat oven to dry. The shriveled brown apple became the deep, wrinkled head of the doll. This doll had been outfitted with poofy white hair, a bonnet, and a calico dress over a pipe cleaner body. “Ain't she cute?” Selma shrieked.

“She's great. What will you do with her?”

“Oh, probably try to sell the darn thing on *Swap Shop*.”

As Wayne looked at the shriveled apple face, it started to look a little too real. The whole day had come to a miserable end. He was forced to admit that his old grandma couldn't help anymore, even though her ring sat on his finger, even though she still loved him. “Well, Grandma, I just stopped to say hi. I'd better get home.”

“Okay, honey, you be careful driving on those slick streets.” Selma stood on the porch, poking her big head out and waving as he drove away. The streetlights had switched on in the early dusk of winter. Christmas decorations were still hung on the lampposts on Main Street. Driving down the street, Wayne felt that there wasn't another person in the world. And, seeming to agree, the foil angels bowed their sad golden heads against the winter wind.

III.

Friday and Saturday nights were set apart from the rest of life in Iowa. Even though they are often boring, these two nights held the potential for adventure that might bring danger into a too-safe world. There are two types of danger—physical and mental—and both were always available, even in a town of six thousand. As for physical danger, the most likely was to smash up against a wall after driving dead drunk, which many did with great abandon in Iowa. One of the most popular attractions at the county fair each year was the Highway Patrol Drunk Driving Booth. The booth featured a slide show of the most gruesome accidents caused due to alcohol. An inordinate number of the accidents involved train collisions in which the car was sliced like a loaf of bread by the train. It always seemed that a lot of lives could have been saved by outlawing the railroad. Also popular at the Highway Patrol booth were the classic snowmobile decapitation accidents consisting of drunken snowmobilers who didn't see the barbed-wire fence and *riiiiip,* there it goes bouncing down the hill.

Although few in Iowa would have admitted it, mental hazard was more probable than physical injury. Unlike the ripped throats and severed limbs, the external effects of mental trauma are subtle. One sees only a smoothing of the personality take place, a sanding off of the temperment's rough edges. With each inward slash, the human becomes calmer in appearance, slower in movement, softer in speech. Each emotional wound takes away a unique characteristic and leaves something closer and closer to a blank emptiness within. Iowa society strives toward comfortable uniformity, and emotional torture is an effective tool in slicing off extremities. So clean, and no stitches needed. And on these two nights when dramatic change was possible, Friday and Saturday pushed some further outside, while luring others permanently back into the fold.

Carl was standing in the shower. A long, hot shower. He was lathering his body without feeling it. He ran the soap obsessively under his arms and in the crack of his ass. He liked it less when he had to wash around his dick because it hardened and excited him and washing was serious, not meant to be sexual. Carl feared stinking. His brother stank atrociously, a sweet stench rising from him even when clean. They could never figure out that stink, but Carl decided that he would never risk it. Sometimes Carl's skin was raw from the washing, but still he continued the hours in the basement shower stall by his room. He loved it there, anyway. The tin walls were his private sanctuary where he turned slowly, displaying his magnificent body for all to admire. In the tin room, he was no longer stupid, no longer doomed to work in a Safeway. But he was not free. Not free to let his hand explore as it liked while he washed. Not free to think clearly whose mouth he would have liked to substitute for the hand. Not free because of memories of a brother who was too free, who had suffered.

All over town, young men's bodies were being prepared for the weekend, and Eric was also passing the time bathing. But for Eric, this was an unusual experience, a disliked experience of sloughing off the oily sheen of his white skin. Eric liked the comfortable dirt to pile up on him, so on the rare occasions when he felt the necessity to bathe, he turned it into an aesthetic experience. The bathtub was filled with strange-smelling oils and spices. The stereo blasted out Simon and Garfunkel while he imagined himself in an exotic Turkish bath, attended by beautiful girls. In Eric's naïveté, he never realized that the attendants of Turkish baths were actually hairy brutes who delivered more of a beating than a massage. Unlike Carl, Eric was not afraid to pay full attention to his genitals, even to the extent that nothing else really got washed. He was also not afraid to imagine the mouth of his girlfriend instead of his hand rushing up and down on his red cock. Eric poured handfuls of hot, soapy water over the fur that encased his stomach, getting off on seeing the hair rush from side to side like seaweed. He lay back and let his hand tremble around his balls and then work the dripping head of his cock slow, real slow, baby. Eric would finish his bath and wait upstairs in his room for his girl, his woman, his sexy morsel to arrive and service him. He would wait while the shreds of come dried and crinkled up in the sleek hair of his legs.

A third figure also prepared in a bath. Not so young. Not such a beauty. But a romantic figure. Mr. A also floated in a bath, a corpulent island of pale skin dotted here and there by a red blemish and brown hair. There were no plans for the night, or the next night, or any night, so he resolved to stay in the tub all weekend as an experiment. Mr. A would conduct a scientific study on the prolonged effect of normal tap water on human skin. Perhaps, he thought, it would be a wonderful youth cure, hydrating away ten years. Perhaps, though, his skin would actually dissolve, leaving only the internal him finally leaking out, unrestrained by an outer sheath. Whatever the results, he knew that inevitably the weekend would progress in the same way as all the others. Tortured or just bored, he would get out the big decorative candle from under the bed, grease it up, and shove it violently into himself until the relief came. Mr. A knew that the staff at Kmart carefully watched his purchases in the home-decoration department. Why, when he started, Mr. A was purchasing candles so tiny that they could have been used on a birthday cake. Then the tasteful cream-colored tapers. "But now," he thought, "my Lord, it looks likes I'm buying for the chandeliers of Henry V with these massive black brutes of wax. That is for later. Wait. For now, I will float."

With the soft lapping of the water, Mr. A began to hum a slow, dirgy kind of tune somewhere between a prayer and a pop song. The humming echoed in the hard empty corners, bouncing off white porcelain surfaces. The water washed over his face in a wave and then again as he sank into the depths of the tub, the water unable to sustain his bulk. The song was taking shape now, even underwater, and the tones were beginning to attach themselves to words as the room grew fuzzy, finally disappearing. In the haze, Mr. A saw a boy, a naked boy spotlighted from behind on a stage. A terrible, tawdry kind of stage such as he had seen in Minneapolis, and this boy was singing into a microphone, singing in a dead voice:

Come on, baby, come on.
I'm waiting for your love, baby.
Come on.

Oh, baby,
it's been too long,
baby. Come on.

Because if you don't come now, baby, I'll wait for you your whole life. Got my ice pick in your brain, baby, and I can wait. I can wait. I can wait as long as it takes, baby.

Come to Daddy, baby.
Come on, baby, come on.

Mr. A's lungs screamed for him to surface, but his blank eyes just stared through the water at the fluorescent ceiling light as the boy's voice took him farther and farther down a road. His fat body rolled back and forth slowly in the bath like an overloaded tanker. Mr. A was far, far away from the world now, and the weekend had just begun. As he surfaced, he pulled in breath with a noise that was both a gasp and a sob.

Highway 71, which ran through town, seemed slick and cold to Wayne as he swung his red car onto it and headed to the south side of town. On Friday night at 9:00, the streetlights glared orangish and the cars had begun to travel the circuit back and forth through town, their wheels cutting slushy lines in the snow. The drink of choice for the last few weekends had been Strip-'n'-Go-Nakeds, a noxious concoction made of equal parts vodka, beer, frozen lemonade, and lime soda. The drink had an unequaled ability to cause teens to black out major parts of the evening and to lie in a darkened room for the majority of the next day. As Wayne poured out a Strip from the silver thermos, he pushed in the unwieldy eight-track tape of David Bowie's *Heroes* and heard the song slash out from the car's scratchy speakers, "We can be heroes—if just for one day." "Strange that David Bowie could wear dresses and eye shadow and be a star," Wayne thought. "Strange that, when you get on TV, you can do anything and they can't touch you."

Wayne passed by Main Street, nearly deserted as usual, and through the old section of town that was built around the railroad station. It was easy to envision the excitement that must have welled up in this town on a weekend night fifty years ago: big, furry men knocking 'em back at the Twilight Lounge. Strange couplings arranged in bars and greasy restaurants like the one where Selma had once worked. The old Red Door Restaurant was a filthy place and Selma had a thousand stories to tell about it. Selma worked there after she had left Glen and his brother with their alcoholic father in Sutherland, a town even smaller than Cherokee. Selma worked as a waitress, carrying a meal for four at one time, plates of hot beef sandwiches lined along her arms, little bowls of green beans clutched in each hand. "Oh, that filthy goddamn dive!" she would exclaim at the slightest urging. Her best story was about the sheet of tin that wrapped along the edge of the long counter, extending a few inches down along the front. One night, late, after all the customers had left, Selma was sitting at the counter having a piece of cherry pie. Selma's tired eyes wandered down to the tin strip, drawn by a slight motion. Selma couldn't believe what she saw, couldn't explain the constant waving motion at the edge of the tin strip that looked as if it had been lined with velvet. Thousands and millions of tiny black legs waved a welcome to her, jutting out from behind the counter. Her hands were drawn down, unable to resist the sight that disgusted her and, as she touched the tin strip lightly, it fell away from the counter, releasing a flood of cockroaches and water bugs and silverfish and other assorted monsters such as couldn't be believed. Selma screamed, falling backward in the insect tidal wave that must have been building for years and rushed from the restaurant, vowing never to work in the restaurant business again. "Those filthy goddamn Greeks owned it!"

The filthy Greeks may have owned the place for a while, but they were driven out, like every other intruder. The Jews came, but no one would give them a job, so they left. The blacks came and were not even allowed to get out of their cars. The Chinese doctor was hired by the Nut Hut before they realized what he was. (What kind of name did they think Wong was?) Only the Germans and the Irish and the cold white Nordics were allowed because they did not see themselves as German and Irish and Nordic. They thought of themselves as just American, or relatively American, compared to the dark skins of eastern cities. They forgot what they were. They believed that they had always been Americans. If the others came, they'd know what to do.

They make us uncomfortable. We don't know why, but we don't like those people, and that's all we need to know. Protect the family, protect the kids. From everything different—even slightly different.

Wayne passed the river that flooded Selma's neighborhood each spring and took the road into the Fishman Addition, a little housing area composed of straight rows of prefab houses sitting south of town. Pussy's neighborhood. As a hood, Pussy smoked, drank, and embraced anything she was told to keep away from—such as getting fucked regularly and thoroughly by one of the town cops. At nine o'clock, Pussy had long ago finished her showering and makeup. As a hood woman, her hair treatment and makeup were vitally important to her look. Every other Tuesday night, she gave her hair a wash with the shampoo from the special bottle filled halfway with Johnson's Baby Shampoo and halfway with peroxide. She let the mixture sit on her naturally mousy hair for fifteen minutes—no more—and then rinsed thoroughly. This routine kept her hair nearly white, except in the sun, where it glowed with a slightly greenish cast. The hair was put around hot rollers first and then blow-dried with a round brush to achieve the biggest of big hair. Although high, Pussy's hair was not dense; you could catch an occasional glimpse of her pink scalp lying beneath the marshmallow covering.

Pussy looked at the mirror with kissy lips, her hair floating around her head. Her stereo was playing

Meatloaf's "Paradise by the Dashboard Light," and she thrust her tits out, swinging her hips, and squirted a breath of Love's Baby Soft right between her legs. The cop loved that sweet smell when he ate her out, and she fully intended to have someone's tongue in there by the end of the night. Her mother pounded on the door. "Turn down that music, you whore!" So she turned up the music and gyrated faster. She would stay here in her room until she heard Wayne's car horn. Pussy wriggled into tight jeans and, just before pulling on her blouse, turned once more to the mirror, saying, in her most seductive voice, "You're the queen, baby, the queen."

Pussy was Wayne's best cruising companion, and they always reserved Friday nights for each other. Pussy's house was especially ugly, with no shrubs or trees on the lot to hide the fact that the house was dumped whole in its present position. Her parents were such freaks that Wayne never went in to get her but honked from out front. Pussy immediately emerged in her thigh-hugging jeans, a tight white shirt, and a hideous parka. Her mother's face could be seen glaring through the triangular window in the front door, her mouth moving slowly and talking about sin, retribution, and Jesus.

"Hey, Pussy," Wayne said as she slopped into the front seat and reached straightaway for the thermos of drinks. "Little thirsty tonight?"

"My fuckin' mom tried to bust me," she said in between gulps. "She heard about the cop and said if she caught me down at the VFW with him again, I was gonna get thrown out."

"She's jealous because she's not gettin' any dick at home," he told Pussy, knowing that any suggestion of her mother and a dick would elicit screams of laughter.

"She thinks she's fuckin' Saint Wet Pants sitting in her cardboard house collecting welfare checks," Pussy shouted, ready for another drink. "I should tell her that Dad's givin' head to that waitress up at the Happy Chef. Let's go! I'm gonna get some action tonight!"

The cruising loop started out by the bowling alley near Pussy's house and extended all the way north to the Kmart parking lot at the other end of town. The north side of town contained all the hangout places: Godfather's Pizza, Happy Chef Restaurant, Dairy Queen, and, recently added, Roy Rogers. Wayne was keeping an eye out for Carl's brown car, and Pussy leaned against the window looking for any boy action that might drive by. They had never discussed it but Pussy knew well enough that Wayne could be only a friend to her. Yet Pussy never dreamed that he would actually touch another man. Maybe she did think of it and found it erotic or disgusting or just strange. Wayne firmly believed that he would never want to have sex with Pussy, but he thought often enough about that cop screwing her and the way the cop's big ass stretched the butt of his pants so that there was a white line at the seam, straining to keep those fat hairy cheeks under wraps while leaning over the bar at the VFW.

"I heard that Miss Socialite Stephanie is preggers," Wayne said, starting in on one of their favorite targets.

"Oh, yeah? Who's the father—our Lord Jesus? She makes me sick with her little holier-than-thou comments about my clothes. She should be more concerned with her ugly hair that looks exactly like pubic hair, if you ask me. She's been porking Tim for years in between going to confession and winning those stupid 4-H prizes. What she needs is a real man. I can just see her if she got a big fat dick between her legs. She'd be testifying and rolling her eyes. Shit, they'd have to call for an exorcist! I'd like to see her gettin' it from the cop. You know, he has this big tuft of hair right where his back turns into his ass that is just perfect to hang on to. Right when he's getting ready to come, I give that a yank as hard as I can. Whoo, does he let out a yell!"

"You're making me sick," said Wayne, wanting to hear more.

"Oh, baby, Stephanie doesn't know what it's like to have a big man rolling around on top of you and kissing you. The other thing I love about the cop is his legs. He has this real soft hair all over his legs, but I mean all over. Kind of like a great big cat. Jesus, that feels great."

"You don't have a bun in the oven from the cop, do you?"

"Shit, no! I'm still taking the pill, even though my mother tries to throw them away every chance she gets." Pussy's mother had joined the Holy Rollers who seemed to be taking over the town. Although there was hardly any sin to root out, these people sifted through every pile looking for it. If there was no sin to be found immediately in Cherokee, they turned to books or TV and shrieked about a movie star's tits or immoral passages in textbooks. *What to do late at night when all the lights are finally out and no one can see and they can feel their dicks between their legs and they know they want to touch it as they grasp the sheets trying to think of family values but they know that dick is down there getting real big, and oh, just a touch, but now can't stop and the pastor is playing with his balls and feels so good, big heavy balls and what would the congregation think, but what about that beefy choirboy and now that finger slips up his ass and the head of the DAR finds herself with one finger in her pussy and another wiggling in her tight butt. There they lay and the fingers are darting and their mouths gaping and what to do, how to stop, how to make the want go away? No turning back but caught now and the juices start to flow, the holes are loose and wanting and there's nothing for it but to give, to give and for her to think of that butch number that works at Safeway and how she'd like to rub, to rub, to rub pussies with her, back in the produce, back by the potato sacks, back by the feminine-hygiene sprays ready to go on the shelf. And there they lay twitching, fighting until the juices spurt out of their holes in a horrible release and the guilt begins. The guilt builds so that tomorrow they will root out the homosexuals, take* Penthouse *off the newsstands, stop that lascivious new sitcom, and be admitted into the House of God.*

"These drinks make me feel good and mean," Wayne fake-snarled, and he could see from Pussy's blurry smirk that she wanted some trouble too. "Let's go look at some cars," he suggested and she snorted. They drove down the highway to Peck's Autos, which stupidly left its lot wide open at night so the cute husbands and wives could admire the Caddies and Lincolns they would buy someday. Motoring around to the far side, slowly passing the economy models to see the real showboats, they felt like priests or mass murderers. They felt like prostitutes or judges. They felt like child abusers or the criminally insane. But most of all they felt like someone had stuck a hand under the skin on their faces and just ripped it back, tore away all the covering from the nerves and they could feel the pain, the lonely rack of their hearts, the pounding between their legs. They could feel now.

"Well, honey, do you think that beautiful white Caddy will be big enough for your giant jugs and all the kids?" Wayne asked.

"Oh, gee, sweetheart, I think I can squeeze my tits in there," she proclaimed sweetly. "But, you know what? I'm a little concerned that with the twins coming, we won't have enough room in back. Let's look a little closer."

They pulled up to the Caddy until the front bumper was almost touching the passenger door. "Can you see now, lovebucket?" Wayne asked.

"A little closer, you fucker! Get me right up on my new fuckin' Caddy!"

The tires screamed as the car rushed forward and slammed into the pristine white door. Pussy let out a whoop. "Show me again, baby." Back they went and in again at a sharper angle, fast, hearing the sick crunching thud of metal folding in on itself. They pulled back to fully admire the ugly black wound on the white door, chrome jutting out, dripping ripped veiny wires.

"No more Strip-'n'-Go-Nakeds, Pussy," Wayne proclaimed, shaking the empty thermos sourly. "What'll we get now?"

"I like Triple Sec," she said, referring to the nauseating orange liqueur that was supposed to be used only as a mixer. Pussy gulped it right out of the bottle.

"No, I'm too wasted already. I'll puke. How about some beer?"

"Okay with me," said Pussy, as she said about any alcohol.

Wayne realized when he drove out of the car lot how drunk he really was. He had the horrible combination of a still-clear head with a disintegrating, rebelling body. His head had already started the throbbing-temple routine from the drinks, and he began to massage the spot on his right temple where a vein bulged obscenely. The loop was slow as they drove along, but then a car rushed past suddenly, too quick to see the driver, and it made him mad. "Why don't they slow the fuck down?" he grumbled. Wayne drove looking intently at the center line in the road and remembering the drunk driving videos from the fair. He imagined a series of disasters that could befall them. Head-on collision—too boring. Bending around a light post—been done. Smashing into a pedestrian—no pedestrians in Iowa.

The Come-N-Go was the best spot to buy beer because they didn't ask for ID, and even though Wayne and Pussy were both now legally old enough to buy beer, they continued to go there. One of the reasons that it was so easy to buy beer there was that Wayne's other "grandmother" worked there. Janine was not really his grandmother, but his Grandfather Harold's second wife. Because of Janine, family relations on his mother's side were strained. When Harold drove a school bus part time, he met Janine (or the Pig, as Ann called her) and soon moved on to having an affair with her when she was a senior in high school. Wayne's grandmother (and not Selma because Selma never divorces, she just kills the bastards) divorced Harold immediately and moved to California, which had always been her dream anyway. Janine was an apparition—over two hundred pounds and the butchest biker dyke you'd ever want to see. She rode her Harley ("Hog") through town in men's clothes and was absolutely filthy. Janine was no longer allowed in Wayne's house ("I don't want that fat Pig in my living room"), but she continued to fascinate Wayne because of the few days he spent alone with her when he was young. On those days, as soon as his grandfather left the house, Janine would get out the porno magazines and sex books and let Wayne read what he wanted. His favorite, driving him into the bathroom to jerk off after every few pages, was *The Joy of Sex*. She once told the repulsive story of using one of the sex tricks (The Whirlwind) in the book on his grandfather. The Whirlwind consists of covering a man's dick and balls with Dreamwhip (or real whipped cream, but not in Iowa) and then licking it off until he comes. "Trouble was, Grandad couldn't keep a boner 'cause it was so cold!"

"Pussy, could you get the beer? I can't look at Janine tonight," Wayne explained and she happily agreed to get a six-pack of Bud.

He shut off the car as she got out and let the cold silence close in quickly. Wayne turned the power to the tape player back on and pushed in another tape, one his mother had left in the car. Patsy Cline. Corny, but somehow just right, so comforting right then. He sang along softly, "I stop to see a weeping willow. Crying on his pillow. Maybe he's crying for me." Patsy was and is an icon, a goddess, every queen's secret drunken persona. Wayne thought of Patsy in that tight lavender dress, finishing up another night at a no-good saloon and going home to her man. Patsy climbed the stairs of the walk-up, opened the door, and found the apartment empty. "No one home for Patsy," he thought.

"Granny says hi," Pussy hooted, startling him. She was back with the beer and had popped one open already. "Nice music. Really puts me in a good mood."

"I want to find Carl," he said, ignoring her.

"Go to the bowling-alley parking lot," she said, excited at the prospect of studly little Carl. "He's always parked out there eventually."

Wayne didn't listen, but drove as best he could, feeling truly ill. Feeling violently sick in a weary, wasted way. "Let this night end," he prayed, but knew it couldn't yet when nothing had happened. Must have an end point. Must have Carl here and try and tonight it will happen.

The bowling alley had closed and the parking lot was nearly empty, but Pussy's prediction was magically true. They spotted Carl's brown Gremlin parked at the far end. They honked and Pussy had her head out the window, screaming and showing her tits while the car spun around on the icy pavement, doing "doughnuts"—so called for the marks the maneuver made. Carl was out of his car when they finally pulled up beside him, and Wayne looked at his solid form, tried to devour it but it was blurry, he couldn't see well and he gulped the rest of the beer.

"Hey, Carlster get your butt in here," Pussy yelled, flinging open the door and leaning forward so that Carl could slip past her into the backseat.

And for Wayne it was like going underwater, silent, and all he could hear was the voice in his own head; a voice but not his own voice that babbled on and on—"He is here now and I can't hear myself, can't hear what makes him laugh but only see a face that is everything in my mind, that opens a catalog of what I love best about him, starting with that white skin topped with gold and moves on to what I can imagine under that black leather jacket and filled-out jeans. I look at you and drink more and make ready, but it's fading, fading from me and I'm not looking at you but the black of your jacket that is the black of my eyelids, closed for just a moment. A rustling and I hear the motor switched off and hear nothing else, hear nothing but the beat, beat, throb of my head. We can be heroes...I remember... standing...on the wall.... We can be heroes...just for one day. Must wake and must see him and talk and make this night work."

Wayne's eyes floated open. It was later but he didn't know how much later but the front seat empty and the windshield were covered with a fine, frosty mist, glass opaque and soft. Pussy was gone but the car rocked, groaned, rocked, and he felt he must look back but no, must see, but no. The form of Pussy huddled on the floor. Her head moved in a rhythm that slapped his eyes away and now to the rearview, can't look, but in the mirror the sight worse because now only Carl's beautiful hard face with eyes closed and face drawn in pleasure. Smeary glossy lips riding a white shaft and the humpf, humpf, humpf of gasped breath, and the voice again—"in ecstasy that I never give, cannot give in this place, doomed to stay and not now and not ever will I, will he. Outlawed and denied my life, my life taken away by this cruel piece of dry land place in the middle of cruel nowhere and no escape. Please let it end, please let this life end for me while I can still bear it, while I can still think, before the last bit is destroyed with no chance. This life will never end but always alone and like Mr. A, eventually pushing the blond wisps, dragging the few strands over baldness, over the stinking rot of my vomit."

"Fuck you, fuck you both!" Wayne heard his voice bubble as he swung out of the door, vomit rushing out his mouth, exploding over his lips and down his front.

So sick couldn't bend, could only fall into it and run, must run from this place and his face was wet with tears and spitting mumbled half-words. Wayne could hear their voices as they chased him and tried to catch him. "Too late!" Too late for all that. The voice whispered a few last words—"Let me fall and end, put an end to all this as my feet rebel and disappear and my eyes make a last crazy arc across the sky as the ground rushes black toward me."

Dark then and then light. Then the light of his house and the sound of a car pulling away as the door loomed and Wayne turned the knob; not look, not care. Into the house and the kitchen and crash went a chair as he stumbled past it, crash and the dog barked and he thought, "All I need!" His father would sleep through a nuclear attack—no danger there. The house was too small for privacy. He heard stirring, knew his mother would come out and prayed that she wouldn't. "Not now," he whispered. "Please not now." To the table and got the case to remove his eye, his eyes, to pull out the little saucers of glass that floated under half-closed lids. A pull at the lid and a sick wet pop and one glass sliver floated into his hand, into the case. Now one more pull and a sharp stab of pain.

He thought he wouldn't look at her and she'd go. "Is everything okay?" Don't respond, just concentrate on getting it out but it had gone sliding off under the lid, up in the top nasty parts of the eye, the sliver wedged and a groan as he yanked the lid of his eye and a sick slide down now to the bottom of the eye socket, this little menace hiding in him. He felt the small lump and thought he could get it if she would just stop, if she would leave. "Honey, let me help you. You'll hurt yourself."

His head heaved to the side and up and his mouth spoke without him, "Leave me alone." A flat dead voice. "Just leave me alone." The world can change with a word, destroyed and remade. Just wanted it to stop.

His mother's face was too hard to look at now. The pain and he could see what she saw, a ruined life, a worthless life before her and only love, only pain. "Tell me what's wrong. I'm not mad. I just want to help."

"You can't help," and he wished his voice weren't rising to an ugly, angry pitch. "Nobody can help me. Just fucking get out of my face. I don't want your help!"

"Don't scream at me. Just come on and go to bed. Give me your clothes, now, they're a mess."

"Don't ever touch me again! You don't want to help. Never have, never wanted to know. I hate this place so much it makes me sick. I hate Iowa and this house and I hate you. I'm getting out of here pretty soon and don't ever ask me to come back." And while he screamed, a separate, parallel voice pleaded in his head with one word over and over, "No, no, no, no, no, no, no..."

The world was gone and his mother's face was gone then but he could hear her voice choking, "You know, honey, you're not the only one who's ever had a hard time. We all do what we have to." A soft black throbbing world had replaced it all, it all. Only the throb and a faint echo of his mother's voice as he pulled himself down the hall toward the waiting bed.

"Please, honey, we have to leave for Canada this week, and I don't want to leave you like this. I'm sorry we have to go and leave you like this, but you know we love you. Please don't act like this. I'm so worried about leaving you."

His growling voice trailed back behind him: "Don't worry about me. I'll be just fine alone."

IV.

It had been a strange, weary sort of time that had slipped past Wayne lately. It was the sort of time that could have been luxurious spent lolling in the summer sun, too lazy even to move; but with the chill of winter still in the air, the hours took on a disjointed quality. Especially in Iowa, where March is so determinedly grim with an icy shell still frozen over the snowdrifts, reflective time alone can push one too deep, take the explorations too far. In March the silence echoed in Wayne's house without the discrete noises of his parents and the dog and the cat. Freedom that should have invigorated him became instead a kind of mourning for something lost and for something yet to occur. Wayne felt that some tragedy had managed to slip past without notice. He felt his heart pound each time he realized his parents were gone, really gone.

Gone to Canada like each year, but also gone for good. Each week, on Sunday, the telephone rang and they talked about the weather, but never breathed a word about things gone wrong, problems left unresolved.

Each year the good-byes in the driveway were traumatic but this year they had had the ring of finality. There are key moments in life and they knew one had occurred. Ann especially knew it while she was packing the brown cardboard boxes with pots, pans, canned corn, soup, clothes, and alarm clocks. Every item that went into a labeled box moved her a bit farther away from her son because this time there would be no coming back to find him in the house in the fall. The three of them stared at each other that day knowing that they had missed a chance. The red pickup was loaded down with all the possessions that migrated each year between Ontario and Iowa, nothing else left but that excruciating moment of good-bye. Wayne wondered how the world could have changed had a flood of words been exchanged in the cracked driveway. There would be no second chance, and each one would remember tiny details from that day. Ann would remember how cold the wind was as it blew a speck of dust into her eye, which made her eyes start to water, which made the real tears begin. Glen would remember looking at the peeling paint around the storm gutters on the house and adding painting to his list of things to do the next year. Wayne remembered how tired his parents looked, how old in the dreary spring light.

To Wayne, the house was more barren than ever with even the little comforts gone. Who would have thought he'd miss the hideous potted plant in the yellow macramé hanger? Who would have thought he'd miss the constant gurgle of the Mr. Coffee machine?

After they had gone, he'd slept in the basement. The basement seemed less a part of the house to him. From the basement he counted the days to summer, the hours to be passed before escape to college. He had begged the admissions office to let him start in the summer session. "The sooner, the better." The closer these changes came, the more terrifying they seemed to him. And a slow ripping sound started in his head the day his parents left. A sound that had softened but not subsided. It was the sound of wet fabric tearing, of opening a zipper, of a blow to the flesh, the feel of taking a good shit. Nothing would ever be the same, and he was glad. Afraid, but glad to be in the house alone, take off his clothes, and lie naked in the living room.

Alone, finally, the night was a mysterious time in the house when anything could have happened if only there had been something to happen in Iowa. Left alone in a house, many men invent their strange pleasures with ropes and bare bodies and steel tools and quiet rituals. That was how Wayne looked at the empty rooms when the sky darkened and the driveway was an invitation for someone to come in. Then, with the gentlest touch, he knew instinctively that the house could be transformed, ruined, remade. He invited Carl and the hoods over, and they loved to drink in the house and get sick, but they never touched. Something about the walls seemed to squash sex. So he stopped eating. For days, Wayne would not eat simply for the enjoyment of seeing his body slowly whittled down. For the first day, he had a pounding headache that could not be relieved by aspirin. On the second day, his head felt hollow, as if it were much too big for the rest of his body and the entire apparatus were in danger of tipping over. And on the third day without food, which was as long as he ever went, his body simply went away. Those third days were when the entire house trembled with expectation because Wayne would have let anybody do anything to his body. On those days, he lay prone on the scratchy living room carpet, naked and waiting for what would never come. On those days, his only company were sounds from the basement, followed by the lights dimming for a moment. And then he would fall asleep to strange dreams. The gnawing stomach allowed only short dreams. Then he would awake again, cold on the floor, listening.

On one particular night he fought off sleep, waiting for a television show he had awaited eagerly for weeks. The show, on public television, was supposedly about pests—mice, rats, cockroaches, etc. But the show was called *The Unseen City,* and it was sure to offer a full hour of scenes from the tawdry side of New York. For Wayne, the city's glamour only increased with dirt and decay. The dirt itself was desperately appealing to a boy whose house was absolutely clean, where the sight of a cockroach would have set off air-raid sirens, where dirt was not now, not ever, never would be tolerated. The show was perfect from the opening shot, high above gorgeous skyscrapers swooping down toward the teeming streets, and further down still, to the sidewalks and burrowing through to the subways. God, what lay below that surface.

The show's first segment dealt exclusively with the subways and stories from the sanitation crews of huge rats and dogs and even the usual stories about alligators in the sewers. But then they actually left the cameras down there. As if on cue, a rat—but no common rat—appeared in the distance. This rat had so much personality. This rat was magnetic, a star. The giant caught the gleam of the camera and swaggered toward it, staring it down, staking out its territory. The face of the rat was terribly animated as it sniffed closer and closer to the foreign object. The whiskery face was alternately coy and sexy, then hostile and demanding. After a long perusal, the rat simply swung its body around, ass toward the camera and pissed on the lens.

The next segment was the highlight. This segment dealt with the horrors of apartment living. It started slowly with a weepy profile of a mother whose baby had been mauled by a rat. Then the cameras returned to the street, and a voice-over narration said, "This is Manhattan's Lower East Side. Life here is a constant struggle for the poor who flock to this neighborhood of immigrants, drug users, and artists." The lushness of those streets washed over Wayne as the screen showed a hot summer night with beautiful dark-skinned men lounging on street corners, hanging from windows, all waiting for something. Then it showed a room with a bed at the center, a small white room, where one of these men lived. The scene progressed in silence as a time-lapse camera with a night lens recorded the man's evening. He lay in bed with shorts and a T-shirt on, falling asleep with only a thin sheet drawn over him in the heat. The parade began. The visitors appeared. First an indistinct black blur across the sheet and it was gone. Then another. Then a little army of cockroaches marched across slowly, right over his undisturbed chest. An enormous inquisitive bug waddled up to his head, taking in the man's aroma. The nasty feelers scratched at the man's neck until an unconcerned swat knocked the bug into the dark. The walls—the walls were crawling, alive.

Wayne's fist was up against his mouth in horror as a rat sat slapping its tail about on the man's leg. The film sped up as great waves of bugs crashed across the man and departed. And the man slept on, thinking of nothing, thinking of sweat, thinking of the raging city.

After the show, Wayne walked over the crinkly linoleum floors to the phone in the kitchen and dialed 1-212-555-1212.

"What number, please?" the harsh woman's voice asked.

"I would like the telephone number for Studio 54, please," he said slowly, drawing out the encounter, listening twice before writing the number onto a slip of paper. As he dialed the number, he could feel the electronic bricks of a magical bridge slipping into place, linking him to the screaming intensity of the city. The first several times there was a busy signal, but on the fifth try a man picked up the phone—"Studio"—and the air gasped out of Wayne in a series of stuttering mutters. Click went the phone. Click went the connection to that beautiful place, and he was returned to the dead silence of a kitchen where he would eat finally—a frozen pizza and Campbell's soup that would lull him to a lasting sleep.

Before sleep, though, Wayne took out the sex magazines. He let his eyes feast on the nude curves of male flesh, thinking of the man in the city, in that hideous room. He began to read another section of the story he always returned to:

He told me one day that he might have to leave and not talk to me for a long time, not even write or call me. I didn't believe it, couldn't believe it, and five years later still don't. The cum is hard to wash out of my bush and still is stuck here and there to my legs. After I'm dry I sit on the sink with my legs pulled up to inspect my ass, making sure it still looks good, looks clean. It all has to be the same because now, five lonely years later, I've had word from him. At least, I think it's him. Just the address of a motel on the edge of town, a room number, a date and time. So it must be him, back but still in hiding, available only secretly. I'll have him. I have to. I wear no deodorant, cologne or underwear—all forbidden long ago. I pull on the white T-shirt, black gym shorts and tennis shoes I know to wear. The shorts are old, too small, and they push my nuts up with the tube of my cock until all of them form a round, obscene bulge.

I know the way to the motel. I've been there lots of times with all shapes and sizes and ages of men that I sell my asshole to for survival money, for a lot of money lately. I don't sell only my ass, of course, but any part of me they want to stuff a cock or a fist into. If I didn't need the money, I'd give it away because it really doesn't matter to me. This body belongs to only one person, and if he doesn't want it, anybody's welcome to it. Last week, three guys picked me up in the woods and we went to this motel. They were three older guys, fifty maybe, with big hairy arms and beer bellies. As soon as we went in the room, they started kicking me in the ass, telling me to get the pants off quick. They kept their pants and shoes on the whole time, just taking off their shirts and pulling their cocks out. With my legs tied up over me, they kept getting my ass looser and looser, with their hands, never their cocks that were only semihard. A long time later, they said I was ready when the one with the biggest hands could shove his fist in like he was prizefighting with my hole. They greased up their still-

soft cocks and the first one slipped his in easily, just stuffing the soft length of it through the open lips. His sweaty, mustached face twitched with concentration and after a moment I felt a warmth pouring into my greasy canal, a flood of hot piss filling me up. The other two emptied themselves, too, slapping me when I'd let some dribble out as they pulled their dicks out and shoved another one in place. I was lying facedown on the bed, with my legs tied the other way now. I lay there a long time as they beat my ass with their belts and hangers from the closet. Finally one slipped under my face, his cock hard down my throat, and I felt a pair of lips on my ass, prying and digging for the hole as the cock plunged over my tongue. Another pair of lips was competing for the prize up my ass, thirsty for the shitty yellow brew inside. The suction at my butt was too much, and as I arched my back the piss enema started to flow out, gushing to the sound of smacking lips and mouths glued to the hole, one after another sucking and pulling for every last drop.

The sleep of that night crept past with muddled dreams, and the dreariness of another day presented itself. The strangeness of these weeks had been compounded by reading and rereading the O'Neill play that the high school drama department was working on. Since the day his family left, Wayne had thrown himself into the false closeness of the theater group presided over by Mr. A. It still seemed ludicrous to him that they should be doing *Long Day's Journey Into Night,* given that all the characters were about fifty years older than the actors. Also, Mr. A had decided that they would do only the last act and present it as if it were a one-act play. In Mr. A's version, emotions that were epic in scope and developed over the course of four hours, over the course of a lifetime in the play, were to be conjured up instantaneously. Yet, the three actors (three because Mr. A had also lumped two of the characters together) went nightly to rehearse in the school auditorium. The rehearsal process had taken on something of a ritual, as if they were taking part in something forbidden. In a way, they were. In a town where emotions were seldom expressed, to weep uncontrollably on a stage seemed obscene. It was addicting to feel in that extreme way. So the three teenager actors converged nightly at 7:30 on the darkened school where Mr. A waited in the dark auditorium, smoking with a wheezy nervousness and pushing the strands of wispy hair back over his bald spot again and again. Mr. A often spent the entire night in the school, sleeping on the ratty sofa backstage and eating bags of potato chips, drinking Coke, muttering and dreaming of Eric.

There had been a definite chill in the mentor relationship ever since Eric's father had snapped about Mr. A's constant presence. Goaded on by the fact that he and Eric were working together on the play, Mr. A had practically taken up residence in Eric's house, coming each night to watch TV until the early-morning hours. He and Eric would sit analyzing the acting in the HBO movies until Eric's father was driven to distraction. Eric's father, the great liberal, the great psychiatrist, finally showed his true colors when, after asking his son about this developing relationship, he slapped Eric and screamed, "My boy, he wants your fine white ass!" Eric, naïve till the end, approached Mr. A about his exact intentions and, in response, Mr. A opened his heart to the boy by silently handing over his black book of writings. It was a tender act, with Mr. A sitting slumped in an armchair, tears streaming down his face while he said quietly, "I trust you, Eric. I trust you to know that people suffer and can be mortally wounded. I trust you so deeply that I am willing to hand over to you the innermost workings of my heart. You can kill me with these scribblings in a book but remember—always remember—what it is to be trusted and loved."

The stupid boy, the still-naïve boy opened the leather cover of the little diary expecting academic treatises about art and love, and when confronted with the undiluted pain of tortured years, vomited onto a page. He felt sick. He was humiliated by finally knowing that he was a stupid boy who had understood nothing. He was embarrassed by the realization that he was desired by another. Eric stormed out of the house that night, striding around the grounds of the MHI, crying quietly, yelling loudly. Yet, after an hour or more of walking and analyzing, he suddenly came to the disconcerting realization that he agreed with his father. Eric realized that he wanted no part of these goings-on, was furious that they even existed in the world. He had seen the heterosexual light; he had accepted his true calling. It was as if, rather than sighting the Virgin Mary, he had seen a vision of a giant vagina floating over the manicured grounds of the Nut Hut. The giant vagina drifted toward him, waving its labia folds, beckoning him in, and, with a great leap, in he flew. Into the atmosphere of HeteroLand, forever and ever. So while they still spoke and saw one another, Mr. A knew that the thing that could have saved him was gone forever.

The cast of the play was composed of Eric playing the young consumptive son, Edmund, Wayne playing the sixty-five-year-old father, grand actor James

Tyrone, and a girl named Lisa playing the mother, a fifty-four-year-old morphine addict. Lisa and Wayne often theorized that the whole production was just a bizarre excuse for Mr. A to see his beloved Eric on stage as a "tragic young artist." Whatever the motivation, it was too late and they were trapped, no longer even trying to struggle. Entering the darkened school, Wayne walked down the hallways that earlier in the day were torture chambers but in the evening looked clean and inviting with their long, labyrinthine curves. Lockers painted a brownish gray lined all the halls, each one serving two occupants that were lumped together by their last names, forming an unholy alphabetic marriage. Wayne had shared his locker throughout school life with Tom, a completely unappealing guy with Coke-bottle glasses and a harelip who had somehow passed himself off as a jock. Tom did get his share of torture, though, because of his harelip. It had prompted one particularly sadistic teacher to ask him, "Can't you fully close your mouth?" After that she tried to assist Tom by pulling down on his upper lip in front of the entire class while the kid stuttered and sputtered and cried until her forearm was covered in spit as if she'd rammed it down his throat.

The school theater teetered at the edge of the building as if it were slightly suspect and put on the perimeter in case of trouble. An enormous room, it was partitioned by two huge hanging walls that could be rolled out to make the space smaller. The stage itself was made of gray concrete with three massive steps up. Even with its sterile design, Wayne saw it as a privileged place where only a few were admitted and, for once, he was a member of the exclusive club. The house lights were turned off when he entered and only a lamp burning on a rickety old table on stage illuminated the expanse of seats. Mr. A's welcoming signal of a red cigarette tip was crouched about four rows back, huddled into the seat as if to hide. Eric sat with him and they murmured on with their conversation, discussing the intricacies of O'Neill's writing and Eric's future as a great actor. Mr. A was a great theater prodigy at the University of Michigan, but had returned to Iowa instead of going to New York or Chicago or even Minneapolis. Wayne despised him for that, hated him for making escape seem hopeless. This man, whom Wayne admired, he also resented intensely for giving in to a shaky respectability and desperation that could only become more desperate with time. When he's seventy, Wayne wondered, would Mr. A still sit here with his latest teenage discovery and with every glance risk being sent off to prison? Just leave, Wayne wanted to say.

With all the actors assembled, Mr. A clapped his flabby hands together twice. He looked at them through his smudged glasses and wondered why he bothered, why he delegated these stupid children to be the messengers of his art. They could not possibly appreciate what he was trying to achieve. He must push them further, he vowed. He must bring them all to the emotional peak that only Eric seemed able to achieve. Tonight, he thought, he would take them to a place they had never thought of going. "You three have embarked on an enormously difficult task. I am asking you to portray characters years older than yourselves, emotionally distraught, physically weak. You are three healthy young people and I have asked you to break yourselves down, feel the weakness that they feel, feel the delirium of their world breaking apart. You must throw yourselves away when you walk onto the stage, and to do that you must reach an extreme. I would like to do a complete run-through tonight, and we will do an exercise before we begin. First you will stand around the lamp, concentrating on it to focus. Go ahead on up."

Eric rushed to the stage, with Lisa and Wayne following a bit slower behind. Lisa rolled her eyes up in their sockets and looked at Wayne. They stood still around the single lamp, letting its brightness burn into their eyes as Mr. A continued: "Let the light become everything, pushing out the world. For Mary, it is the foghorn that both attracts and repels her. For Tyrone, it is the call of past glories onstage, never to be repeated. For Edmund, it is the death that he faces and in many ways welcomes. Look deeper into the light. In a moment, you will try to exhaust yourselves physically to feel the weight that lies on these three characters. Mary's addicted mind, Tyrone's age, Edmund's weakened lungs. You will jump, legs together around the edge of the stage until you can no longer move. You must push yourselves! You must continue on until you are truly spent by the effort. When you feel your legs begin to collapse beneath you, then you know that you are ready to begin. If you are not able or willing to take this effort to the very limits, you should leave now. Take a moment to look more deeply into the light, and then throw yourselves into the physical exertion. Begin."

They began jumping—more accurately, hopping—around the stage, and Wayne knew that if he dared to look at Lisa they would both start laughing uncontrollably. Her slightly-too-tight jeans strained with every hop, and when their eyes did finally meet, her face was blue from trying not to burst out. But on they went, with Eric's hard ass leading the way. As the exercise went on, Wayne started to sweat. He wondered whether this exertion would be different from gym class, or if it, too, would humiliate him. There was a rush that the jocks always talked about after a good workout, and Wayne thought it was stupid that the three of them were trying to use that same feeling. Lisa was no longer amused, but sweating and mad about it, her elaborately curled hair drooping. Wayne pushed a bit harder at the floor with his legs and felt the rock-sturdy stage return the force, propelling him on and jolting his empty stomach.

They had become quiet in their labor, moving intensely in private concentric circles that seemed to stretch longer and longer. Wayne's mind was blank from the effort and only the pull of muscle between his ass and feet was of interest to him. Sweat poured indecently from them, dotting the floor with a soft patter of salty rain. The exhaustion was the opposite of feeling, it created a lack, a void, a blank that could be filled by anything thrust upon it. Around and around the yellow glow of the light they went until Lisa tottered a bit, looking up with slightly watery eyes, and leaned against the wall, trailing her fingers along its roughness. Her face look violated. A girl who had her father, a doctor, excuse her from even taking gym class—and now she poured sweat through one of her best sweaters. They began.

Wayne did not feel and did not think and knew somehow that this was called acting. His lines tumbled slowly or quickly out of his mouth as he concentrated on a cramp in his leg. Actors clear away every bit of themselves to leave a clear screen for the audience to project their own feelings on. This clear screen could slap someone or cry or simply sit there, and the result would be the same. Wayne tried to cancel himself totally, pushing at the edges of self that tried to intrude as he listened to Eric dredge through one of the long, dragging poems:

"Be always drunken. Nothing else matters: that is the only question. If you would not feel the horrible burden of Time weighing on your shoulders and crushing you to the earth, be drunken continually.

"Drunken with what? With wine, with poetry, or with virtue, as you will. But be drunken."

Wayne felt his mouth go flap, flap, flap with response, but saw only the soft curve of Eric's neck in the dim light. Wayne smelled Eric's sweaty neck, pungent across the table. Wayne could smell all the odors of Eric's damp body under the plaid shirt and tried to differentiate between the strong acidic smell of Eric's armpits and the blunt clean smell of Eric's hairy stomach, crotch, and ass. He looked at Eric and tried to remember that he was playing Eric's father, all the while getting an uneasy erection. This was the one who could have been possible—much more possible than Carl—but Wayne had lost him; Mr. A had lost him. Emotions were mixing sickeningly together for Wayne. Real life and stage life both seemed false to him. He tried to clear his mind again. Tried to feel something, reaching down through the porous concrete of the stage into the bedrock, and farther yet to where all the world's feeling must boil in a huge whirling pit far beneath the surface. One day there would be a volcano of emotion in the Midwest, bursting out hideous feeling from the pressure. But for Wayne, only a numbness persisted.

Then the numbness shifted slightly, turned into a feeling, and Wayne believed that there was only one emotion: a certain intensity that was the same for despair or joy or love or hate. There was only one emotion that flicked on like a switch, lighting a sign that says, "Feel, feel." Wayne thought that the actors were just dead machines that moved a leg or an arm or cried from a valve in the eye while pretending to sit hearing and hallucinating foghorns. Wayne sat there feeling an intense focus on Lisa that could have been mistaken for concern or interest, but was really only attention. He paid attention.

In the midst of the play, Wayne felt it was too real, even as his mouth moved slowly, and he looked up into the dark and hated Mr. A. The old lecher made him sick, sitting out there enjoying the show. Three people put together will naturally start to tear at one another, one ripping at another as soon as they turn their back for a quick embrace with the third and then back they whirl to begin the war again. There was something warped about the play, Wayne thought, something that fit too well. He refused to put his face on Eric's and take his father's face for his own.

The day before his family left, Wayne had felt he must do something rather than watch television and wander aimlessly about the house. In a matter of hours, he knew his parents would leave, and nothing would ever be the same, and that day was the last slim opportunity for change. "That goddamn truck is idling fast again," his father had said irritably before going outside and opening the hood. His father was out there, clanging and adjusting, and Wayne felt that, if nothing else, he must go and stand by him for a few minutes.

"How's it going?" Wayne asked, pretending to care.

"This thing's a lemon. I'll tell you that," his father muttered without looking up.

A deep, deep silence. Hard to break a silence like that, but Wayne tried tentatively. "You know, I never asked you what you thought about me going to this theater school."

"Your choice," his father said without looking up. "Whatever you want to do."

"Yeah, I know, but I was just sort of interested in what you thought."

His father's voice was starting to sound a bit irritated. "Well, I think there are plenty of good schools in Iowa without running to the other side of the country. I also don't think you'll make much money. But it doesn't make much difference, does it? Will that change your mind?"

"No," Wayne said, irritated himself. "No, but I just thought we should talk for a change. Seems like we haven't had much to say for a while."

"Takes two to talk," his father said.

"Yeah, but sometimes it's hard. Sometimes it's real hard for certain people. It's hard to talk when people don't want to hear it."

Wayne walked back into the house. He vowed that he would never try again. He would just get as much money as possible out of this man and never try again.

And Wayne's mouth flapped out somebody else's words and feelings. Lisa slowly wandered onstage and drifted to the left, drifted to the right. Wayne didn't understand what the tears coursing down his face were for, who they were for. He just felt the one emotion and looked at Lisa's dead clear eyes as her mouth slowly formed each word:

"After I left her, I felt all mixed up, so I went to the shrine and prayed to the Blessed Virgin and found peace again because I knew she heard my prayer and would always love me and see no harm ever came to me so long as I never lost my faith in her.

"That was the winter of senior year. Then in the spring something happened to me. Yes, I remember. I fell in love with James Tyrone and was so happy for a time."

For a long while, they stood there, bewildered, not knowing what to do now that it was over. Mr. A stood and said, "All right. Everyone have a seat out here," and then waddled forward to sit on one of the concrete steps at the front of the stage. Wayne and Lisa sat next to one another and Eric a row forward.

"You've done wonderful work tonight. All three of you. Lisa and Eric, I have no notes for you. I can only hope that you can maintain what happened here tonight. Wayne, I don't want to say that you weren't wonderful, but you do have one very specific thing to work on. Tyrone is a grand actor, a man about town. He takes his image very seriously. He cannot seem weak in any way. I'm afraid there is a certain weakness in you that you must hide while onstage."

"What do you mean?" Wayne asked in a flat voice.

"I mean that you must be very masculine while playing this character," Mr. A continued, a bit nervously. "I mean that you must cloak some of your natural mannerisms because they do not fit Tyrone's character."

"Oh," Wayne said. "Can you show me?"

"It's something that has to come from within," Mr. A replied.

"I don't really understand it," Wayne said. "Just show me. I'd like you to show me how to be masculine."

Mr. A's voice was pinched now, "Wayne, actors must take direction. It is their job, and they must not be affected personally by criticism."

"It doesn't bother me," Wayne replied calmly. "I just want you to show me how to be a man. I thought that if anyone could, you could really show me how to be a man. I mean, who could do it better that you, Mr. A? Who could be more of a man?"

"Look, Wayne," said Mr. A's withering voice. "If you don't want to be a productive part of this cast, then I don't think you should be a part of it at all."

"You're right," Wayne said while getting up with his coat and starting to walk out of the auditorium. "I think that maybe you should take over my part. After all, you're already the right age. And, most important, you're such a man, such a big macho man. You can probably even show Eric a thing or two. About being a man."

V.

"It's the best," Carl said as he and Wayne sat uncomfortably in Wayne's ugly living room. "Mike told me he's never gotten any this good."

Carl's lips and face were moving, but Wayne already felt strange, unable to concentrate, even though they hadn't taken the acid yet. "That's the way it is, though," Wayne thought. "That's the way it is when you're about to do it and it feels like it's already happened."

The town hushed in anticipation of a rule about to be broken. Almost like the New Year's Eve countdown. All the lonely souls were counting down...10, 9, 8...sure that something momentous was about to happen. Surely there would be an earthquake, or the president would be shot...7,6,5...Selma felt like it was gonna rain; she could feel it in her bones and the arthritic joints of her fingers, and Jim said, "Somethin's gonna happen."

Selma felt horrible; she felt like the worry was going to creep right out of her forehead with nothing to do about it…4,3,2…so she kept walking in to the living room to look at the TV, to see if there was a test pattern or an announcer's voice. The Catholics at mass felt it, too, and were mouthing the words along with the priest because they knew either a miracle or the end of the world was at hand and their arms were flying faster and faster as they crossed themselves. All over town, the invisible network's wires were humming because someone's gonna do it, someone's gonna do what they shouldn't, someone's gonna make them all sorry.

The doubts began for Wayne, as they always did with drugs, right before he took the thing, with it sitting like a little work of art in his hand. This acid was called Green Pyramid and looked like a little shard of triangular green glass, ready to stick in the throat or pierce some interior organ. He and Carl had planned this for weeks because it took time to get drugs in Cherokee and, finally, it was Friday night and the drugs had arrived and Wayne thought, "I don't want to do it." The artistic green acid looked more menacing somehow than the other kind dripped on paper with a little cheery Mickey Mouse or Superman. "Okay, I'm taking it," Carl said suddenly, impulsively, and gobbled down the green splinter before Wayne could protest. "Now I have to take it," Wayne groaned inside. "Now he's going to trip and how can I leave him alone? How could I leave Carl?" So the pyramid sat on Wayne's tongue for a moment until the Coke rinsed it down into his stomach. He could feel its movement as it fell and shattered down his throat, landing dusty in an empty stomach and then moving aggressively to points unknown.

They had planned the music in the house carefully, concentrating mostly on Bowie, but the real plan was to go outside as soon as they started tripping. "I feel high," Wayne said, laughing, as soon as he took the drug, and Carl grinned back. They lay there, quiet and expectant as the minutes ticked past. Ten and twenty minutes passed as they lay waiting, saying little. Then, twenty-five minutes, and Wayne watched Carl's flesh zooming into close-up sharp focus. Then, thirty minutes. Wayne's thoughts converged and trembled as he watched Carl. Wayne knew why the trip was a mistake as he looked at Carl's white skin. Wayne wondered how he would keep the firm walls standing that he had constructed inside himself to hold him back. A glance and they could crumble as they nearly did now. Carl sat in an orange vinyl beanbag chair, flung back into it so that his jeaned legs were scattered across the floor and the yellow and black T-shirt sank onto every rippling smooth curve of his torso. Wayne kept thinking of running his tongue over the ridges between Carl's navel and his chest, felt his tongue working at the inside of his cheek, wanting out.

"I'm going to the bathroom," Wayne said, with his voice as flat as he could make it. The bathroom was small, small around him with the light looking very flattering on his face. Yes, quite attractive, he thought as he examined his face and, most particularly, his eyes closely in the mirror. Wayne was impressed by his new look. As a tribute to Bowie, he had started wearing two different colors of contact lenses bought from a mail-order company in Vermont. One eye peered out a bright, unholy blue while the other pouted with a dark pine green, and he knew that Carl, as he hallucinated and spun, would look at these eyes as if they were ideas. Carl would stare more intently, not able to help himself as he drew closer and closer to Wayne's face until lips joined in the most natural way, as if no one noticed. Carl would be so unsure of what was real that he wouldn't hesitate to do anything. This was Wayne's plan, and he nodded, looking at those two blazing eyes, thinking "Tonight, tonight."

Wayne had a low tolerance to most of life, including liquor and drugs, so he was feeling the acid strongly. The minutes ticked away in the bathroom as he tried to compose and ready himself for the evening. The bathroom was done up in faux-pine paneling with lemon yellow cabinets. "Shit brown and piss yellow. My father, the decorator," he muttered. Everything had become too sharp in the middle and vibrated at the extreme edges. There were miniature peaks and valleys in the paneling, and he knew that if he stared long enough, without trying, he could see tiny towns and cars driving slowly through veiny streets. Wayne knew if he looked at the shag carpet surrounding the toilet, it would turn, without effort, into a sea anemone with a thousand legs waving, hello, hello. But too soon for that, so he stared back at his eyes of different sizes and shapes.

Wayne thought, "I have to get out of this bathroom—no avoiding it." But his cock felt shriveled up between his legs, and Wayne wanted to feel sexy. He wanted to feel ready. Just a few minutes more is all it will take, he thought. Wayne reached under the counter, thinking that a few pages of the porn story would loosen him up. Those last intense pages would be perfect:

Tonight the motel is different, less barren even though the same aluminum-sided little cottages still hug the highway. I go straight to cabin seven, avoiding the motel office, but wait outside for a while, rubbing my aching dick and balls through the shorts and feeling the soft, stubbly hairs coating the inside of my legs. The shorts are struggling to keep my dick confined, to keep its greasy head from poking out the leg hole. I keep rubbing, pushing at the flesh of my tits and ass thinking of the man who is waiting for me inside that room, wondering if he rubs his strong arms as I rub mine. My ass contracts, relaxes, hungry for him and that meat.

I can't stand it anymore and walk to the door that stands slightly ajar leading into a dark room. When I enter, I see that the only light in the room comes from the bathroom. A long slice of light silhouettes my father standing in the middle of the room, waiting for me to service him. I'm across the room without knowing how I got there, and my face bows to rest on his strong chest, tears streaking a wet path down the smooth curve of naked flesh. His body has grown while he has been gone, and I explore the expanse of the tits and arms, amazed that the shape of him could become even more beautiful. My tongue works over the pecs and up into the sweet brush of his pits to clean, to take his smell and taste into me. I feel I must remember everything, in case I never have this chance again. Finally, I find his face, and my tongue moves to suck the bristles of his black mustache and the strong sweep of his nose, moving my tongue up his nostrils, cleaning the man who owns me.

Dad's tongue moves into my mouth, thick and tasting of rum and Cokes, cigarettes. My T-shirt begins to rip at the seams from the force of his strong hands. My shorts are torn down the front, and my cock leaps out. His tongue never leaves me as he maneuvers me into the lit bathroom and into the waiting tub of water. The beauty of his face and body hypnotize me, having forgotten how beautiful a man can be. I strain to see his cock, but it's covered in tight white Jockey shorts, his rippled stomach meeting the waistband with a few dark curls peeking over. I remember the days I would go to the laundry basket while he slept and pull out old, dirty pairs of underwear, smelling the aroma of his cock and balls and the sweaty juice they'd left there.

He pushes me under the water, wetting me all over, letting me up with a gasp only when he's satisfied that every inch is soaked, prepared. His brass-handled razor is on the side of the tub, and the hair between my legs is removed with long strokes of the silver blade. My balls lay fat and bloated on the exposed flesh, and he takes the few hairs off my legs and stomach as well. Then he gathers both of my hands in his strong grasp, holding my arms over my head with one of his hands as the other removes the hair from my pits. My body is bald again, like so long ago, and I thank Dad, thank him for caring for my little body.

His tongue has filled my mouth again while his fingers fill my ass, slipping in one, then two and three, forcing apart what is his property. He lifts me from the bath, dripping, and carries me leaning against his neck to the bed in the mostly dark room. My dad says nothing. I say nothing. His body has always told me everything I need to know, and he's telling me what he wants now with his ass steaming and ripe, hovering over my face. I bury my face in the ass, cleaning and sucking the wrinkled hole surrounded by what seems like miles of white flesh. I would be happy if this is the only thing I saw and tasted the rest of my life—the singular smell of my dad's ass waiting to be cleaned and gradually letting my tongue farther and farther up his red chute. He opens his ass to me, lets me eat as much as I want.

Suddenly he's shifted, and the long brown rod shoves down my throat, his balls ballooning over my nose and his sac hairs trailing through my eyelashes. I've opened my throat completely, encasing his thrusting dick, working my throat muscles to massage the deep veins of his meat and urge him deeper into me. His voice is deep and soft, not talking, but making animal sounds and grunting in pleasure as he roots his son's face. His hands are working my tits, pulling them and massaging the muscles underneath them. The harder he yanks at my brown nipples, the more I open up to his controlling groin. His eyes must be examining the changes in my body, nude, hairless, and rocking in response to his thrusts. Never have I felt a sensation like my father's mustached mouth moving down on my hairless dick while his cock is stuck halfway down to my lungs. The bristles of his lip torture and tease my just-shaved groin and he pulls my legs back, exposing my meaty ass. Oh, Dad, eat me, chew me up and eat me and take me wherever you want.

His tongue has opened my ass to the point that I feel turned inside out, and he pulls out of my throat to reposition himself, his glistening marble-white body making him look like a sculpture poised above me. He greases the folded, twisted muscles of his long arm, flexing his torso for me to admire. And now it comes, the five-year wait over at last, and I open to my father, give him this body to destroy or love or sell on the street as he wishes. His fingers push away the walls of my outer ass, demanding entrance to the gleaming red walls inside. Five long, graceful fingers angling in, followed by the bulge of his palm and wrist. Inside me forever, I give myself to you. His brown-black eyes look directly into mine while he pumps and smacks my hole, which has become my whole body.

My cock strains up in spite of the pressure, leaking, jumping. Dad repositions his huge cock over my face with much of his arm still inside me, and I see again the greasy length of his pole, the raging head beating and demanding attention. He shoves it back down my eager throat while my hungry mouth and tongue chew at the hairy base. I'm full, completely possessed by this man, and we're no longer two people, we're a unit made of two strange men, two lovers, two brothers, a father and son. His cock expands, stretching my throat as he explodes his cum directly down into my stomach. I arch up, his hand falling from my ass as the juice flows out of my cock for what seems like hours.

The soft fur of his groin is still grinding against my face when I fall asleep, thinking, "Dad's back. Dad's back."

Wayne's hands trembled a bit when he had finished the story. The pages wavered as he tore each out of the magazine and crumpled them. "What are you doing? What are you doing?" a voice whispered harshly in his head. "Just cleaning up," he whispered back and flushed the pages. Flush after flush as the flesh was swept away and the words smeared and the ideas were relieved. "It's just filthy in here," Wayne whispered and then continued, "I hate housework, but I just have to tidy up a little. Have to clean up this filth." Wayne walked stiffly to the living room, only three steps from the bathroom and two steps from the kitchen, dick hard as hell, not trying to hide it. Carl was feeling the acid like the big time as Wayne filled their glasses with Coke, playing the mommy, playing the hausfrau here in our comfortable, respectable little home. That is my husband, Carl, over there. The one listening to the music. Oh, I agree, I can't stand this music with all those guitars. David Bowie. Yes, the one who dresses up. Giggle. Giggle. Let me tell you about this particular song, but let's talk quietly because it's one of Carl's favorites. Here's the record jacket for a special long version of it. This tune is called "Heroes," and I must admit I like it, too. Let's listen for a moment. What do you think he means about dolphins singing? Why does he say nothing could keep us together? It's a positive message, though. I feel sure it is because he says that we could all be heroes. Sometimes I think of us in our cozy little house here as if we were the kings and queens. As if we were the kings—the heroes—who could win.

Over and over so long that the beanbag chair started to pulse with it and if it exploded with all those beans on the floor, OH, WHAT A MESS. I have tried my best to house-train that chair, but you know how pets can be. They take over your life. Having a pet is like having a child. A commitment. I'll have to ask my husband to take the chair out for a walk. Honey, has the chair been out tonight?

"Carl, how do you feel? Do you feel really high, because I feel a little bit too high." Wayne wobbled a little as he paced about. "Do you think it's time to go out?"

"Yeah, right after this song. This is my favorite of the whole album, I think."

"Carl, this is the *only* song of the whole album. It's this one for thirty minutes, and I have to say it's driving me a little crazy. I mean, I like it and everything, but don't you think that a half hour is a little long for one song? Does it drive you crazy, too, or am I too high?"

"Have a cigarette," Carl said, real slow. "You'll feel better."

It was good advice. Wayne did feel so much better once he had a sturdy Kool cigarette in his mouth and felt the numbing menthol spreading over his face, freezing it nice. "You know, you're supposed to keep Kools in the freezer. It makes them better."

"Who told you that?" asked Carl from his permanent supine position.

"My mother. You look like someone took all your bones out. Why don't you stand up and put on *Scary Monsters?* I know you like *Heroes,* but *Scary Monsters* is really his best. I'd have to say it's my all-time favorite record ever made."

"I don't think I can stand up," Carl murmured.

"Oh, come on! I feel great," Wayne yelled, leaping over the inches/centimeters/miles to Carl's beanbag chair. Wayne grabbed his arm and pulled him up, strong and easy. Carl's body bent like a spring and then folded up, his face grinning uncontrollably while they laughed and Wayne thought, "Time to move away now," because the feel of the wiry hairs on the firm forearm nearly did it, almost did it. Then they broke away. Carl was whooping and doing a cute little rain dance while Wayne hit the record changer. "That's really a great rain dance," Wayne commented. "Is that real?" Stomp, stomp went the piston legs. Carl was doing that real rain dance around the giant lima-bean-bag chair, which loved it, loooved it and had started to wag its tail in time. "Carl, I swear if you don't stop, you'll drive that lima bean crazy!" Carl was sweating profusely from that damn dance of his and the shirt was sticking to his back, crawling up a bit in back so that Wayne could see the wet brown hairs that started just above his waistband and tingle-tangled their way down to between the asscheeks.

"Did I ever show you this" Wayne asked as he dragged Carl into his bedroom. "Carl, stop dancing because I have to show you this," he said as he pushed Carl onto the bed and got out his notebook with the photos of New York. "Look at this," he said, handing it to Carl.

Carl peered at the book and rolled over onto his stomach with it. Wayne almost gasped at the sight of his ass in those jeans, the curves of the sturdy athletic ass. "What a sight!" he said, not able to restrain himself.

"What?" Carl asked, still poring over the book.

"New York. Can you believe it?" Wayne sat on the floor beside the bed, close to Carl's face and looked at the book with him. "It's the coolest place on earth. The biggest city. The best city. I'm going there."

"You're going to college in Pittsburgh," said Carl.

"Fuck college! I'm going to New York. But not to do stupid things like go to plays. Just to walk. You can do that there, you know. Just walk, and the whole place is so amazing that all you need to do is walk around for fun. So I'm going. Why don't you come, too? I don't care about college, and you're not going anyway, so why don't you come, too?"

"To New York?" Carl asked, not sure what this meant, whether this was really a possibility.

"Yeah, because it's expensive there, so we could share a place and have stupid jobs." Wayne was close now, and there was something that could have been a scream or a laugh or tears starting way down deep inside him.

"That would be great," Carl said. Carl's eyes were closed and his hand was limp on the book.

Too much, too, too, much. A little alarm was going off inside Wayne, and he knew that it would be easy to kiss and easy to believe and easy to love. Too easy and too dangerous. He must wait. Not quite yet.

"Carl, it's time to go," Wayne yelled over the music. "Carl. Carl. Carl. Carl. Carl. I just got this feeling. Like it's time to go."

Carl opened his eyes and stretched luxuriously. "You're right. I think we should go. I'm wearing a jacket. What about you?"

"Yes. I'm wearing my jean jacket," Wayne said as he carefully turned off the stereo. "I'm putting two beers in this bag for us to take in case we get thirsty."

"Good," Carl said, and they stood concentrating with all their might on what they could be forgetting. "I'm set," Carl said and led the way out the door, pulling on his black school jacket.

The air was so warm around them. Spring and balmy and almost beautiful in the night air. Looking at the car, Wayne said, "I don't think I can drive. I can barely walk." The cement of the driveway had turned sponge, sponge, spongy and the air all too silky, and they swayed in the luxury of it all.

Carl was delighted with the turn of developments and said, "We'll walk. What'll they think of that? We'll walk, like we're in New York already."

Into the street and into the night went the explorers. Granny was waving good night from the window, and the wolf was stirring in his den, knowing that new meat was ready for roasting. The little boys—the intrepid explorers—walked into the street and up the block, for there were no sidewalks in Iowa; walking was as forbidden as that. They thought they could hear the dark windows of houses slamming down as they passed; they thought they could hear the squeaky locks of the window latches pushed into place against the invaders. "It's a big world," they thought as one. And now two innocents drew a bit closer to one another in the face of a huge black sky and silent houses. Their knuckles brushed; fingers explored tentatively before Carl jerked a bit, drew back, and Wayne's body froze to stone one limb at a time. He felt his feet turn to clumps of ice while his crotch still leaked and itched. Wayne's face had returned to the mask. Wear that happy mask—polish it up and wear it well.

The windows were still slamming in rhythm and Carl said, "I think we should run. Let's show them." And with those words it lifted, the mood pulled away, and the boys were young and strong as they sprinted down the street that bordered the town. For a moment, they wavered between the cardboard houses and the empty fields full of tamed beasts and barbed-wire fences. It all rushed along like water in a spring river, trout whipping their tails in a frenzy and water crashing, cascading through the rocks. Their legs flowed out in a flood before them, sweeping the strong bodies on as they raced past houses, raced past the old folks' home, raced past the last slamming window and into the fields. Fields that had just shed their snow and come up with weeds, awaiting the annual wheat and corn. The smell of newly plowed fields rose up about them in a mist revealing layers of scent from the pungent fertilizer to the flat dirt to the mustardy smell of old bones buried way down deep.

"Better now," Carl said, staggering in the field.

"Much better," Wayne said. Their eyes joined. Wayne's eyes were irresistible with their strangeness, and Carl heard the words of the music come again, again it welled up and the silly lyrics sang, "I, I will be king and you, you will be queen." King and queen and heroes just for one day. Wayne's face had dissolved away until only those ever-different eyes remained, glaring in the field. Two strong boys moved a bit closer and with each step the town shuddered and Selma whimpered in her sleep. These bodies—these boys—moved so that fingers intertwined once again because not real now, not boys now but eyes and Carl thought, "They are only eyes. Only eyes." Here in the ashy field they moved yet closer with heaven trembling above, and here in the ashes of all that past, their bodies touched gently together in a full slam of flesh as lip touched lip touched tongue. Wayne felt his whole body wet with the slickness of Carl's tongue that reached inside him and a warm, wet cloth rapped around him. Safe, oh, safe. The taste of each other was not exotic but better; the taste of each other was mundane and natural. This is one moment. One moment. Remember. This meeting of flesh that stretches on and on is but one short moment. Immerse it in a protective casing and preserve what little happiness there might be in soft lips meeting briefly.

Wayne tasted Carl's mouth and thought, "Yes, it's all possible." He kissed around Carl's face slowly, licking the stubble on the classical chin. Wayne put his hands against Carl's chest for the first time, the first time ever, and knew that everything was worth it if this would just continue. The heat of Carl's chest was shocking to Wayne's hands as he ran them lightly over the smooth, dreamed-of areas. So much to touch, so much to explore, as he thought, "Remember everything." Wayne's hands lifted the shirt, tasted the damp, sweaty skin. He tasted the clean, salty water of this man, his lover. Wayne pushed his face further, up into one of Carl's armpits and felt the muscle of the biceps drape over his nose. Wayne had never realized that these smells, these tastes, were actual, attainable things. Wayne smelled an odor in the brown hair so personal that he knew, by having Carl's sweat in his nose, he owned him. "More importantly," Wayne thought, "he owns me. Do what you want with me. Let me give you pleasure."

Carl's strong arms surrounded him, taking control of his head and pushing him down as Wayne's tongue lapped frantically. Do what you want. Do what you want. Wayne was kneeling in the damp open field and knew that escape was near, that the key had begun to turn in the lock. As Wayne undid the buttons of this man's pants, he rubbed his hair and face all over Carl's crotch. His heart was down here. Wayne could feel the blood pulse through Carl as the stiff cock beat against his cheek. Don't forget, my boy. As he pulled the white underwear, limp with sweat, away from Carl's groin, Wayne looked up. Wayne looked up to all that hope, the future in one face. Wayne's eyes put off looking at the treasure of Carl's cock to see his face one more time before he proved his love.

"I can't," Carl said as their eyes met and wall after wall of glass righted itself and took up a sturdy position between them. "I don't want to," he continued. And now he had moved back, and Wayne knew the little dream was over. The cornstalks still rattled of their own accord in the fields and the moon vibrated at its edges, but Wayne knew that the moment was over. That all hope had passed. He thought Carl a very simple, stupid boy who stuttered the words again, "I can't."

"Then don't. Don't worry about it," Wayne said coolly, kneeling in the reeking field. He felt the world fall away and couldn't remember what Carl tasted like and couldn't remember what his armpits smelled like and couldn't remember the feel of the boy's tongue in his mouth. Wayne stood up vertebra by vertebra and walked back toward the fence and the asphalt and the flat houses of the all-too-near streets. The earth in the field pitched sickeningly, roughly, and Wayne wanted nothing more than hard pavement beneath his feet. The ground was cracking and quaking, swallowing up farm animals. Wayne concentrated very hard on getting to the fence. "Let's walk some more. We're too high."

Their bodies were old and frozen and brittle where they had been warm and supple a few seconds before. The houses engulfed them as they marched their stiff way down the streets where everyone had gone to sleep. The town drew itself back around them too quickly. The town was dead and waiting. Rushes of quiet whistled in a high, high, pitch through their minds. As they wandered down another aimless street, Carl asked Wayne, "Where are we going?"

"Nowhere," Wayne said and led them farther down the middle of the deserted street. The minutes and the blocks were ticking away, pulling them on. Wayne saw a house, a typical ugly house with aluminum siding painted white and a lawn where grass had never bothered to grow. Snarling and lunging at the end of its chain was a huge German shepherd. "The cop's house," Wayne said as he felt his slack lips moving on his face. "Let's go in and see if Pussy's there. You'd like to see Pussy, wouldn't you, Carl?"

"I'm not going in there with that fucking dog. That dog's a monster. Let's go."

"No, no, no, no," said Wayne, sitting down just beyond the reach of the dog's chain, watching it lunge and snap desperately at his face. The sharp, frothing rows of teeth were wonderfully abstract, and he scooted forward a bit farther, making the margin of danger sharper and sharper.

"Wayne. Please, let's go," Carl whimpered.

"Carl, I'm communing with nature right at the moment. Having a little Dr. Doolittle experience. Trying to have a talk with my friend here. Cool out." This insolence had incensed the dog, which backed up and lunged forward with all its might. Each run of the dog ended with a painful yelp as the choke chain took hold and jerked back on the animal's neck, snapping the body around after it. The frenzy of fur and white teeth and motion clicked by in stop-motion through Wayne's tumbling mind. "Carl, this dog doesn't like you. We might as well go."

Down the streets they proceeded, with the snapping and howling fading slowly behind them. They believed they were the only people still awake in Cherokee, maybe in all Iowa, until they turned the corner sharply and found themselves confronted by the mass and weight of a house all too awake. This towering house was ablaze with lights from candles and fluorescents and flickering yellow bulbs. This house was on fire with light on the otherwise-black street. There on the intricate porch of the blazing mansion sat Mr. A, swaying and waiting on the porch swing with a tall cocktail in his hand. Wayne presumed that the cocktail was a mint julep and thought of Mr. A there in a hoopskirt waving to the gentlemen callers. But rather, Mr. A sat there with his fat, hairy legs sticking out of gym shorts—no shoes—and the bulges of his torso covered by a brown terry-cloth bathrobe. They walked of their own accord but felt drawn toward this sight that was not a hallucination.

"You guys are enjoying the magnificence of nature that is the Lord's great creation," Mr. A called out, beckoning them onto the porch. "We are all kindred souls on this night."

"We're just walking," Wayne said as they stood stiffly against the rail. "We were running, but now we're just walking."

"Yes, you certainly are," Mr. A said as he swung up off of his seat. He was close now, close enough to smell the Zest soap and sweet perfume mixed into the knots of his hairy body as he said quietly, so quietly, "And walking is a man's sport. Come on in for a refreshment. We'll break bread with the Lord."

Wayne didn't look at Carl, felt no need to look at him now as they walked behind Mr. A through a short hall into the immaculate living room, painted grandmotherly white. White walls and white lace slipcovers and white lamp shades and white curtains and a wood floor so black that it looked like a snake pit. Great dark waves swept across the black floor, scaring Carl, scaring him to within an inch of his life as Mr. A handed him a Coke and gave him a shove, the lightest of shoves back into a rocking chair where Carl lay slack and dazed. "Just lie there, Carl. Relax. Don't talk. You're so boring with your clothes on." Carl could hear the words and stared at Mr. A and shook his head a little, trying to clear his vision, trying to decide what might be real.

Turning to Wayne, Mr. A said directly and loudly, "I have something to show you."

"What are you going to show me? Where's it at?" asked Wayne.

"In the basement," Mr. A answered with a wink. "You know what a basement is, don't you?" Mr. A was leaning against the mantelpiece and had taken a little marble bust of Beethoven off the shelf. He was caressing the statue's face, stroking its hair and holding it in front of him so that he could address it directly. "It's under the sea, under the Black Sea where the Lord creates a world so strange and beautiful that we are never allowed to see it. Deep down where light no longer illuminates His creations, the Lord has made life that would make you tremble. He has creatures that could make you scream. Let me show you."

"What are you going to show me?"

"The sea, my boy, the sea. I want to take you on a barefoot walk over the warm, smooth sand beside the sea." Mr. A was looking kindly at Wayne, easing the confusion.

"The sea? Where is it?" Wayne asked as the entire house seemed to rock back and forth a bit.

"Underwater. Let me show you," said Mr. A, opening a door and descending the rickety stairs, the rolls of fat rippling under the fur of his body. Mr. A's voice trailed behind him: "It's important, my dear boy. More important than your young mind can possibly imagine."

Wayne followed not Mr. A but the image of the man's legs, thinking of his own tongue wetting that fur and turning it blacker and winding upward. The boy forgot revulsion, forgot that revulsion existed and thought only of hair. Wayne looked back at Carl but could not see him so well, could see only Carl's outline pitching about recklessly in the chair. Carl was the blurred outline of something moving too fast, a movement machine that shook its parts until it finally just fell apart, staining the white walls. A movement machine where bolts joined limbs and a steel rib cage dripping with flesh.

When Wayne reached the basement, he saw only a white hall with a door open at the far end. Dim light there and a gaping blackness beyond the door that he slowly approached. Wayne counted each step and tried desperately to measure the distance zooming in and out of forced perspective. The room, which took exactly five months, three days, seven hours, and two seconds to reach, was so dark that entering it was like falling down forever. Letting your body drop endlessly. Wayne leaned against a hard wall that sometimes he could not feel, but he pushed desperately against it. Mr. A's voice came through the darkness sounding amplified, sounding as if the man were speaking into an antique microphone. "There is so much to tell you," Wayne heard the voice say. "I have so much to say to you and so little time. You must not be afraid and you must not think. Never think when it's important. Bring your hands to your face. Run your fingertips over your young face. That is a beautiful, precious thing you feel. Something not yet ruined. Something that can yet be saved. Run your hands down your unspoiled young body. Feel what a perfect creation you are. I will not let them have you. I will not let them hurt you. Late at night when the terrifying hours swirl about you, you will hear my voice floating down from between the buildings and you will feel my arms around you and you will never be afraid again. There is so much I cannot explain, cannot say, and I wish I could spare you that pain.

"Lie down now. I want you to look forward, straight in front of you, as my lips brush yours and you are not alone. Look forward and let yourself see it. I will not leave you. As long as you can hear my voice, you are not alone and you are safe. You're seeing a great many things now as you slide forward. Many things pass before they are recognized, partial. Let them slip past and down this road. Do you remember the way? Do you see the scraps of meat and the long-gowned ladies nodding as you pass? Don't look away; this is yours. It is night now, past day, and the trucks are in long white rows. Little caverns, alleyways, and that smell rising from the dark, damp pavement. Drag your fingers over the greasy street and bring the odor back. The flesh dropped from gleaming hooks by men not knowing this street. For what it is. Late at night with doors opening slowly, almost there. Down the aisle as the incense rises from meat burning in trash cans afire. It falls, the rain, and rises, the smell. Home now and safe and you can hear my voice and you will never be alone. Look forward now and lie down. When you leave, I'll lay you in my lap, so light, stroking your hair. And those folds and folds of fabric slipping from my shoulder as I whisper and tell you as it goes. When you leave, my voice will not stop, and you will hear it and be safe. You will hear my voice shake with anger as I walk those streets, holding you still. I will hold your light body high above my head, screaming and screaming through the night. They will hear because my voice will not stop and they'll toss and turn restless in their beds as they hear me calling in the night. You will be safe and I'll grind your body carefully, sprinkling it in their mouths as they sleep. They'll taste you and know you as I do. Unignorable, we infiltrate their very flesh. And as they talk to me, try to quell my rage, I'll see you in their eyes, laughing inside as you rip slowly in their churning stomachs. And they'll think it is my anger, those screams, that they can no long bear. But it's you and we have them. And those nights the chunks of flesh I kick from my heavy path are theirs and the dogs and roaches consume them, not you. Because you're safe and you hear me as I laugh and scream. I wish I could save you from the pain. Lord, let me save him from the pain.

"But no. Lie down. Lie down now because it is they who will die—not you—in their hate and their shame. We walk and you hear me now. I will not leave you, and they will never rest again."

A match flared from miles away, lighting first one candle, then two more. In the limitless room was a Victorian bed swarming with drapes, and on the pitching elegant black wood floor stood a man. In the raging silence stood a man who was now bare to the world, who had taken off the cloaks and scarves and stood exposed, drawing Wayne on with his eyes. "I want to show you the Lord, my boy," Mr. A said, staring into a monstrous mirror mounted on great claw feet. He did not look at Wayne but at his own image, his own shocking whiteness interrupted by the coursing black hair that wound up from his groin to cover his stomach and chest and armpits and back and legs. Mr. A looked only at his own image as Wayne crossed the room toward him. "Look at what He has created," Mr. A said as he drew Wayne in front of the mirror, his furry arm around the boy's shoulder.

Their eyes joined first in the mirror and then turned to one another as Wayne's lips found their way through the currents of air to the wetness that waited. The wetness covered and filled him for a second time that night as Wayne's mouth was engulfed and he felt soft hands moving gently over his body, exploring him. Wayne dove through the soft wet seaweed and let his hands feel this foreign shape, this forgotten sculpture lost at sea. A brief moment, a moment as brief as with Carl, but which did not end when the lips separated. There was no violation, no betrayal here. Mr. A's black eyes stared still harder, and he whispered in Wayne's ear, "Look at us in the mirror. Look at the strange and beautiful creatures the Lord has created. Creations never meant to be exposed to the harsh light. Creations that can barely survive the harsh light of day. I have shown you the way of the Lord." Once again, their lips joined as Wayne felt the hands, the hundreds of hands spreading over him, bringing him farther underwater, caressing him and building. And now he felt a surging. Wayne felt his body break high above the water into a brilliant warm light. Wayne lay easily in Mr. A's arms as the man told him, "Now leave. I must stay. Too late. But you must leave this place forever and spread His glorious word."

The bright light of day reflected off Wayne's red car sitting at the edge of town. Wayne sat in the car packed with possessions he no longer wanted and felt the summer heat of Iowa pressing down.

In town, everything was as usual. In town, everything was as it seemed it always would be. Selma sat in her kitchen and Jim sat across the table from her. They had both taken toothpicks and were scooping the grime out of the crack in the table. Selma was mad as a hornet, and when Jim said, "Not the way it used to be," she rushed out instead of hitting him. Selma slammed the metal gate and stood in the backyard looking at the squirrels and sparrows and her beloved blue jays. Her red hair destroyed the peace of the scene as she stood there reworking a poem in her head about losing a loved one. She would write it down later on one of her lined tablets with her usual doodled illustrations running alongside. She thought about her grandson's graduation, where she felt so proud that her stomach lurched and cried inside her. Selma wondered why everyone had to leave. Glen and Ann off to Canada even before Wayne's graduation, her other kids in Denver, and now her grandson gone. Gone forever, she knew. So she went inside to write down the poem rattling around in her.

Looking back at Cherokee, Wayne wondered if they would all stay and wait. Ten years from now, would Pussy still lean against the bar at the VFW on Friday nights? Five years from now, would Mr. A still be gazing at a boy in the soft light of the theater? Four years from now, would Carl be bagging groceries at Safeway? Three years from now, would Mr. Zelle still be determinedly fucking a woman? Two years from now, would Eric still be mouthing the words of playwrights he didn't understand? One year from now, would the hard earth and the cruel wind still feel the same?

What Wayne couldn't imagine that day was that in ten years absolutely everything in the world would change, and that Iowa would seem bearable, even wistfully quaint. That is the hateful part of memory, its selective desire to soften some things while grinding others deeper and deeper into the flesh. That is why we must forget our past, forget our loves, forget that people continue on once we leave them.

Wayne's tear-streaked face looked one last time at the valley and wondered why he cried for people sure to pass completely from his mind. He pushed the battered Patsy Cline tape into the stereo and laughed as her voice wobbled out of the speakers, "It's you that I am thinking of.... As I read the lines that to me were so dear... I remember our faded love." Wayne moved the car quickly, efficiently, onto the highway and headed East. And he had to admit that there was a certain beauty in the lushness of the green corn and brown wheat and a horizon that was far, far off.

Back

I.

The passengers of the plane pressed forward, their waists straining against seat belts, as hard rubber wheels grabbed hold of the runway to slow the plane's massive bulk while leaving the fragile bodies inside to hurtle forward at their earlier velocity. For even the most jaded traveler, there remains the unspoken tension of these uncontrolled moments between flight and rest. Then, within seconds, tightened jaws relaxed gradually as body and vehicle moved back into sync and the small jet taxied toward the terminal. The scratchy amplification of the stewardess's voice finalized the trip: "Welcome to Sioux City, Iowa."

Even as the plane came to a halt, images remained in Wayne's mind of a jet that had gone cartwheeling in flames down this same runway several years before.

Filtered through the media to a television set in Manhattan, the event had been both immediately experienced and distanced by the repetition of the video running on the news again and again. Sitting in front of the television, Wayne had felt so far from Iowa, so distant from events here, particularly because there was seldom national media coverage of stories from Iowa. But no matter how deadening the coverage of the disaster became—experts explaining the mechanical aspects of the crash and locals expressing the emotional devastation—each report with its vaguely familiar landmarks and accents had pulled at Wayne's heart a bit. "So far away," he had thought. Many other passengers in the plane played these same disastrous images inside their heads and were relieved as the jet finally pulled to a stop.

It had become uncommon for Wayne to find nature waiting directly outside the door of a plane. Ramps into the terminal were to be found even in poor countries like Egypt and Turkey. He felt a rush of excitement when the stewardess threw her weight against the locking device and flung open the door, allowing a blast of sunlight and air to enter into the cabin. In the interior plastic dimness, the light coming through the door was blindingly white, and Wayne leaned back a moment as more anxious passengers began to get out. The hard-looking little man sitting by the window in a stretchy suit and a precarious toupee grunted at Wayne. Standing up but not moving into the aisle, Wayne provided the minimum amount of space required to let the man heave free his black salesman's case. Wayne resumed his seat. He waited, prepared for what was to come. Looking down, he took stock of himself, worried as usual that what he was wearing was inappropriate. But there was nothing shocking in his appearance. Modest jean shorts and a white T-shirt with sneakers could hardly shock someone even here in Iowa. His body was not terribly muscular, but Wayne could finally look at it and see that he was no longer fat. Daily exercise had finally convinced him that the fat was gone. Yet he made a series of remembered gestures, sucking in his stomach to tuck his shirt tightly into the pants and then pulling the waist up to hold in any remaining flab.

Throughout the flight, and particularly now as he moved toward the door, Wayne felt the uneasy sense of recognition in strangers' faces. Perhaps these unremarkable faces were long-forgotten acquaintances who recognized him. He had never gone to a class reunion, never responded to the silly invitations that somehow always found their way to his apartment every several years. He imagined that attending class reunions would be unsettling, trying to look through the layers of flesh to the remembered person who still lay within. Returning home was a little like being famous, he thought with the arrogance of those who never remember but expect remembrance from others. In honesty, none of the other passengers on the plane—mostly businessmen—looked familiar to him. The connecting flight in St. Louis had been mostly full when he got on, but the passengers' faces remained remote and uninterested as he had boarded. Such was the anticipation of returning to one's birthplace that there is a sense of knowing everyone. It's a disappointment when one is met with complete disinterest, particularly in Iowa.

He thought, "Let me just wait here for a moment. Let me take one more minute to get ready for this." As he had sat on the flight, Wayne had meant to prepare somehow for this arrival. Instead, he leafed blindly through *Vanity Fair* and British *Vogue,* a perverse thrill running up his spine at seeing friends pictured in each. An addiction to celebrities, like all addictions, retains its hold even at the most inappropriate moments. So he had traveled, wrapped in the cold glamour of pages smudged with ink from his fingers which traced famous faces. He stuffed the magazines in the seat back, feeling some revulsion for them in this setting. At the same time, these vapid publications held memories of long, involved trips to beautiful places with Jack. Many twelve- and fourteen-hour flights had passed with the two of them poring over every word in *Town and Country,* lulled half-asleep by prescription medicine.

People continued to squeeze past Wayne to the exit. After a few deep breaths, he followed them through the blinding white door.

Ann was pressed to the window inside the terminal, her heart beating fast. She swore under her breath about the airlines, always late, schedules always wrong. Her fear was that he hadn't been able to catch his connection in St. Louis because the flight from New York had been late. She knew that much from talking to the woman at the TWA counter. Seeing Ann's face starting to get red and hysterical, the woman had calmly checked the computer and told her that the flight from La Guardia had been forty-five minutes late. Ann thought she couldn't stand having to wait here for hours for the next flight. Who even knew if there was another flight today?

So she pressed harder against the glass, blotting her tears with a Kleenex. The tears were automatic, somehow; she didn't sob or feel sad, but just continued to cry. Each person getting off the plane seemed to lessen the chances of Wayne being on it. At the same time, she thought, "What if I don't recognize him?" This was a recurring fear she experienced, a guilt. What a horrible thing that would be, not to recognize your own son! Ann knew that a lot could have changed in the two years that had passed since she had actually been able to hold her son, touch him and kiss him. He had told her that his hair was very short, and she feared that he would be withered by what had gone on. She knew that she had changed. She had hardly eaten during the last few months of Don's life, and now her clothes hung on her. Her pleated acid-washed jeans were from a thrift store in town, and her T-shirt had an awful picture of a flower on it. Not that she cared. Ann hadn't cared for a long time what she looked like. This morning, though, she made an effort. She had put on makeup and carefully blow-dried her hair. Sometimes it still surprised her to look in the mirror and find her hair completely gray because it was still thick and unchanged in other ways. It actually looked pretty good, she thought, without the permanent that Wayne had always hated so much.

Ann groped in her purse for another Kleenex. It was packed methodically, and her hand recognized each item in a checklist that periodically ensured nothing had fallen out. She held the purse so tightly that it made the muscles in her neck ache and the lines around her mouth twitch slightly with tension. Here on the top was the hairbrush and the slip of paper with the arrival time and number of the flight carefully written on it. Beneath was her lipstick and a leftover pack of the Canadian cigarettes she had developed a taste for during her years there. The American variety tasted too weak now, like smoky air, but she considered both ridiculously expensive and had been planning to quit for some time. At the bottom of the purse was the zippered bank-deposit bag she used for a wallet. Years of avoiding business taxes had required not only two sets of books, but the necessity of thousands of dollars of cash kept outside of bank accounts. She had taken to carrying the money with her, thinking it safer in her purse than in a house that could be broken into or could catch on fire. The necessity remained even now that the business had been sold, as part of the bargain with the new owners was that half of each payment be made in cash. She felt the $2,531 through the fabric of the bag and relaxed slightly. Ann had always worked, so she had little fear of getting another job if she needed to, but she did want to provide for her son. Finished with her habitual check, she pulled another Kleenex from the side pocket and added it to the moist one in her hand.

Ann studied the stream of passengers walking down the silver stairs that had been pushed up to the plane. She started for a moment as a youngish man with dark hair got off wearing a suit. "That's not him," she knew. "He doesn't look at all like Wayne." Most of the men were wearing suits, and she had seen Wayne in a suit so seldom that she had a hard time thinking of how one would look on him or what type he would wear. She was still trying to imagine whether he would wear a suit and tie when another man walked from the plane. Her breath stopped and she began to work the wet Kleenexes into a tight, tight ball in her hand. The two tissues began to break apart as she kneaded them harder, barely breathing. Her son was walking off the plane, and she recognized him completely. But at the same time, she felt that he had changed so utterly that it couldn't possibly be the same person. There was something about how he looked—too studied, strange—that made him seem unreal. It was as if the window were a TV screen, and she was watching a movie about people getting off a plane. His clothes weren't particularly unusual—just jean shorts—and his hair looked more military than anything else. No, it was his face. Even from this distance in the blinding sun and with the black sunglasses covering his eyes, she could tell that her son had changed more than she thought possible. His face had become something like a mask. Her tears had stopped with the fascination of the thing. First of all, he was no longer a boy in any sense. Nor a young man. He looked infinitely old in a way that had nothing to do with lines in the face. She could feel from here that this was a person who had seen too much, who had been through something too soon. He held himself very carefully, as if something might come hurtling toward him and mow him down. Her son was afraid and jerked his head, startled, as he walked past the stewardess who had probably just said good-bye. His long path down the stairs was taken carefully, and he would slow occasionally to bring his hand up to his face and push the sunglasses back on his nose. What had happened to him? Of course, she knew all too well.

Wayne felt the heat hit him and wrap its wetness around his body. One never remembers fully the humidity of the Midwest in the summer until it actually touches your body. This had always been a mystery to him. Why, in a place so far away from water, was the air so wet and heavy? Space became thick here, and Wayne shoved through the air walking down the precarious steps toward the terminal. He tried not to look at anything. He felt he couldn't just yet, and that it was better simply to walk without thinking about what would happen. He thought that he would look at the color of the terminal building instead. It was a sort of beige Sheetrock. The building was very, very flat against the blue sky, and he tried to remember how the old terminal had looked. He remembered the smelly coffee shop that had been stuck on the side and was now remodeled with tinted glass windows. He also remembered the control tower, which now sat desolate at the side, rendered obsolete by the imposing new tower with exposed beams and a boxy gray top. All the while the heat pressed down, increased by the roar of jet engines that pushed the sullen air against the terminal.

The terminal was icy cool, with air conditioning blowing at full blast. As Wayne walked in, he slowed again with shock. He couldn't figure out where his mother was, and in his disoriented state, he wandered to the side and pulled off his sunglasses. This was a mistake, he thought. Too much, too soon, and he wished that he hadn't drunk so steadily on both flights. The changing temperatures and the harsh taste of liquor in his empty stomach had started the familiar throbbing of his right temple and a dull pain as he ground his teeth together. Suddenly she was there with her arms around him, her cheek against his, holding on tight. Her arms were like a vise around him. He still couldn't fully comprehend what was happening. Her hands were behind his neck, kneading and pulling. When he looked down into her eyes and kissed her, he could feel everything beginning to slip and fall, so he said, "Don't say anything here. Let's not do this here. Wait and let me get my suitcase."

Wayne pulled away quickly and walked across the

room to the conveyor belt, where his suitcase soon appeared. All the while he tried to think neutral thoughts: "How far to Cherokee, and how long will that take if we drive at fifty-five miles per hour, and is that still the speed limit, and is the speed limit the same on interstates, freeways, and regular highways? How much does gas cost now, and will it take more than one tank if the trip takes approximately an hour and a half? Don't think and count backward from ten. Don't think and figure out what time it is now in New York." He made a soft choking sound as he noticed that a security sticker from Air France was still on the handle of his bag. Memories began to crowd closer still. He grabbed the bag wildly and pulled it from the conveyor belt, bumping into a businessman as he brought it around. Ann was at his side and they walked quickly out of the terminal, Wayne tugging the brown case along beside him. Time was very slow as the glass doors slid open and the heat rolled toward them again.

Wayne wondered how long they had been sitting here in the car, crying. Neither had said anything when they had gotten into the infernally hot car, but simply sat, reached for one another, and began to weep. Now it came again. Wayne could do nothing but rest his head on his mother's shoulder and let the sobs take over. Ann patted his head, the pain hunching her shoulders. She was alarmed by the gasping sounds he was making. She had never heard him cry like this, never heard anyone cry like this. It was a horrible sound, and she wanted it to stop. It was more physical than emotional, something like throwing up and laughing at the same time. She wanted him to cry, but not this sound, almost like a seizure. It scared her.

She pulled him up and said the only thing she could think of, but what she instinctively knew he wanted to hear. Those simple words: "It'll be all right. Everything will be all right."

Wayne felt his emotions subside a bit, and he could stop gasping for breath. He had always hated the way it felt to cry so violently, to cry at all, really. Because the strange thing about crying is that you can see yourself doing it. At least Wayne could. It was always as if he were standing outside of himself when he would cry, controlling it, modulating it. Perhaps from the years of drama school, he had learned that emotions are something separate from us that can be used as well as felt. That inside/outside sensation was deeply disturbing to him. He wondered if he really meant it anymore, or if this was simply his new normal state. Perhaps for the rest of his life, he thought, he would simply break down with no more concern than another person would have for a yawn. Because so far, in these last months, none of these crying jags had relieved anything. They never brought forth the expected revelation, only deep exhaustion and a momentary numbness.

The motion of his mother's hand on his head slowed his tears. A while later, he moved back fully into his own seat. Dramatically, Wayne repositioned his sunglasses, knowing the glamour of tears rolling from beneath black glasses. He smirked a bit, embarrassed, and said with a small smile, "Well, look at us. The two widows!"

And suddenly it was something wonderful for them to hold each other's hands. It was something Wayne had never felt before about any relative, particularly his parents. There was that deep, deep bond always counted on, but never there when he needed it. His mother and he giggled a bit hysterically as they wiped their eyes.

"I don't know about you, Mom, but I could use a cocktail," he said as he reached behind the seat and pulled a flask from his suitcase.

"Did you take that on the plane with you?" Ann asked, shocked at the silver flask covered with a brown leather sheath.

"No, I checked it. They have drinks on the plane. Want some?" he asked, taking a shot of the vodka that was very warm, almost hot by this point.

"I don't think so." Ann felt as if she wanted to scold him but decided that she shouldn't. "Good thing I'm driving."

"It is a good thing because I don't know if I'd remember the way, even if I was sober. Maybe we should go before we start up again. Does this thing have air conditioning?"

The route toward Cherokee flowed through Wayne's memory, immediately bringing small recollections with each turn of the road. This path was a progression of smaller and smaller roads beginning with the interstate and ending with Highway 71 right into the center of town. What Wayne didn't remember and had no sense of experiencing before was the physical beauty of the place. After the car, which Ann described as a "mini-van," passed the Sioux City mall and began to move into farm land, Wayne lay back against the seat to look at his surroundings. The vast panorama of flat earth, puckered occasionally by a gentle valley, was soft with green and gold and a newly plowed brown. In July, the moist richness of the soil had peaked and remained lush, waiting for the scorching days of August to arrive.

Stiff fields of green corn were outnumbered by miles of wheat rustling back and forth like silky golden moss and seaweed. The impression was heightened by the air conditioning in the car that cut off all outside noise. The entire view took on the unreal quality of a glass-bottomed boat opening onto an underwater vista brightened by refracted light. In the heat of the afternoon, cows would stand still and then slowly dip their necks to the hay, or simply shake their heads as if confused while chewing their cud. Sometimes tractors passed through the fields, cutting intricate designs into the furry thickness of the crops or pulling wagons stacked with bales of hay.

During a long-ago teenage summer, Wayne had worked baling hay on a similar wagon. A complex, threatening machine attached to the tractor would cut the stalks and digest them, finally belching out the neatly wrapped rectangular bales. At this point, the young men and women would grab the heavy packages by the twine and, with gloved hands, stack them neatly into a towering pile behind them. Many days the heat and wind would whip dust and shards of stalk into a whirlwind around the sweating young bodies. As the sun beat hotter, the men would take off their white shirts and tuck them into belt loops, allowing the gold dust to coat their bodies, broken only by a long rivulet of perspiration running down a strong back. Sometimes the women would work in just their bras, beautiful, also, in their strength. Particularly graceful and dangerous were the long hooks used up front to grab and throw the bales backward, where they would be positioned more carefully. A long arc of thick arms as the hook flew forward and then, in a moment of sheer force, the strong forms would rear back to bring the weight of the bale flying over their shoulders. Plenty of times, those hooks had missed their targets. The bale had flown back with such force as to knock someone down to the waiting wheels below. Brutal accidents. Still, Wayne wished it were harvesting time now so that he could look for the gleaming dim figures moving in the clouds of dust.

These fields were not so different that the fields of Provence, he thought. He had flown halfway around the world to look at fields like these. The difference being, of course, the towns of France which held three-star Michelin restaurants and jaded New Yorkers tired of the Hamptons scene. And with each town the highway intersected here, the illusion of beauty was shattered because rather than ancient stone houses, these towns were dominated by hastily built convenience stores with tin sidings. The trees had been cleared, and the sun beat down without relief on the deserted streets. Only occasionally would you see someone walking stiffly from their house to the promised comfort of air conditioning in a car, sickened by the feel of the asphalt giving way underfoot as the sun returned it to a molten state. After dark, the teenagers would venture back onto the streets to drive laughing and looking for underage beer. After dark, the older people would sit on their porches or perhaps stroll down to a neighbor's house. But for now, with the punishing sun at its afternoon peak, they took shelter and left only a hush.

But then the car would move back to the relief of the open fields. Wayne tried to look at Iowa with fresh eyes. A decade had cured one pain, he realized, because Iowa no longer held the pain of home. New York was far away now, but waited for him, unconcerned by his absence, and knowing that, inevitably, he would return. There was plenty of pain there, waiting and able to reach out carelessly and touch him even here. Concentrating on the view before him, Wayne looked up to the sky. Iowa's sky is not a penetrating blue, but more like a chalky white sheet hanging very near the ground. No clouds dotted the sky today; but there was a very distant tail emanating from a high jet. Iowa's skies are well traveled, more so than the ground. One could almost always spot a plane or jet crossing silently through the air. There was a relief for Wayne in not being on that jet, running away again to a foreign place that only intensified the feeling of loss.

"You know, the countryside's really beautiful here. I don't remember it this way."

"Neither do I," Ann replied as she lit a cigarette.

"What do you mean?"

"You've probably been here in the summer more recently than I have," she said. It was true. For more than twenty years, Ann and Glen had left for Canada every April and hadn't come back to Iowa before November, even December some years. She thanked God every day that she would never have to go back to that damned country ever again. That might not be possible, though, seeing that Ann had become a Canadian citizen. But at least she would never have to scrub dirty cabins, wash hundreds of sheets, or be nice to the guests. Ann looked at the fields with a certain fondness today. Her memories of the country landscape were deeper and more complex than Wayne's. Ann had grown up on a farm, and for her to look at the wheat or a cow or a tractor was not to look at that real object, but at her father. While she had loved him and nursed him to the end, Ann's hands tightened painfully on the steering wheel as she thought of what he had done to her young body. "Selfish," she thought. Selfish was the way to describe every man in her life, including her son. It was hard for her to think about Wayne that way because she loved him, had missed him terribly. But down deep she knew that Wayne grieved only for himself, couldn't feel her pain. Instead of following the thought further, she reached over to hold his hand.

"At least the camp sold," Ann sighed. "Twenty years of work for two hundred thousand dollars."

"I didn't think you'd get that much. He held on to it for too long." Wayne had begged his father to sell the business for several years while the few fish left in the lakes disappeared in the polluted waters and business began to decline. "So how much did you have to pay in taxes?"

"Almost half. Can you believe it?"

"But you never have to go back to that place, Mom. You'll never have to see it again."

"Neither do you. You don't have to go back, either." Ann's voice trembled a bit. She should have waited, she knew, because this was a tricky subject, but it just came out. "Don't go back," she wanted to plead. "Don't go back to that place where so many bad things happen." But she didn't say more, and she turned the car onto Highway 71, where the sign pointed toward Cherokee.

"Here we are. The beautiful town of Cherokee," Ann joked nervously, worried at what Wayne would think of how the town had changed. She herself was shocked every time she came back and saw the town shrinking gradually, closing in on itself. The south end of town, where they entered, had been a thriving shopping area in the seventies. Empty now, these buildings had once been a precursor to the strips of fast-food joints and convenience stores now located at the opposite end of town. Beyond these empty buildings was the chain-link fence guarding Wilson's packing plant, or "The Pack," as it was known. The Pack always had the ominous look of a prison, and its smell left no doubt as to its purpose. Especially on hot summer days, the stench of chemicals and rotting blood would rise up from the place and drift toward town if the wind was right. People would slam down the windows of their houses, even if they didn't have air conditioning. "The Pack's stinkin' today," Ann said as she angled the air vent down away from her face.

Wayne almost laughed as he smelled the overripe sausage odor and wondered what his mother would think if she knew what he associated the smell with. If he closed his eyes, he could see the greasy cobblestones of the Meat District in New York. In the summer there, too, the old layers of fat accumulated in cracks and crevices no matter how many times the streets were washed with rain, would start to heat up and throw off the stench of decayed meat. The Iowa odor was worse, though, as it mingled with chemicals and was sharpened. The Meat District's smell was everlastingly wrapped in a cloud of sexual abandon, adventure. Wayne felt for the first time since the plane had landed how very far away he was from home. There was a distance beyond miles in this smell—a distance between minds that could never comprehend the rough beauty Wayne had come to take for granted in a cruel city. From the first time Wayne had walked through the streets of New York, he understood absolutely everything about them. There was no mystery there, only an addictive pull.

"I don't know anybody here anymore," Wayne

mumbled as the car rolled past the houses along the south side. "Where is everyone?" he wondered, looking at the empty lawns with an occasional sprinkler watering them. In front of a green house squarely positioned on its ungenerous plot of grass, a little boy was hopping back and forth in the spraying water. The boy, a skinny six- or seven-year-old blond, looked bored and chewed on his lip, as if he'd been there for hours. The sprinkler swung around in circles, and each time the water approached him, he would tense slightly and then hop halfheartedly in the air as the water hit him. There seemed to be little point in the jumping as it only brought him more directly into the path of the spray.

"Do you know who has a little boy like that now?" Ann asked, enjoying her pronouncement. "No, two little boys now."

"This is going to make me sick. Who?"

"Your old friend Pussy. She just keeps having them. I see her every so often up at the store, and they are absolute brats, running around and screaming. And there she is, walking around like she doesn't have a care in the world. Very skinny, now, though."

"Pussy, skinny?"

"Can you believe it?"

"No, I can't. I also can't imagine her knowing what to do with kids."

"Obviously, she doesn't know," Ann said with satisfaction. "That's the problem."

The density of the houses increased slightly as they passed over the river and Locust Street. Wayne didn't want to cry, but shrank inside as he looked down the street where no one lived anymore that he knew. "So how's Grandma? Does she know I'm here?"

"I haven't been up to visit her very many times

because she doesn't know who I am. I did tell her you were coming, but I don't think she understood. You can decide when you want to go. I don't want it to upset you, though."

Selma had returned to the Nut Hut after finishing off another husband and witnessing her son's death. Selma's past visits had been marked by a lot of screaming, but this time was deeper, more permanent, because of her silence. One thing Selma had never been was silent, but as she sat with Glen slipping away in the hospital, she had quietly started rubbing the knuckles of her bony fingers, looked at nothing and, finally, was gone. No response, no sound.

For several years now, Wayne had sensed that something was changing with her. Selma had been always been a prolific letter writer and had focused her correspondence on him after he left Cherokee. That he seldom wrote back never seemed to slow the weekly letters that were always variations on a theme. The letters were written on a formula that began with two or three paragraphs about the weather, then a solid two pages of neighborhood gossip, a paragraph of complaining about Glen and Ann going to Canada, and then a little poem at the end. The poem was illustrated in the same blue ballpoint that produced the looping cursive text. His favorite had gone:

> I wish I had a spoon
> as tall as the sky
> so I could taste the clouds
> slowly floating by.

In the past few years, the letters became increasingly infrequent, only tucked into a wildly inappropriate card at birthdays or at holidays. Instead, there were occasional manic phone calls during the day when Wayne was trying to do business. Assuming that there must be an emergency, Wayne always took the calls only to hang up a half hour later, bewildered by the rambling conversation. Not yet, he thought. Don't think of it until tomorrow.

The streets leading to Wayne's house were slightly less barren than on the south side of town. Trees shaded the simple boxes here and there in the late afternoon, and Ann pulled the car under the oak tree that protected part of the driveway. The pine that had sat proudly in front of the house was gone, leaving the picture window gaping openly onto the street. "What happened to the tree?"

"Your grandpa pruned it his last summer and cut it so short it just dried up."

"Kind of like him," Wayne thought, hauling his suitcase in the side door of the house into the kitchen. Ann stood stiffly behind him, knowing what he thought of this house, what he thought of being here. Ann recalled two years ago when Wayne had stood with her in this kitchen to tell her he was gay and was never coming back. She still remembered his words: "This place is like hell for me." Yet here he was, owing his return to a series of unforeseeable events that had changed the world. Wayne also recalled his last visit here. How he had sat in this kitchen with the yellow cabinets and the green linoleum floor talking with his mother. He had waited until his father had gone out of the house and, in a shaking voice, told her that he was gay and that Jack was his lover.

Wayne turned to Ann and hugged her, remembering

her response that day. "You were pretty great the last time I was here," he told her. And she had been, saying that she had known for years and that she loved him, that it made no difference to her. The other thing she told him was a mistake, though. Ann had offered to tell Glen. "Let me tell your dad," she had said and, in his fear, Wayne had agreed. Glen's response had been a lasting and absolute silence. As had been their pattern for years, father and son avoided a confrontation and were left with nothing.

Ann was already putting on coffee. "Should I sleep downstairs?" He picked up his suitcase.

"Wherever you want, honey. I made up the room down there, and it'll probably be cooler."

"Okay." Wayne dragged the luggage down the steps and into the cement-block room decorated with a yellow-gold carpet and brown-fringed lamps. He sat on the bed next to the suitcase, slowly dragging the zipper around its periphery to open it. Grief is a private place, an isolation from the world, drawing one back into the same room over and over again to replay experience, to make sense of what is incomprehensible. One forgets for a moment and lets he pain slink away but then, with a musical phrase, a word or a gesture, it comes running back greedily to feast. Wayne could feel his body lying down, his sunglasses pushed up on his head as he let his fingers feel blindly through the clothes inside the luggage. The sensation was like a children's museum exhibit, where the kid would bravely plunge a hand into a felt box to discover common objects made foreign by lack of sight. He let the tiredness take over, feeling as if it would never leave. This was the fatigue felt by prisoners, the sick, the hungry, by those who have seen too much death. Wayne's fingers felt past cold metal buttons, soft cotton shirts, and the wadded balls of socks. In their detached state, they could have been knives or hammers, faces or bodies, skin or paper. Tunneling onward, he felt a cold drape of silk cover his hand. The gauzy insistence of its touch swirled around his hand, a soft eel making love to his fingers, caressing his palm. The ugly tan walls of the suitcase were a reliquary that in medieval times would have held hair, teeth, or toenail clippings. Thirty years ago, Beuys would have filled it with fat straining against a sharp wire binding and resting against soft felt. Today's reliquary is filled with old clothes, expensive or cheap, that have shrunk away in horror from the ever-diminishing bodies of their wearers. Today's magic objects are catheters, vomit, needles, bandages, shit, bedpans, and pill after pill after pill wrapped in anger and resignation. A modern-day Beuys might lay a shit-stained sheet from a body no longer in control in a glass case echoing with all the political chants, all the impassioned rhetoric that had not been able to save Jack's life.

Wayne's hand returned again and again to rest in the lining of Jack's dove-gray Valentino suit. "Too tired to cry," his mind whispered. Instead he let the coolness of the silk soothe him. Like many of Jack's beautiful clothes, Wayne had begun to wear this suit because it became too large for his lover's withering body, shrinking uncontrollably. The two had become frantic while the disease whirled unpredictably through Jack. So they had become good customers at Bergdorf's and Barney's and Brooks Brothers. They had refused to give in to the idea of tattered jackets hanging like banners over Jack's body. More and more money flowed into perfect-fitting suits and trousers that a few months later looked like jokes, too large for a tailor to take in. When the drugs no longer worked, clothes continued to pile into their apartment closets. Their world miniaturized as shirts, trousers, jackets, suits, underwear, and belts shrank inexorably toward children's sizes. A new set of friends began to assemble: the gay salesmen who searched heroically for smaller sizes, the woman at the pharmacy who mixed special makeup to cover the spots, the nurses who knew how to make the injections hurt less. It was both moving and horrific that death had become a way of life for so many in the city. They depended on the small kind acts that they encountered in a city that didn't know what else to do. People would look at them in the streets with eyes opened wide in empathy, silently saying, "We know, we know. We're sorry." Wayne knew that it all still waited for him and, thousands of miles away, his pain had been taken up by the thousands and thousands still struggling just to live. He had just walked away from it. He had turned away from friends who lay in hard hospital beds. He had clenched his teeth walking onto the plane today and wondered who would already be gone when—and if—he returned. Not yet thirty…those words reminded him of another injustice to chalk on the wall with the endless others. Wayne had never dreamed that he would have to touch death so intimately before he reached thirty.

And the years began to fly through his mind, beyond control. "Oh, God!" Wayne whispered. "Oh, God, please, no!" Sitting on the balcony of the Hôtel du Cap, sipping a martini, and they both knew it was the last. They knew that this would not, could not, happen again. Jack had worn this very suit on the deep blue nights as the warm breeze of the Riviera blew up from the ocean and they were silent. All the tables were silent looking out over the gardens. German and English and French voices would hush in respect for the spectacle of roses stretching to the sea as the light faded and faded for hours. As the sun sank over the far hills of the Alps, they had casually held one another's hands and known that this would never happen again. Wayne let himself think back to that hotel, a place where nothing bad could happen, where hushed servants assured that the world would stay away. Those last days among roses and the sea and the great lawn of the hotel that rolled down to the waiting ocean. In the distance were the lights of Cannes and St. Tropez; in the other direction lay Nice and Monte Carlo. Through those days, it felt as if the names of the towns alone were enough to save them. Even the hideous streets of Cannes were a comfort when turned into twinkling lights across a bay. As night came on, roses released their last burst of fragrance, as they do at dusk, and they knew that this beauty could not save them. That suits worth thousands of dollars could not save them. That all the money and all the love in the world could not save them. And they gave way to that. They knew they must abandon hope then. They gave way to the sweet last days when everything becomes a dream. Before the more mundane grip of illness closed in, they painted themselves as characters from a novel and escaped. If we are not real, we can't be destroyed. So, late at night, they would drive to Monte and stand in tuxedos at the roulette table. They would drink Chartreuse in the lobby of the Hôtel de Paris. They would speak languages they didn't really understand and the roulette wheel would spin and spin while they stood in tuxedos, dying. Two boys, two American boys trying not to die.

Wayne pulled the suit out and on top of him, letting the smells engulf him. He could see his lover's deep brown eyes with the impossibly long black lashes. He could see his lover's body, strong as it had once been. Wayne let the smell of Guerlain cologne take away the pain, let the smell of Vetiver bring back Jack's touch on his arm for a moment in a warm beautiful place by the sea. Lost now and so far away. Jack had the habit of trailing a finger up and down Wayne's arm as he went to sleep, some lovely little gesture remembered from childhood that could encompass everything one loves in a person. Wayne refused to believe that the world was unchanged without Jack. Nobody had ordered a martini tonight at the Hôtel du Cap. No one had the audacity to try on the most expensive suit in the store. No one was baking Greek pastries in the Village. No one loved Wayne quite that much anymore. He trailed his finger up and down his arm, drawing a rambling line around the elbow. One sensation that becomes a person. "I love you," Wayne murmured as his finger traced a line around his elbow. "I miss you."

And the house in Iowa was as quiet as it had ever been. On so many adolescent evenings, the hush of Iowa had seemed oppressive, maddening. Wayne would have welcomed a siren or traffic or pounding music or a scream. Tonight he felt he'd heard enough screams, danced to the tireless beat of enough songs, run through the streets one too many times as the sirens wailed; so he took a deep breath and welcomed the velvet gurgle of small sounds. The wind had died down in the wheat fields and kids had come in, tired and ready for supper. The heat of the day rose up into the deepening sky where a sliver of moon was already bright. It was quiet and cool and peaceful. As he drifted toward sleep, Wayne could hear a car engine turn off, a door slam. Someone else was home. Tonight Wayne was glad to be so very far away from home.

II.

The page's white margins were darkened by a population of inked figures. Each drawing or doodling of men, flowers, houses, trees, geometric shapes allowed another diversion before writing. The paper had also become bowed in the center by the sweat of a hand pressing down. The paper no longer looked quite fit to hold words. Wayne colored in a triangle with black ink and wondered how to begin, what to begin. Without a subject fully formed and waiting to emerge from him, Wayne could rarely just sit down and begin. Rather, a subject would build up inside of him for months and take on shape during sleep or sex. After this long gestation, Wayne would simply let it flow out, shaping the words as they tumbled effortlessly from him. He hadn't written in months. He had always found it difficult to write when not in New York.

Something about New York had always inspired him to write. In the city, writing represented a way to retreat from the world into a place where there was no excuse for a disturbance and no way to be reached in an apartment where a doorman stood guard and an air conditioner blotted out noise. On those city mornings, he would get up, have coffee, and read the *New York Times.* Then the phone and answering machine would be turned off before he sat down at the computer. Several hours later, he would look up and know that the writing for the day had been done. Here, in Iowa, there was no computer, no *New York Times,* and it was the early evening.

The computer problem was significant because Wayne's handwriting had always been terrible—his hand clenched torturously around the pen so tightly that it would be bent by the end—forcing Wayne to print slowly if he couldn't tap quickly along on a keyboard. Throughout grade school, Wayne had tried to loop the lines carefully along the dotted blue guides in his training book. The stiffly formed cursive letters always looked uncomfortable crouching there. To achieve the effusive style that was considered desirable, one's hand needed to fall into the stream, giving in and moving with the currents of dispatch, not getting caught up in an eddy of letters but cascading from word to word. Somehow the computer alleviated the problem. Words and phrases would appear preformed, fashioned on the screen by the tracings of his fingers on the sympathetic keyboard. Words would turns to phrases and, unforeseen, pages surfaced. The machine contained an enchantment that recast it as something more than a series of electronic circuits, converting its mechanical proficiency into a human tool. Wayne missed the computer's soft murmur offering counsel and the way its tone harmonized with the torrent discharged from the air conditioner. The white noise was needless in the damp hush of this bunkerlike basement. Here Wayne was left without the tools that held the city in abeyance. Here walls were already erected and, although they might be infirm, there was slight chance for agitation. But in the untroubled Iowa night, Wayne lowered his pen to a fresh sheet of paper and thought he might as well try.

The night rushed in jagged waves around Patrick as he opened the second tiny brown vial of coke in the bathroom stall. What would be a miniature if it were just any bottle is large when it is a vial containing a substantial amount of drug. Patrick noted that it was 3:30. A transitional hour, marking either a shift or a progression. Either make the shift of going home when most bars close at 4:00 or progress to establishments that draw a less-distinct line between the long hours of night and dawn, the spoiler. This was such an establishment, perched on the sharp edge of residential Manhattan, where the river drew an array of those who searched through the night. They searched for what? Unimportant. They searched. They probed the murky, subterranean sphere for sex, drugs, love, companionship, and other less-tangible goals. Ten years before, the clubs had been a fusion of all of these elements. Now the arenas were more clearly delineated. For example, this club might have been the Hellfire had it operated in a less-constricted era, offering diversions for both men and women interested in pain, bondage, and other specialized sexualities. In the present, it attracted gay men on weekends, straights on weekdays, and facilitated introductions, rather than intercourse.

What it retained was the aura of abandon, the promise of losing control, and that quality was central to the allure of New York nightlife.

Patrick sat backward on the toilet and, after wiping off the tank cover, poured out two fat lines of powder. He noticed the usual messages scratched into the metal walls, from boring ("For good head...") to titillating ("Shit slave humbles before Master's ass...") to cryptic ("I'm looking for you.... Meet me here at 1:30"). There was a queue of men waiting for a stall but Patrick assumed that if there was anything these boys would understand, it would be the need for a good fat line of blow. Waiting for a stall was a common activity in this club and others of its ilk, demonstrating that the stalls were more like temporary private rooms used for any number of projects—sex, urination, defecation, or getting a satisfying amount of coke up your nose. Patrick leaned down to the enticing white lines. There was some giggling from the company outside in response to the atrocious snorting that issued from his stall. "Sounds good, baby!" Wetting his fingers in the waiting club soda, Patrick sniffed a few drops of moisture up into his nostrils—douching, he called it—and chuckled himself upon hearing, "You're ready now, baby!"

Patrick had long charted the course of coke highs and knew exactly where he was at in tonight's experience. After a few hours, the high had become less luxurious, lacking the potency of the first rush. Now, as his body adapted to the drug, he felt edgy and short of breath. This was the time when a lot of the drug was necessary, fast. So, in a move both correct and dangerous, Patrick snorted one more line for good measure and was pleased as he felt it explode against his brain, his skull tingling. Now was not the time to become aware of the pounding heart or the short breath nor the inevitable drain that could last for days afterward. This was definitely not the time for those thoughts. "Work that high, baby," called out the voice, shriller now, and laughter from others echoed off the bathroom tiles. He tapped the vial down on the porcelain and was comforted by the solid mound left. The drug built and crested in his head, drizzling down the back of his throat as it wound through his system. Patrick didn't care how tonight went, just so it continued. That is the important thing—to continue, carry on, linger, remain, stay. Dipping one's finger into the darkness is pathetic. Better to persist until hitting rock bottom; that's where the discoveries are.

Leaving the stall, the men in line cackled, knowing. Patrick playfully checked each face and body, fixing them with a hyperactive stare as he passed. "Were you boys talking to me? Sorry to keep you all waiting," he growled in a voice made more nasal and husky by the drug anesthetizing his throat. "Nowhere in the world could you find more ravishing men than in New York," he thought. He paused momentarily where the door frame narrowed the space, taking advantage of the closeness to rub a tall black man's crotch that strained to burst through a worn pair of jean shorts. The man was neither appalled nor enthused, just blank.

Moving on, Patrick knew he would have to execute tonight exactly perfectly if he was going to have sex. It may seem as if sex were the only logical goal in an SM sex club. But there are many breeds of night creatures, magnetically drawn to the powerful emotional games played late at night and the extremities of existence never found in the day. Many did look for sex, but many just passed the night as they could. Drugs, a particularly prominent and requisite part of the gay world, could make one horny as hell while making erection unfeasible. The advantage of SM sex is its purity. Scenarios can be formed from carefully prescribed rules that have nothing to do with erection or coming. The extremity creates an open-ended situation which may not require the closure of ejaculation.

And so this world is a charismatic lure for those who cannot go home. Suddenly possibilities exist in the form of a cock, a lunging hand, or a piercing scream. These acts can uproot the too-solid foundations of life. Even those businessmen and secretaries who will most likely return to their natural, antiseptic environments promptly on Monday morning can call their safety into question. It is possible never to return from a trip here, to be lost irretrievably into an addiction. What is not commonly accepted, though, is that to be lost is also to be free. And one could plunge endlessly into the eyes of many of the men lounging against the wall, fall into the emptiness that depicted not pain, but a throwing off of pain; not suffering, but a rejection of the suffering world around them.

Descending gouged, pitted stairs, the music pounded aggressively into Patrick's ears. There is only a partial recognition of the music in a sex club, and it often seems to be coming from a far distance. The muffled quality allows it to be truly a backdrop; but, even so, snatches of clarity occasionally break through. "You cannot touch reality...you're living in a fantasy..." This club had been open for more than a year, but Patrick had never visited it before. It had been on the edge of his mind several times, but somehow he had never gotten to giving the West Side address to a cabdriver. The space was enormously impersonal and must have been a truck garage. That coldness was now important to the carefully cultivated ambience of brutality. If masculinity means playing at being hetero, few of the men here worked toward that. Rather, they were gay men playing a game, exploring roles which they created in this concrete bunker that could serve as sound stage and set. The renovation from garage to nightclub consisted mainly of throwing up a few black walls to separate the coat check from the bar from the stage from the sex room. You could almost feel the lumbering movements of the truckers who had once parked their rigs here, near the river, always near sex. How many of them had parked and then walked across the highway to the piers? In those days, the piers would have been alive with sex. Everything was alive then. The men would have slid out of the trucks, unsticking their dicks from sweaty underwear, wanting to toss off a few loads before going home to wives and girlfriends—a few stinking loads thrown into mouths and asses that waited patiently by the river. Then they would attack. The mouth that had, moments before, been an object of desire would appear accusatory in their panicked minds. Then fists would strike out, trying to erase what was true, what was undeniable, what would always win out. Maybe their rage at hidden desires was not sated even then. Maybe, after emptying their dicks, they would rampage down the streets with blood-spattered bats. Finally exhausted, they would take their bloody hands and stinking cocks back to women who chose to believe, who bought into a debilitating lie.

The crowd tonight was altogether more healthy in its sexual persuasions, and the club had a welcoming feel for all of its industrial environment. The men tended to be talkative. This subset of the gay world knew itself well, and friends were made easily after seeing one another week after week. Coming to these spots was still an act disavowed by many gay men. Sleazy, they would have called it, as they made their way to summer houses featured in decorating magazines. Repulsive, they would have spat, while all the while they yearned for it. Every gay man yearns for the release of anonymity and pure physical pleasure unencumbered by the constraints of love. And while they sit smugly over foie gras at La Grenouille, the images hover above ruby-red banquettes. Images of degradation and exaltation. The gay men order stuffed zucchini blossoms, but they wonder whether a fist would really go up their ass, whether handcuffs would ache after hours of wear. The gay men who sculpt perfect hairless bodies for themselves open their throats to chardonnay and wish it were piss, wish they could give themselves fully and utterly to another man in the way unique to their breed. Tonight the men in this industrial wilderness in Chelsea enjoy themselves heartily because they know that there is relief in acting on impulse and stepping over the line. No going back. No return.

Patrick walked, glided, leaned against a wall and moved on again. He wound deliberately through the maze of rooms, not ready, not quite ready, to do anything but move along. "Aaah!" he moaned as he leaned against the stage and felt the drug boost incredibly throughout his entire body, lengthening and pulling at him. His torso felt miles long, unwieldy and dangerous. His legs were sharp spikes dug into the ground for stability. He trailed his quivering fingers along the edge of the stage, studying the soft emanation of light from the strip of glow tape that marked the border and guided the performers safely in the dark. Onstage, a man in a black leather hood had been hooked to a giant torturous wheel that waited, still now, for its orders. The wheel also had a slightly ridiculous game-show quality to it, as if one could spin the naked man to win a refrigerator or a mobile home. The man on the wheel had an overly muscled body, Patrick thought. His true body was hidden by layers of muscle that served as a defense from anyone seeking to touch the vulnerability that he sought. He lacked the normality, the everyday quality in his body that drove Patrick wild. The man on the wheel hung slack against the restraints lifting him from the ground and securing him for use. The wheel was tended by two men who conferred about the next course of action. Patrick wandered in a circuit around the stage, trying to hear what the two wheel men were discussing. The music drowned them out. "Gonna set you free... Rock your body... The music gonna set you free...." One of the men stepped away from the wheel as the other started to turn it slowly, steadily. One picked up a whip as Patrick lost interest, getting ready to move toward the bar with the slaps and screams building predictably.

Nearby, a less-predictable scene presented itself. On a lower platform, adorned only with a rough sawhorse, teetered an unlikely creature whose birth was possible only in a club such as this. This woman—and Patrick assumed it was a woman—was sheathed wholly in white vinyl. After taking in the entire form of her, Patrick decided to begin once again at the feet to try and fully comprehend this creation. The feet, in and of themselves, were a study in perversion. The white heels were cripplingly high, causing her constantly to sway to and fro, in danger of imminent collapse. The shoes were met immediately above by the legs of the bodysuit, which encased the thick body underneath. The only real clue, and it was hardly conclusive, as to this personage's sex was the swelling in the suit's chest area. As to the head, this was the area that crossed some boundary, moving the look far beyond the possibility of simple fashion. Large, frightened eyes stared out from the cutouts in the white hood. The eyes were garishly made up with false eyelashes and powder-blue shadow. The stare of those eyes made Patrick feel as if he were going to hyperventilate. This was an animal. Humanity had left the eyes that stared out so intensely that one could almost ignore the huge ponytail of straw-blond hair exploding like a volcano from a hole at the crown of the head. The creature's eyes were suddenly obscured as an unnoticed attendant grabbed hold of a milky vinyl arm and threw the form over the sawhorse. In its own way, the look of the dominatrix was even more radical. She was extremely short and wore a tweedy suit with a tailored skirt. There was an English aura to the mistress, a short Vita Sackville-West just in from the garden to adjust her pearls before picking up a riding crop and getting to work. The first strike of the crop on white vinyl was the most shocking for its lack of sound, only a muffled thud and a far-removed groan from inside the sack. As the blows increased, the high heels became more and more precarious, with only the sawhorse preventing total collapse. After some time, the maitresse simply walked away, lit a cigarette, and began to chat with a group of unimpressed women to the side. The slave, beyond standing, slumped farther forward and shook its ass in appreciation.

"Is your name Patrick?" The voice startled him and

he turned to a nondescript, skinny young blond with wire-rim glasses. He wondered why anyone would wear wire rim glasses to a place like this. The face made him slightly nervous because he was sure he had never seen this person before.

"Yeah, that's my name."

The guy had a strangely nervous way of hopping slowly on one foot. His voice was smarmy. "Did you go to Carnegie-Mellon?"

"I'm sorry, but I don't think I know you," Patrick said, and started to turn away.

"Oh, yeah, you remember me," the guy said, and introduced himself. Patrick had a bad habit of not listening when people told him their names. If fact, his memory was very poor in general, and he still had no recollection of this wispy blond at college. However, his interest was reignited when the guy lit a joint and offered it to him.

"Thanks. I could use some. I think I might be a little too high."

"Me, too," said the blond. "I just did some crack. Usually I like to snort heroin, but tonight I bought some crack over by my house. I live on East Fourth."

"I've heard a lot of people died last weekend from heroin. You should be careful of this new batch on the streets; it's supposed to be very pure." Patrick had never taken heroin, but he saw it as the most extreme of drugs. His estimation of the blond grew slightly now that he knew him to be a junkie. "Thanks for the smoke. I'd give you some coke, but I just did the last of it," he said, lying.

"That's okay," he said, somewhat cooler. Patrick noted that the guy's hopping dance had increased. "Well, uhm, I have to go to the bathroom. Just wanted to say hello. See you around." Then he was off.

"Coke whore!" Patrick spat, walking away from the stage where the man revolving steadily on the wheel was developing an irregular pattern of red whip marks on his body.

Too, tttttttoooooooo, high. Peeeeeeeeak. "Jesus Christ!" Patrick muttered as he flung himself onto a bar stool in the nick of time, just before falling over. He pushed his back hard against the bar, harder than he realized, and had the distant sensation of the vertebrae of his spine grating against the counter edge. At this apex of the high, he had no sense of and no regard for his body. A constant grinding of the jaw whittled down his molars imperceptibly, and his tongue followed an undeviating path along the back of his teeth. Patrick's body may as well have been the heel of a shoe that scuds and sticks in whatever lies in its path, milling the objects in the street. With his legs sprawled before him, Patrick attained a precarious balance on the stool while making it appear an indifferent pose. Each point of contact, though, was absolutely necessary to prevent an undignified pitch to the floor. Feeling structurally sound for the moment, Patrick examined his reflection in a mirror facing the bar. His skin was very white and his hair very black, an important contrast demonstrated by everyone from Diana Vreeland to John Kennedy. His eyes were inscrutable, too much, and he tried not even to look at them. These were no longer the shocking two-color eyes he had in high school, created by colored lenses. No, these were real eyes and all the more terrifying because of it. His eyes were blue, but at this instant they reflected no light, swallowed all light, until they appeared an unequivocal black. A rational person would have noted that after taking drugs, the pupils dilate. But in this setting, they appeared malevolent, prone to violence, ready to accept another's violence. He shook his head once or twice. Closed his eyes and breathed. For an unmeasured interval, there was no sound. The mute button had been hit; the soundproof door had closed; the leather hood had been zipped shut. No sound, no light. Another breath and it all came charging back into focus. As his eyes opened, Patrick's hand floated up to his bare chest, framed by the black leather jacket that hung open to reveal his tits and stomach but camouflaged the problem "love handle" area. His chest was lightly haired. From a distance, it looked almost bare. He was pleased with his chest most of all, he decided. In this one area, he was satisfied. Lower, his hips could stand to be thinner but didn't look bad in the long black denim shorts which ended just past the knee, revealing strong calves disappearing into black high-top Converse sneakers. He let his hand run over his chest and stomach while letting the coke take him past a half-understood point. His body was a thing now and he was satisfied. Two entities—him and his body. "You can't hurt me now," he thought.

And then Patrick lost himself. "Yes, yes, what I want. Don't think. Nothing. Don't think. Do." He threw away his body, an object that could be used or not. He wanted the control. "Why don't you do it to me..." the music lulled. "Tell me why...Why don't you do it to me..." He wanted to be controlled by one man. That man stood directly in front of him. "Use me," Patrick thought, as his blue-black eyes bored into the eyes of the man in front of him, and the man in front of him walked between Patrick's legs, walked forward and took control. One person can appear miraculously as salvation, as death, as punisher, as redemption, and this one person positioned his leather chaps right between Patrick's legs. There is no reason to look for the right person, Patrick knew, because when the factors are right, he simply appears. You can walk all night and never find him. But when the time has come, just throw yourself back and let him appear, more complete and perfect than could be planned. "There is magic," he thought. He believed that his want, unleashed by the drug, had conjured up this man, summoned forth a physical incarnation of the emotional flood.

He thought of a book he had read that was a string of commands, imperative sentences for hundreds of pages. "Check this out..." the music said. Give yourself over. At the exact moment of breaking, surrender yourself utterly. Dress yourself for sacrifice and expect humiliation to reveal a path. Move a bit lower than you thought possible. Destroy your physical self as an experiment. Find out how far down you can go. Pray and think religious thoughts at inappropriate times. Think of your parents during sex. Think of your penis during Holy Communion. Pretend to have Tourette's syndrome at an office party. Break down in front of a homeless person. Tense your asshole until it itches while eating at "21." Listen to old disco on a Walkman while crying at a funeral. Close your eyes and disregard the hand exploring you. Find beauty in the ugliest moments. Talk about AIDS while fucking a man hard. Make hatred a way of life. Hate yourself most of all. Sit in church and list every tragedy created by God. Show pictures of your dead lover to potential tricks. Wear expensive suits with no underwear and a buttplug. Go to galleries and tell artists their work is unimportant. Make a mark on your body and see how long it stays. Cut off your long hair. Keep the hair in a glass jar. Cut your fingernails to the quick. Keep the clippings with the hair. Regard everything as a record. See yourself in history. Estimate how much time is left. Be wearing a long skirt and motorcycle boots when you finally break. Curse every writer you have ever known. Have one last drink at Trader Vic's. Don't invite Madonna. In the flash when you are about to disappear, turn to the photographers and scream, "At least I was famous!"

"Stupid, thank God," Patrick thought as soon as he heard the man's voice. This was not an affected stupidity, but the real item. That's what he wanted. Tonight he craved the erotic mundane.

After asking Patrick's name twice, the guy just looked at him. He seemed not to have heard or to be able to understand. His hair was cut in an ugly, slightly-too-long style framing his Italian New Jersey face and mustache perfectly. Patrick let his hands wander slowly around the ample, hairy chest and rub the firm beer belly, asking the guy his name.

"Joe," came the answer. Patrick almost lost control. Could it be more perfect? He hardly dared ask the next question. "What do you do for a living?"

"Construction," came the answer in an almost-retarded, mean-spirited voice. "My body gets real tense from work. 'Specially my shoulders. What I need is a good rubdown. You ever do that? You into that?"

"Oh, man!" Patrick moaned. "Let me take care of your body."

"You like this body?"

"If I were to put together a picture in my mind of the perfect body, it would be yours. Your proportions are magnificent because you're not too tall. The rest of you? It'd be hard to say which part turns me on most. The chest, maybe. The arms, maybe."

"What?"

"I said I love your body and I want to take care of it," Patrick said, kneading the man's shoulders.

"Mmmm, that's what I need. Wanna come give me a rubdown for a couple of hours? That's what I need. I'm kind of sexed out, but I need somebody to relax me."

"Let's go, man. I don't want to waste one minute I can have my hands on your incredible body."

"What?" Joe asked as they walked out.

Patrick was talking, talking fast, but he had absolutely no idea what he was saying. "So fucking high," he thought, and heard Joe say something. "What'd you say," Patrick asked.

"I live in Brooklyn. You mind?"

"No, I don't mind."

"Good, I'm gonna pick up some ribs in Chinatown on the way. Hungry?"

"Hungry? Are you kidding? Do you want some coke? I'm gonna have a little more." Patrick opened the vial as they were driving down the street, but Joe seemed uninterested. Patrick was talking again, about massage techniques, mapping out exactly how Joe wanted his body handled.

"You know, this is great, Joe. Because when I do coke, I feel really horny, but I can't get a hard-on; so I really appreciate the chance to just make your body feel great. It would really turn me on to start massaging you right away when we get to your place, even while you're eating. I mean, I could even start on your feet while you're sitting there eating. Would you like that?"

"Yeah, I guess." Joe was driving down the Bowery toward Chinatown. Patrick was sort of praying that they weren't actually going to a Chinese restaurant with

him in this condition, but he had given way. He had given in to whatever happened. He just wanted to give.

The streets of Chinatown were mostly deserted at this hour, the neon lights flooding color over the empty pavement and random groups of young men. Always atmospheric, it was threatening when empty and quiet. The rules changed. Patrick was rubbing the length of Joe's hairy arm when they pulled up in front of Wo Hop. "Get me an order of spare ribs," Joe ordered, casually handing him a ten-dollar bill.

"Oh, you want me to go in?" Patrick was in no condition to go in to a strange restaurant at the moment, but was also completely at the service of this man.

"Yeah, man, you think I'm gonna leave my car on this street? These Chinks would swipe it in a minute."

Walking down the steps, teetering slightly, Patrick pushed open the door to Wo Hop. As he had feared, it was mobbed with people. Having given his order, he stuck near the cash register and tried not to sniffle. When he heard the door open behind him, his entire body tensed tighter. "Two cops, two greasy fuckin' cops, wanting fried pork, just like Big Daddy up in the car. Man, hurry it up," he thought, looking intently at the menu. The cops couldn't have cared less about the wired-up little fag next to them, though. They were thinking about grease. They were thinking about pork. They were thinking about fried wontons. They just wanted their food and didn't give a fuck.

There was a shrill building of voices in the back of the restaurant. At one of the tightly spaced tables sat a towering black drag queen, hair teased to the ceiling and piss drunk. She looked disgustedly at her food and pointed an imperious finger to it. She flicked at the pieces of pork with her long red claw. The waiter was having none of it, "That what you order."

"I didn't order no dog-meat salad, baby," said the drag queen, putting her hand on her ample hip.

"That pork. That good."

"Get me some chicken foo and take this back to the soup kitchen." The drag queen must have been well over six feet before the heels, and her legs seemed to take over the entire restaurant. Her calves were the size of small children. Most of all, her face was one of those expanding faces; the more you looked at it, the bigger it got. Now she took another slug of beer and seemed to resign herself to the food.

"That good. That what you ordered."

"Oh, run along, Ling-Ling, and get me some duck sauce," she shrieked, and started eating.

Patrick could smell the pork in the bag as they crossed the Manhattan Bridge and traveled past Williamsburg and Park Slope. He could tell they were going a long way, farther than he had been in Brooklyn, but he could also tell it was too late. There was nothing to do. Nothing that could stop this. He had no interest in Joe's descriptions of the Italian, black, Jewish, Puerto Rican, and Irish neighborhoods. "Creeps," he thought. "Sexy, stupid pigs." He ran his hand over the jeans that kept him away from Joe's hairy flesh. "Man, I can't wait to get my hands on you. You're the best."

Pulling up later, he didn't know how much later, Joe turned off the engine in front of a depressing-looking two-story suburban house. The sun was beginning to come up, and neighbors were coming out of the house next door. "Get down," Joe growled, pushing Patrick toward the floorboards. When the neighbors had gotten into their car and left, Joe said, "Okay, hurry up and get inside."

Joe followed Patrick up the flight of stairs with his ribs. As the door opened, the house revealed itself to be extraordinarily ugly, neat, and mundane. "Perfect!" Patrick thought. "Better and better."

Joe told Patrick to take off his clothes in the kitchen and put them over the chair. Joe paid no attention to this disrobing, made no comment, but pulled off his own jacket and proceeded to dump the ribs onto a plate. Patrick continued to stand naked in the middle of the kitchen as Joe sat down heavily at the Formica kitchen table. "So get to work on those feet," Joe mumbled through a mouthful of ribs.

Patrick had imagined this but never done it, never known how to get to this point and make it real, not an act. It was real, he knew. It was really happening. The erotic tension of it, the perfection of this guy's attitude, made him short of breath. Squeezing beneath the table, he began to unlace Joe's shoes and carefully pulled them off. He also carefully removed the gym socks. The feet didn't stink. Running his hands over them, Patrick was unsure whether or not he wished them to stink. From above came a disembodied voice: "So how you like those feet?"

"Beautiful," Patrick whispered as he rubbed each toe separately, thoroughly. He examined them carefully. The toenails were cut short, and each toe had a short tuft of hair. The arch of the feet had longer, silky hair that merged at the ankle into a darker forest hidden by the jeans. There were hard calluses on the heels, and he made a mental note to work particularly hard on softening them with lotion or oil or his tongue.

"What's your name?"

"Patrick," he said, without wonder at being asked now for the third time.

"Let's go in the bedroom," came the voice. "I want you to get to work."

Joe's bedroom was as ugly and as neat as the rest of the house. Macho guys were often rather babyish about their surroundings and neurotically clean. The house had obviously been furnished at thrift shops and garage sales. Joe lay a towel on the bed, saying sternly, "If you use any of that cream on me, don't get it on the sheets. And stay away from my asshole—I don't like to get fucked or nothin'."

"Of course," Patrick said, unable even to imagine fucking this guy. He watched from the corner as Joe got undressed. Joe's body was the most beautiful thing he had ever seen. It was perfect in its mixture of muscle and fat. He had a rather hairy chest and a firm, bulging stomach. His dick was unremarkable and soft. The arms were defined naturally, by work rather than a gym, just as Patrick liked. But it was particularly his legs and ass that drew Patrick forward as Joe lay face-down on the bed. This man looked as if he were wearing a pair of hair pants. His totally smooth back sloped down to meet a clear line of hair beginning at the top of his buttocks. Soft, thick black hair that covered both asscheeks and became impenetrable toward the crack. The strong legs were similarly covered.

Patrick gasped as he straddled Joe to begin to work on the shoulders. "What'd you say?" Joe muttered.

"Your body is perfect. It's the sexiest body I've ever seen."

"Oh, yeah," Joe said, sleepy and bored. "Not too hard and take your time. I want a real thorough rubdown."

Patrick had finished the remainder of his coke in the bathroom, and the drug exploded once again against the back of his head, focusing all of his perceptions closely on the flesh that he touched. While thoughts raced through his mind, his physical attention was focused completely. Do a good job, do a good job. He wanted only to please this man, and he tried his hardest as his fingers firmly but gently worked the smooth layers of muscle encasing the back. In its way, this was a totally nonsexual act. Patrick tried to think of it in that way. He tried to think of it as a job. "I have a job to do. Do it well." This job was to make a man's body relax as deeply as possible. He would work as long and as hard as was required of him. Doing a good job was the reward. Being allowed to touch this flesh was the reward.

His hands moved silently along the back as Joe started to snore. Asleep, no attention paid to the efforts. It was assumed that he would do a good job. Time has no meaning when there is no sound. And there was only silence and a softly sweating man beneath Patrick's hands. This man in his silence commanded a respect that had nothing to do with stupidity and taste. Patrick wanted to lose himself in this service. And he had lost himself. He heard his thoughts tumbling along: "I'm gone. There is nothing left of me and if I concentrate, if I focus myself completely on his masculine pleasure, I can disappear. So beautiful...absolute normal perfection."

Patrick didn't understand the dual thoughts that raced through his mind as he worked down along the side of the hairy asscheeks. Stroking the sleek coat of hair with his hands, he continued down the legs and began working the feet with cream. There were two separate minds within him. Two minds that sat beside one another, pouring out thought. The one thought of nothing but loss. In that mind there was only pain and memory. In the other mind, there was only attention and a growing void. This was the mind that he strove toward as he lowered his tongue onto Joe's foot, distantly hearing him moan. With the smell and taste of the foot, pain retreated a bit. Sucking on a toe, Patrick could no longer see fevered, pleading eyes looking at him. Chewing lightly on a callus, he no longer felt the empty bed waiting at home.

The coke was surging through him. His throat and face and teeth and nose were completely frozen numb. Yet, in his brain of loss, there were shots of bright light ricocheting back and forth, reflecting off one another and building brighter. The lights were thoughts. The lights were feelings. The lights were sensations. The lights were words: "Leave me now. Please, my darling, leave me now. We will never again find one another, so leave me now to end in some way, to finish in my fashion. Love is not sex and sex is never love. So I humble myself. I offer myself as a tribute to your memory, which I beg to leave me now. Each night I will lower myself toward a waiting man who is not you. These men are not you, and I do not want them to be. I want only an infinite succession. I want only a row reaching toward oblivion when I can no longer think but only perform these services. I can no longer see your pain. I can no longer see your wasted face and body and the intricate swirl of lesions. You are gone, my darling. You have left me now. I no longer feel you. I no longer see you with me. There is only absence. Now is the time for my pain. I paid tribute to your pain, and now my time has come. The glory of my pain blossoms within me, limitless in its blinding power. I walk alone in a dim room, pacing. There are no tears here. There are no tears for me. I am alone. My tears for you are dry, and I have none left for myself. I am alone. Each day I will scoop out a bit more, until only the fragile pristine shell of walking death remains, and they will pass me and say, 'Where is he? Where has he gone? What is that pale shadow that moves like stale breath against the wall?' I am gone now, darling, and so are you. That is our bond. That is our marriage. That is our pact. We are, each of us, gone. Gone, darling. Gone."

Joe's front side now appeared to Patrick. It was less erotic than the back, but his job was not to judge, only to service; so his hands and lips lowered themselves to arms and pits and nipples and stomach and legs and balls, and he wrapped his hand softly around a throbbing cock. "Is this what you want?" he asked Joe, begging. "I want to do what you want me to do." There was no answer from Joe's snoring lips as Patrick worked his hand slowly up and down the cock. Only one mind now, only the empty mind, only the mind that holds nothing and is hard, hard. With hardly a groan, the cum boiled out of the cock.

Patrick sat there on the edge of the bed, looking at the sunlight piercing the drawn blinds with increasing strength. In the weak light, the body beneath his hands was even more mundane. It was even more glorious to him in its imperfections revealed by day. He knew there was no need to say or do more. There was no task left but to leave silently. That was an important task. Simply to leave.

So he did, after roughly pulling on his clothes. Patrick walked out into the blinding summer morning with the drugs still racing, demanding attention. This was New York. This experience was New York, and it was cold, mean, and he was tired of coming back for more. He was cold even in the sun as he walked down streets that became larger and became highways, and he looked now at the ocean. He found himself at the ocean—or rather, across from it—separated by innumerable lanes of traffic and a sign that said, "Welcome to Sheepshead Bay." It took some time to find a path across the lanes of traffic and then to pull himself over the low wall to the sand. The sound of the water was more imagined than real with the roar of cars speeding past, but the thought of it calmed him. The sun had warmed his numb body, and sweat was pouring down his back, soaking into the porous leather of his jacket. He let the jacket fall to the ground, and then stepped out of his shorts as well. He didn't bother with the sneakers but walked quickly up to his waist into the water. It was neither cold nor warm, filthy nor clean. It simply surrounded him and erased the lower part of his body. He looked down and his lower half had disappeared into the slow-moving waves. "Good," he thought. "Gone." And he moved forward slowly, away from New York. He moved so that he could feel each inch disappearing. Now only his head remained above water. He turned to look at the city, but it wasn't there. There were no skyscrapers or neon signs. There was only the concrete wall dividing the thin strip of sand from the road and the brownish-gray houses on the far side. He did not fall, he let go. He released himself into the water carefully. For an important moment, Patrick was not sure whether he was above or below the water. Then, closing his eyes, he knew he was below and moved his lips steadily, saying, "I'm gone, I'm gone, I'm gone, I'm gone," until finally he was.

Wayne looked up from the pad, feeling dazed and sick to his stomach. He hid the pad in his suitcase and slowly walked upstairs to where Ann was watching television. "Hi, honey. How did your writing go?" Ann's eyes looked swollen and red.

"Pretty good, I guess. Not too cheerful."

"Hasn't been too much fun here, has it?"

"Hasn't been too much fun anywhere, lately," Wayne sighed, sitting in the recliner.

"Tomorrow's Friday. Maybe you should call up some of your old friends. You might get a kick out of seeing them."

"I don't even know if they're still here."

Ann stretched and yawned. "Well, I know Pussy is still here, and I saw Carl the other day."

"You didn't tell me you saw Carl. Did you talk to him?"

"No, I just saw him driving along. I should have honked at him."

The two sat quietly for a few minutes, watching the ten o'clock news. The drought. The president. Ann had woken up enough to bring up something that had been on her mind for a while. "What do you think we should do with your dad's ashes? Since there wasn't a funeral, I hadn't really made any plans; but I guess we should do something with them."

Wayne looked at the brown wood box that sat in the living room. "It is sort of morbid to just have them laying around," he said. "With some of my friends, we scattered the ashes. Do you want to do that?"

Ann chewed on her lip, deciding not to cry. "Can we do it together? Just the two of us?"

"Sure we can, Mom." Wayne went over to hold her hand. "But in a few days. Okay? I just need a rest from all this for a few days."

III.

Wayne had expected more resistance from Ann the following morning when he announced that not only was he going to go visit Selma alone, but that he was going to walk to the Nut Hut. Surprisingly, Ann approved on both counts and told him the walk would be good exercise. Ann had never had a great deal of patience for Selma, and her new role as the old woman's sole caretaker was not one that she cherished. On the other hand, Ann had long ago realized that certain things must be done without reward. She walked Wayne to the door and kissed him, as if he were off to school, and returned to washing dishes.

Most offices open at 9:00 or 9:30 in Iowa, so the streets were still at 10:00 when Wayne left the house. Those who were weren't working, or worked at home, tried to run their errands before noon, when the heat of the day built to its height. Wayne was already sweating a little bit as he strode down the street in his summer "work clothes." This was the outfit he would always wear in the city during hot weather if he needed to do business. In Manhattan, as the heat climbed in July and August, the unfortunate workers stuck in the city would affect a disdainful country look. Busy executives would appear to have just popped in for a few hours from Long Island. For Wayne, a slightly tattered white button-down shirt from Brooks Brothers established that he was serious. A pair of knee-length stone-colored shorts from J. Crew stated that he didn't work in an office with a dress code. Most importantly, though, was a pair of brown loafers worn without socks. The idea of not wearing socks had been something of a revelation to Wayne during college; and, although he wouldn't go so far as to do it except in the dead of summer, he cherished the casually sexy way a man's foot sat naked in the leather confines of a shoe.

If he was feeling fat, Wayne would let his shirt flap around untucked. Today, though, he felt extremely thin, almost gaunt. He knew this wasn't true from looking in the mirror, but still he had decisively smoothed the shirt down past a black lizard belt and positioned the all important sunglasses before leaving the house. This morning felt like the day after. The day after what, he didn't know. Perhaps it was similar to the day after drinking excessively or snorting coke, when one is embarrassed at having revealed too much the night before. It is on those mornings when a person feels thin, exhausted, and, perhaps, a bit glamorous. On those mornings, Wayne would glide past the doorman and raise a limp wrist disdainfully into the air for a cab. Those were dangerous mornings, though, because a cycle could begin to form, one that would last for weeks or months. On those—and these—mornings, it was just as easy to have a drink or do another line or head back to the sex club for a few more as it was to settle back into the controlled way of life. Wayne wasn't sure of the Iowan equivalent, as drinking and drugs lost some of their appeal in these settings and readily available sex was far away. While Wayne walked through the still-damp grass of his lawn, he wished for a day without emotion and knew it was not to be.

In a little paper bag from a New York bookshop, Wayne carried a gift for Selma. Really, it was more of a crutch for himself. The thought of seeing Selma without her talking nonstop was so intimidating, so foreign to the nature of the gabby old woman, that Wayne had decided he would read to her when he had run out of things to say. So he had found a beautifully illustrated version of *Alice in Wonderland*. The etchings had the perfect mix of English morbidness and charm. Maybe, he believed, the echoes of the old story would reach her and, if not bring her back, at least provide the comfort of nostalgia. He had spent some time in the store after finding the book and had felt the need not only to look at the illustrations, but to run his fingers over them, tracing the outlines of the figures. His hands had almost tried to thrust into the pictures to grab the familiar characters. The White Rabbit with his watch. Alice as her overgrown limbs stuck out of a house's windows and her skinny neck popped through the chimney. The Cheshire Cat, of course. And the Queen of Hearts. Wayne had felt obligated to buy the thing after rubbing the Cheshire Cat so hard the ink had smeared. He didn't know if he would give it to Selma though.

Wayne was the type of person who liked the presents he picked out for others so well that he would often keep them for himself.

By car, the route to the Nut Hut is indirect, winding around the large wedge of uncleared woods that still stands near the center of Cherokee. The continued presence of this area, somewhat wild but not nearly a wilderness, is due to the railroad tracks that pass through it. Although only a train or two a day now used the tracks, roads still respectfully kept their distance. The trains carried what trucks declined to: poisonous liquids, scrap metal, and squealing pigs. The tracks cut decisively across highways and fields without a care for more modern traffic and then returned to their private route. The railroad always creates secret places that are mostly the domain of children and gay men. Children fit through the snug openings in fences and groves of trees separating houses from the tracks. In these wooded places, children create traps of branches pulled sharply to the ground and fixed in place by a piece of wood that, stepped upon, releases the branch for a vicious slap in a face. The cruel zeal of boys for these traps and other instruments of torture is limitless. Along with other boys, Wayne had often dug shallow pits filled with glass or sharpened twigs that were covered over most inexpertly, but with the real goal of harming others. This pointless violence had a relationship only later understood. For these protected, secret lands are also privy to sexual exploration. Young boys immediately become erect upon entering their wooded dens filled with snares and pits and the promise of ripping skin that is, for some reason, always associated in primal ways with sex. Sometimes the boys simply jerked off onto the dirt, wiping their spunky hands on leaves afterward. Other times, though, there would be a group of randy boys that let a little hand touch newly hairy balls or a little ass rub against a sharp poke. Seldom do these furtive experiments reach fruition, but they are begun here in the woods and, many, many years later, they would be remembered.

Gay men, like little boys, know how to reach forbidden places and squeeze through the tight openings that block passage. Wayne and other gay men always remembered the childish adventures and the lure of the woods. In cities around the world, as one approaches a park or wooden area, men begin to appear. Five blocks away from the park, they are businessmen and students and unconcerned strollers. Three blocks away, they begin to reveal their purpose with quick looks at the other men narrowing the distance to their goal. A block away, the veil begins to slip. Perhaps a tie is loosened or a few buttons undone. Upon entering parks around the world, the men no longer have names or occupations or any sense of the continuing business of life. Here, among trees bordered by self-created paths, the men search for one another to slam against a tree and tenderly caress. When Wayne wandered through a strange city, he, too, would invariably find himself gravitating toward the safe lushness of close-planted trees that could provide a refuge. Of course, safety was not the point. No, the violence of the pointed sticks, the danger of traps expertly set—these were the lure. The leafy trees were nothing but an exciting trap, made no longer by a tied-back branch but of sharp steel and hard fists and still-mean boys.

So, on foot today, Wayne followed a more direct path than the winding streets. He headed toward the train tracks at the end of Jeffries Street. Only on some blocks were there sidewalks. On others, he was forced to walk on the edge of grassy lawns while an occasional car passed by. Wayne wondered what these people thought of him as they drove past or glanced out of their windows. Maybe they didn't think of him at all, and that would be the strangest thing here, he decided; not to be considered at all, just to be another person walking along a street in the morning. The calm of each neatly positioned house and mowed lawn and singing birds drove New York farther and farther away. Wayne had felt a certain amount of panic when he woke this morning and found he didn't have to care. Writing and finding a job to supplement writing and worrying about Jack or grieving about Jack—all these tasks of living had vanished. The deep pains remained in the pit of his stomach, but the everyday nagging cares couldn't seem to touch this well-ordered life. Even as he walked away from his mother, widowed and alone, and toward his grandmother lost to insanity, Wayne found he didn't care. Having seen the loss of so many other people who had only twenty and thirty years of life, it was difficult to care deeply for the pain of those who had the luxury of sixty or seventy years. An old woman had just pulled into her driveway as Wayne was passing her house, and Wayne heard her keening, whining voice needle into his ear, "Young man. Young man. Would you be a dear and pull up my garage door for me? My rheumatiz is giving me such a time!"

Even as he walked up her driveway and pulled the door up for her, he wanted to scream at her self-satisfied face: "Fuck you, you shriveled-up old potato! You've had your time. Go die! Go die! Did you care when you heard about all the faggots dying or did you just turn the channel to *Jeopardy?* Die or suffer, but don't ask me for help. Why don't you stay inside if you're so fucking feeble? Why don't you lay on your BarcaLounger and tweeze the whiskers out of your butthole if you're too fucking fragile to open the door?" Wayne held close to his chest an inexhaustible reservoir of hate for all those millions who hadn't bothered to help, who were glad that their sons weren't fags, and if they were, it was probably better that they die.

The old woman, now that the garage door was open, had decided not to pull in. Instead, she was bobbing her white head and heaving herself from the car with a tiny bag of groceries. The plastic bag contained a small container of skim milk and one peach. She zeroed in on her target now that Wayne had made the first gesture of obedience. "Oh, you are such a dear thing. You really are. Would you mind just helping me carry this inside? My rheumatiz gets so bad with this humidity. Who are you, dear? Do you live in the neighborhood?"

As he reached for the groceries, Wayne smiled behind the dark sunglasses. "I'm the fairy with AIDS that lives up the street. Actually, I don't have AIDS yet, but I probably will because I liked getting fucked up the butt by somebody who died of it."

The old woman grabbed back her groceries with a little shriek and leaped with newfound agility into the car. "Don't touch me!" Wayne could hear her screeching as he continued on.

Jeffries Street ends at the point where it intersects the railroad tracks. One can either turn left or right onto another street, or continue on a diagonal by walking alongside the tracks through the woods. This area was small but significant, as it served as a dividing point. On the other side of the woods was Highway 71, the main thoroughfare of Cherokee commerce. On this side, by Wayne's house, were the quiet neighborhoods and grammar schools bordered by fields. For Wayne, a number of personal landmarks lay just past Highway 71's four lanes on the other side of these woods. The high school, Carl's house, and the Nut Hut formed a neat package of experience that waited in a direct line. As he stepped onto them, the tracks formed a passageway or a tunnel, a way of going from here to there. Wayne looked behind to make sure no trains were coming, but also to look back down the shady path of trees leading to his house. He expected that the old lady had called the cops by now and wondered if he would see flashing lights or hear sirens. Maybe she just had a heart attack. "Die, Granny, die!" he shouted, laughing as he turned away. Pushing his sunglasses firmly into place, he began walking down the tracks, stepping from wooden board to wooden board while trying to remember what they were called. "Trestles," he wondered, knowing that was wrong. "Slats," he thought. That was closer. He didn't really give a damn, but still, what was their name? The boards were positioned so that he had to take uncomfortable half-strides to step on each one. For a change, he tried to take them two at a time and found that too wide an interval. Switching back to a shorter gait of abrupt steps, he continued on the straight line that took him quickly into an area out of sight of the main streets but still connected to the backyards of houses.

The transitional distance into the woods was bordered by some rickety garages and abandoned cars. These were the types of garages filled with items that were no longer used, but not yet trash. Items like car batteries, broken lawn mowers and sewing machines—too substantial simply to throw away, they had to prove their worthlessness over a waiting period. The aging process also seemed to rot the garages from within as boards popped out at strange angles and paint peeled endlessly from doors that were never shut completely. Wayne couldn't remember whether there were rats in Iowa, but if there were, you would find them in these shacks that leaned in on themselves, joints supporting one another like a house of cards. You might find an old set of china with faded patterns and cracked saucers. You might find books no longer meant to be read. You might find, as Wayne once had, a box of pornography hidden by his father. Wayne knew that it was his father who had put the box of dirty magazines in the garage all those years ago. He was sure of it. And it wasn't the idea of dirty magazines that had so thrilled the teenager because Wayne's father had always left *Playboy* and *Penthouse* lying around the house. What had made Wayne feel faint, had made his crotch ache, were the magazines that showed men with men. Wayne no longer remembered what the men looked like or even what they were doing. But there were men having sex with other men, and the fact that his father hadn't thrown away those magazines, had carefully stacked them in a box with his hands touching the images of men, had lingered in Wayne's mind. Perhaps it had caused him to hate his father a little bit more, to hold him responsible. Wayne thought that some of these garages probably held such hidden treasures, too, but he feared the rats and bugs too much to explore.

"Dead," he thought. He let the flat word bounce on the canvas of his mind with little effect. He added to it.

"My father is dead." Wayne thought, "It's truly shocking but I don't care." Once more he tried. He actually visualized each word, drawing them out in his mind, and added an image of his father's face. "My father is dead." Wayne gazed inward at this accusation, acclamation, statement, and the only response he could find within himself, he spoke aloud: "Yes, my father is dead." Without a twitch of his face or a tear in his eye, Wayne walked on.

The shacks thinned to dusty ditches lined with green trees, an area where one expected to see hoboes making a campfire. Hoboes, the more picturesque precursor to the homeless, were favored characters in the 1940s and 1950s. Fred Astaire and Judy Garland came to mind. "We would ride down the avenue, but we haven't got a car!" Wayne had never actually seen a hobo and suspected that, like gypsies, they had never really existed. Selma had always been afraid of the gypsies. "Bud told me there's a whole caravan of gypsies camped outside of town. Lock your doors tonight!" Although Wayne had never seen a hobo or a gypsy, he suspected that they were similar to the homeless over whom New Yorkers stepped quickly and guiltily on their way to work. He was not so terribly proud of his reaction lately to the homeless people he encountered. For most of his life in New York, Wayne had given money to the people who lay sprawled on the dirty sidewalks. This past year, though, he had started to cross the street and avoid contact with them. If asked why, Wayne thought, he could think of three specific reasons. The first was that many of the homeless people had AIDS and, seeing them, he was forced to think of Jack, forced to think that death was easier for some than others. The second was the man perched on a curb, wizened and red from the weather, who had glibly proclaimed Wayne a faggot. He had simply been walking along when the man had yelled, "I wouldn't even take money from you, you faggot!" So Wayne knew that even the weakest saw themselves as stronger than he was, and what could be his response? Should he walk over and kick the shit out of a man starving in the street? Finally, there was the man without a shirt who lay on Sixth Avenue and wailed in a voice that rose over the traffic and music and rumble of the subway, "Please help me. Someone please help me. I'm so hungry. Please, please help me." That wail contained the despair of the world, the imperative to take some action, and Wayne found he could no longer take action.

But there were no hoboes, no gypsies, and certainly no homeless along the tracks today. There were signs of activity, though, on the slats or trestles or whatever they were called. Mysterious piles of rocks, twigs made into designs, and chalk marks that made perfect sense to a six-year-old dotted Wayne's path. In addition, a dead bird had been balanced carefully on one of the tracks, supported on either side by pieces of wood that ensured the specimen would achieve maximum splatter effect when the next train went by. Wayne imagined that this bird would be carefully checked several times today, with great trepidation, by a band of boys. Looking up, Wayne saw a ragged-looking kid beating a branch against one of the tracks in the distance. Wayne continued to walk quietly and steadily, so as not to alert the boy to his presence. The branch was a substantial piece of wood, and it was difficult to tell whether the object of the violence was to damage something lying on the track or to break the wood. In mid-swing, the boy caught sight of Wayne walking toward him and stepped back a half-step, letting the wood thud down onto the train bed. Their stare held as Wayne approached.

"Hi," Wayne said casually, looking down at the piece of wood between them. The intensity of the sun was such that he could see through the boy's yellowish hair to his sweating scalp. The boy's face was deeply tanned, but the sun had not yet been able to transform the clammy white skin beneath his hair. It was not the playful sort of hair that one wants to muss and cluck over. The boy carried with him the sullen look of an unwashed child who had spent too much time alone.

"Hi," said the boy, who was not sure whether to be afraid of this unlikely adult walking on the tracks or to take advantage of some company. The boy felt all the treasured objects in his pockets, taking comfort in their presence. There was the bright pink rabbit-paw key chain, the gold ring, the nail clippers, the five dimes, two quarters, and three pennies. His hands reviewed the items continually, keeping guard.

"What're you working on?" Wayne asked as he tapped the branch with a brown Cole-Haan loafer.

The boy stepped forward, proprietarily regarding his branch. "I'm cleanin' this off."

"Is it dirty?"

"No, I mean the bark. You know, like it's skin. I'm taking it off."

"Oh," Wayne said, noticing that the beating had begun to split the bark off at one end. "Pretty big branch. What are you gonna do with it?"

"Don't know. What are you doin'?" countered the boy, beginning to get wary of this inquisition. He held tight to his rabbit paw and rubbed it for luck. He was rubbing the rabbit paw so hard that he could feel some of the hair start to pull out of it.

"Just walking."

"Why?" asked the boy, not afraid now and openly curious as to what this all meant. The boy had never seen a person like this before, with soft brown shoes, no socks, and big black glasses covering his eyes. The boy could also smell a strong perfume coming from the man, but not sweet like a girl's. This perfume smelled...he couldn't think of a word. It smelled green. "Why're you walking?"

"I just wanted to walk."

"Where to? Don't you have a car?"

"My mom has a car," Wayne said, moving slowly past the boy. "I'm going to the Nut Hut."

The boy's eyes opened very wide, looking at the man with the black sunglasses on. The boy could see himself reflected back in the glasses, twin images of his tanned, skinny face. He leaned over carefully, keeping his eyes on the man while he grabbed hold of his branch. "Are you crazy?" he whispered, backing away.

"Not yet," Wayne answered. He lowered his sunglasses and stared straight at the boy. Wayne knew what his eyes looked like on days like this. They looked somewhere between blue and gray, with a shininess to them, a flat sheen. He squatted down on his heels to be at the same level as the boy, "Not yet." And before the boy could respond, Wayne was already walking away. He thought of how this little exchange would be translated in the boy's mind into something significant: either a secret or a story to tell other kids. After walking a minute without looking back, he heard the pounding resume on the tracks.

The railroad tracks emerged once again into the larger, unprotected world as they crossed the concrete strip of Highway 71 and into the center of town. Here, as the woods thinned, was a busy intersection that had gone through many stages of development. Wayne's earliest memories of this intersection were of the A&W Drive-In, root-beer floats, and hamburgers. Now the drive-in had been replaced by a Safeway store where Carl had once worked—perhaps still did work, for all Wayne knew. The dislocation of being in this setting stopped Wayne. He would take another step and his stomach would begin to churn more and he wished he could sit down and take a shit. Wayne forced himself a few more steps before knowing he really had to stop. The sun beat so bright. "The eye of God," he could hear Elizabeth Taylor's wavery voice say. Wayne was able to step behind a tree before he started to vomit and it rushed from him. All the swirling confusion poured past his lips onto the gravel and he closed his eyes. "Must not give in because that will be the end of it," he knew. "Must not let this take me over. I know where I am. I am...I am two thousand miles away in a flat state, in a town of six thousand people. I know this place, and it can't affect me. I know what I am doing here, and it is a formality. It is temporary. It will end."

Wayne forced his eyes open and focused on whatever was in his view. Facing the grocery store was a photography studio. He looked at the faces in the display window. He studied the faces until he could work up a mouthful of spit and send it flying onto the sidewalk. Another spit, and he reached into his pocket for some gum. "Always have gum," he told himself. After adding a second piece of gum, he felt ready to step onto the sidewalk and walk toward the window. Photography studios are always sinister, and this one, in particular, had an eerie quality, enhanced by the elaborately framed portraits in the window of high-school seniors, brides and grooms, families at Christmas, and babies with tortured expressions of glee. Each shot was carefully posed in front of seamless blue paper and lit in such a way that the eyes seemed like black bullet holes in the face.

Unlike in Manhattan, Wayne waited for the light and crossed Highway 71, passing the moderate activity of the Safeway store. All the grocery stores here had a little coffee shop in them, haunted by old people with no other way to pass the hours. Selma had been the queen of these coffee shops, knowing everyone and eating jelly doughnuts by the hour while gossiping away. Sometimes she brought her knitting or a pad and paper in case she needed to dash off a poem that came to her. More often, though, she would just throw back her candy-red hair and yell. Selma's conversation could be followed throughout the store, and it made no difference to her whether she knew the person next to her or not, the stories would be the same. Much to Ann's horror, Selma would also holler out a shopping tip if she decided it was necessary. "Hey, sweetheart! Don't buy those bottles of Coca-Cola! I found a dead baby mouse in one of those once!"

Wayne continued to walk, slowly, but still making his way along the street. His head had begun to throb from puking. The pounding began in the same spot it always did, and he rubbed his right temple in slow circles. Another day of tears, and he wanted it just to stop. He wanted all feeling to stop inside of him so that nothing could ever pull at his insides again. At the same time, he feared that this was coming true. Because with each pain, and each remembrance of pain, another part of him closed off. His outer edges became more brittle, like something cooked for too long.

Wayne rubbed harder at his temple. This feeling of being outside oneself and disconnected from the decisions of daily life made Wayne think of a marionette. That's how he perceived the changes in himself—a marionette marching blankly into the next battle. That sense had begun before he left New York. As his friends had rallied round to comfort him, he looked at them and saw the same detachment, the stillness of too much suffering. All these brave people who had worked so hard finding a way to survive. All the world had given in. And just as an individual has a pain threshold that, surpassed, triggers a state of shock, so the world, too, has a breaking point. It would pass someday but, for now, there was only a cold resolve to keep on, to stay in the same parade as the other toy soldiers trying to enjoy what was left.

Wayne realized he had been staring straight ahead at Washington High School without recognizing it. Another large building had been added to where the parking lot had once been in front. This building blocked the low line of tan brick that followed the hill; and, whereas the earlier building had moved horizontally, this was a vertical structure. Four stories hardly makes a skyscraper, but this was imposing all the same. There were no windows that Wayne could see. It reminded him of a fortress, like the New York Telephone building in lower Manhattan that appeared to be a prison because there was no discernible way in or out. Now that summer vacation had arrived, there was no activity around either the new or old building. The students stayed as far away as possible during the summer months. Wayne felt the same way. He felt that he didn't want this building to have control over him. He didn't want the memories trapped inside those walls to come flowing out. Instead, he looked up. Wayne looked up the hill knowing what he would see, and he looked up anyway. There, in the same place with same dull brown paint, was Carl's house.

It had been incredible how Wayne's obsession with Carl had faded almost immediately upon leaving Cherokee. Wayne had found that there were literally thousands, maybe millions of Carls waiting in gay bars around the world. This army of Carls waited, muscular and young and helpless, in every bar Wayne entered. In fact, in the very first gay bar Wayne had gone to upon arriving in Pittsburgh (which was conveniently adjacent to the university) he had met a young man with shaggy gold hair and an athletic chest. This young man, whose name was immediately forgotten, promptly bought Wayne a drink, took him home, and plucked his virginity like an unwanted hair. This young man was replaced by another and another in an endless parade that seldom slowed to allow for more than a fuck until Wayne met Jack. But even though Wayne knew that, physically at least, he had touched and licked and had hundreds of men who surpassed Carl, a jolt of desire rapped around his groin looking up the hill to that familiar house.

If there were a gay bar here, in front of Wayne, he would have gone in. Although he loved to drink, there was a deeper addiction for Wayne that was enhanced by liquor. Wayne felt the pull of gay life that continued on without him. Right now, he wondered, how many men are having sex in New York? He recounted the spots where, even now in the early morning, men would be having sex in the city. Most mundanely, in their bedrooms. Or talking on computerized phone-sex lines. Eyeing one another in a hotel bathroom. Inching closer over the hot tiles of the steam room. In the back of a Times Square movie theater. Squeezed into cramped, dirty booths of a bookstore. Lying exhausted in the sex clubs that never close. Or picking up a drunk in a gay bar. Having been a participant, Wayne could not and did not want to withdraw. Because the life of sex continues and if you are not in the loop, you may miss that one incredible fuck that finally sates your appetite. You may miss the most perfectly formed dick. Someone else will get your due. Wayne wanted Carl—or any other man—but he also didn't want it to start here. Wanting gay sex in Iowa is worse than sex on coke—you can't deliver the goods.

The town swimming pool was still closed at this hour, and the parking lot was empty but for the beat-up car of the maintenance man whom Wayne could see making long brush strokes, cleaning the pool in preparation for the hordes of kids who would arrive promptly at 11:30. The freshly painted white wooden gate was pulled shut over the refreshment stand that would later dispense Sno-Cones and frozen candy bars. Wayne's favorite as a child had been the Froz-Pop, the length of frozen syrup packed in a plastic tube that is pushed out into a waiting mouth. Forgetting the refreshment stand as he started to climb the hill that would lead past Carl's house and onto the grounds of the Nut Hut, Wayne looked back to the maintenance man. The man didn't look bad from here with the muscles of his back bunched up under a white T-shirt to pull the long broom across the pool floor. Wayne thought that even looking at him was a mistake—a mistake to start any erotic feeling here that would only lead to frustration and late-night trips to the forlorn gay bar in Sioux City, if it even existed anymore. No matter what had changed for Wayne in distant cities, nothing had changed here. The possibility of man touching man here was remote, and Wayne refused to give way to the pitiful yearnings of a teenager. It was an earlier life, he realized, one that could only echo now but not touch him. Those echoes and dim images could be strong, though; and, looking at Carl's house again as he ascended the hill, he wondered what had become of the beautiful boy he had desired so much. No matter how many other Carls might wait in smoky bars, now that he was in Cherokee, Wayne let himself think of the sensation of silky flesh running smooth beneath his fingers, of a body's weight as it pressed down upon him, of the soft battle between tongues.

Carl's driveway was empty, and the house showed no signs of life. It had been so many years that he couldn't recall the furniture as he tried to look through the front window into the living room. This was not the time, Wayne thought, and what would be the point anyway? "Don't do this to yourself," he said walking away, although a little slower. There were so many lives here that had continued on without him, lives that hadn't entered his mind after he left. Pussy. Carl. Even Mr. A. Wayne had simply tossed their lives to the side, and now he didn't know how to pick them up again. He didn't want just to ask, just to find out. He wasn't sure he had enough inside him to reestablish the broken bonds or even to explain his life to these strangers. Wayne kept moving along the path toward the Mental Health Institute, forcing himself to think, not about Carl, but what waited ahead for him. When he reached the top of the hill, he could see the large suburban houses, including Eric's old house, sitting easily and smugly on plots of well-tended green. He had heard from Eric, even bumped into him once in New York, barely recognizing the balding man. Eric told Wayne that his family had moved to Minnesota and had sold the house in Cherokee. Now strangers lived in these houses, Wayne thought, and felt mildly annoyed. Very little remained here except for the landmarks of memory. The actual life of ten years ago had moved on inevitably. Daily life is smaller than people living in certain homes. It is smaller, more specific, even than sexual relationships and marriage. An entire way of life is defined by the most mundane of rituals. When you get to a fork in the road, you tend always to turn one way, even if both directions get you to the same place. Before leaving your house, you look in the mirror to check your hair. You prefer one of the grocery stores. You always put your keys in the left pocket. Your right shoulder always itches. You sweat for a few minutes after dressing. All of these acts, these gestures, create rules holding daily life together. So important but so individualized are these rules that home is no longer a home to a long-absent participant. Soon enough, though, the patterns of life in Cherokee would yield, incorporate him, swallow him up. "Be careful," he thought. "Don't fall into it."

"Maybe I'll check in," Wayne said to himself as he considered the serene Nut Hut park before him. The grounds made the prospect of a stay at the institute seem quite appealing. Earth swelled in waves of green patterned by ornamental trees and curving paths, and there was a constant rustle as summer breezes floated among the living chimes of leaves. The air, the light. These are the things most striking to one entering this sanctuary. The air moves constantly so that even on the most stifling day a cool rush of wind from beneath the trees wraps around you, cooling the hot back of the neck and drying the fevered brow. Surrounded by the moving air, taken up by it, Wayne stopped to sit on a bench placed beside a sprawling, elderly tree. The wizened fingers of its branches nearly touched the ground on the left side and, on the right, lifted slightly to form a welcoming marquee containing the bench. Looking down the alley of trees lining the main road into the institute, Wayne admired the clarity of light moving from open lawns to be broken into smaller beams by branches and reflected upward again into a general glow above the grass. While birds sang and squirrels fought in the trees, Wayne recalled places similar to this. The DuPont estates outside of Philadelphia. Loire Valley chateaus. Hudson River mansions.

Leaning forward, stiff today from travel, Wayne stretched his legs. The fact that so much suffering was housed in this park only heightened its beauty. This place existed in spite of it. Just as the serenity of estates and chateaus and mansions belied the trauma of the lives within them, the lushness of the branches over Wayne refused to acknowledge pain. The range of color and texture in one living thing can be overwhelming. Wayne touched the bark of the tree. "Let me look so closely at this thing that I will understand it," he thought. "Let me really see something." First of all, the color was not brown. Trees are not brown. They are black and green and often ooze a golden sap. Trees are not smooth. They are furrowed and rasping and contain deep rotting holes that sometimes traverse the entire trunk. Trees are not individuals. They are a community of life containing ants and birds and squirrels on the outside and termites and grubs and worms burrowing deeper within. Trees are not silent. They groan so sadly at the base and snap angrily and sing in a shrill voice with their top branches. Trees are not silent. They talk about their pity for things that can run and leap and are not planted as securely as they. Trees are not isolated. Their roots extend far deeper into the earth than we know; not for water, but to reach out to one another and drape their living cords of wood over one another, ecstatic in the darkness. That is what Wayne sensed most strongly, concentrating on this tree—by looking and touching and smelling this one thing, he could experience the entire lawn. When he stood and walked, he could feel the roots of the tree form hard curves beneath him.

A part of the land was the building that sat upon it. Diverse levels of chimneys and garrets rose into view above the treetops and, after a short walk, a small city came into view. More Victorian than medieval, more curious than frightening, the complex set of buildings was composed of medical facilities, recreation halls, administrative offices, and dormitories. The dormitories were actually called wards, Wayne recalled from Selma's earlier stay here. There were wards for violent and nonviolent, criminal and noncriminal, male and female. The entire feel of the place reminded Wayne of Woolf's description of Orlando's palace:

The great house lay more like a town than a house, brown and blue, rose and purple in the snow, with all its chimneys smoking busily as if inspired with a life of its own.

There was no snow here, only the waxy deep green of leaves and grass, but the place summoned forth an atmosphere of great hearths and heavy tapestries.

Wayne entered through the imposing stone porch that protected those emerging from cars during bad weather. The vaulted ceilings of the reception area were humbled by framed artwork made by patients. The art, which tended to the sunny side, also included some examples that might well be represented by SoHo galleries. Running off the reception room were a series of imposing wooden doors, behind which, one assumed, must sit administrators and doctors making decisions on everything from invasive brain operations to sanitation systems. At the end of the hall lay the first real sign of the institution's real purpose, the first symbol of the less-than-ideal lives lived here. A large metalwork door with a lock led to an elaborate staircase reaching up into the wards. The woman behind the desk was eager for some break in the day's already-considerable boredom. She walked from behind the desk to where Wayne still examined the art and asked in a big, generous, Iowa voice, "Can I help you, honey?"

Wayne was glad for the fat woman in the white dress. Her bright red lips were messily drawn on past the confines of her actual mouth, and the flesh was pressed out from her badly assembled teeth. Her cheeks had been created from the same pot of color and sat like twin wounds on her face. All in all, though, she was reassuring, cheerful. Wayne couldn't imagine her wielding long needles or sizzling electrodes. He looked to her green eyes that darted about, eager to help. "I'm here to see Selma Leary."

"Oh, Mrs. Leary! Are you a relative, sweetie?"

"I'm her grandson."

"She will be just thrilled to see you," the woman trilled, maneuvering her bulk back behind the reception desk. "Let me just write out a visitor's pass."

"How is she? My mother told me she doesn't talk or know people."

"Sweetie, I'm not her doctor, so I shouldn't say much. Against the rules, you know. But just remember, they may not be talking, but that doesn't mean they aren't listening. She'll know when you're with her." The woman squeezed Wayne's hand and gave him the red visitor's pass stamped Ward 2. "You just go right up those stairs to the first door on the landing. Show this to the nurse, and she'll find your grandma for you."

"Thank you," Wayne said, not wanting the exchange to be over yet. With each reluctant step toward the metal gate and the buzzing sound that released the door, he felt farther from his body. In these situations, he always watched from somewhere else, from a safer place. The sharp antiseptic smell of hospitals and gay bathhouses rushed up Wayne's nostrils while he climbed, one slow step at a time, to the second floor. Another woman at a table waited at the next landing. Her presence was less reassuring. Her flat face was the same beige color as her frizzy hair, and she sat at the desk with her head propped onto her fist.

"I'm here to see Selma Leary," he said to the woman, who didn't move her head but just glanced at his pass.

"In through this door. She'll be in the dayroom. All patients are there until lunch. Better get a move on—no visitors at lunch." Her voice was surprisingly high—shrill, even. She hit a button next to the door, opening it quickly.

There was nothing to do at this point but proceed, so Wayne carefully moved inside, expecting to hear shrieks and babbling voices. There was hardly a sound. A slight murmur came from down the hallway but the prevailing mood was of forced tranquillity, of resignation. Hope had given way to something more comforting in the pea-green walls dotted with framed pictures of Jesus and tattered sofas here and there in the hall. Bright sunlight poured through the barred windows and heated the interior of the ward, which overlooked the lawns. This was a stuffy, permanent world where air conditioning or heaters ran, no matter, because the seasons slipped past quickly in minds waiting to rest.

Down the hall, one could see a larger room positioned off to the right. Wayne made his way down the hall, the sound of his shoes on the tile floor louder than it should have been. He turned into the dayroom without looking at it. Without really looking, he could see that it was a large room with an imposing bay window which had been partially opened, although the same steel bars guarded against escape. Sofas and armchairs were supplemented by folding chairs surrounding card tables ready for a game of checkers. Wayne let his eyes take in more, beginning to acknowledge the people in the room. His eyes came to rest randomly on the women, most elderly, sitting and staring. The first woman tapped her fingers coyly against her cheeks and whispered, "Oooh, Jimmy, ooooh." Her voice lilted incongruously from thin lips, and she moved her fingers to check her hair, in a steel-gray bun. "Ooooh!" the sound was like a train whistle. The rattling of paper drew Wayne's eyes to another woman who was hidden completely by a tattered newspaper. Only her red hands could be seen as she huffed and straightened the paper that she held stiffly in front of her. Every few seconds, another huff would issue from behind the paper, and she would snap the pages angrily again.

Then Wayne saw Selma. It felt to Wayne as if a large

hand had picked him up by the scruff of his neck and shaken him, jerked him up and down to produce the stuttering sobs he tried to control. His grandmother sat—or sprawled, rather—on a tweed sofa near the window. Wayne would have been hard pressed to explain how he recognized her. All the features that made her Selma were absent. Walking to her, sitting beside her, there was no flurry of powdery arms and lips about him, no outburst of strong voice, no smell of whiskey, beer, or schnapps, no blazing red hair. Selma's hair was no longer red-orange, but a desultory gray-white that hung thinly around her long face. Long drapes of loose skin hung from beneath her arms. Her eyes stared at a point just in front of her face. Eyes that had been framed with blue eye shadow were now colorless, except for the red puffiness of the lids.

"Grandma," he said, embarrassed. Why even try, he wondered, but felt compelled to continue. "I'm here."

Selma's eyes were a clear blue as she looked down and to the side. They blinked slowly now and then when they became dry but they looked at a private space, a different world not reached by voices or sight. Wayne could barely stand to touch her. He did not want to touch this living corpse. Instead, he looked for something that would be the same. The hospital gown barely covered Selma's considerable girth and sported none of the decorative spots and stains with which Selma had enhanced her clothes. She had often worn pins, too. Daisy pins at the collar. Leaf pins with sparkly rhinestones. Of course, here, pins were potential weapons, a cheerful sunburst could be used to stab and wound. Wayne continued to search the sagging body. His eyes lingered upon her hands, causing, for the first time, his tears to start in earnest. The sense of being out of his body, away from fear, left him as the sight of Selma's hands made everything real again.

She pulled back slightly when he took her hand, and her strength became apparent as he held on, fighting against her pull. Her pulling away did not stop, did not lessen as the moments passed. But Wayne did not let go and he felt her bony knuckles, kneaded them, held strong to the resisting hand. "I won't let go of you. I won't give you up. I'm here. I'm here with you. I love you and I won't let you go. Don't pull away. I need you now. Goddamn it, I need you now. I came all this way and I want to be with you and hold you and I need you to be with me. Please."

"I've got so much to tell you and I have to believe that you can hear me and understand because I've got to tell you what happened to that little boy who played on your porch with gravel in his hand. I'm not some poem, some card, for you. I'm real and here and I have to tell you some things. I love you so much and now that I'm finally here, I don't know if you can hear, but I have to believe that you can. Can't somebody listen to me? Can't you hear, finally hear? God, I've just lost everything and I won't give you up. I won't fucking give you up.

"Can't you see what I've lost? Your ring isn't on my hand anymore. I wore it every day since I left you, and I could feel it there protecting me, and it would be there like your hand on my hand. One night I looked down and saw my empty finger. I knew that I had finally lost everything. I probably lost your ring in a bar looking at another man, another man whose name I didn't know. Your ring just dropped off me finally. I always had you with me; I always had you touching me while that ring was on my finger. It dropped off when everything else happened. I'm sorry I lost your ring. I'm sorry I lost it. That was the one thing you gave me that I never wanted to lose. I'm so very sorry.

"I loved somebody else, somebody other than you. I could never even tell you his name. You could never know that I loved this man—a wonderful man—and he loved me, too, and now he's gone, Grandma. I don't have him anymore, and I don't know what to do. I just don't have anything left. There's nothing for me, and that's why I need you so much to be with me right now. Please. Please stop pulling away from me. Don't you know the feel of my hand? I can see your hand and it's the same hand, the same gangly old hand. I have to believe that you know I loved you and that I had to leave here.

"Don't you know why I left you? Don't you know why I could never come see you? They would have killed me here. They tried to kill me already, before I left. When you would look at the news, didn't you know they were talking about that little boy on your porch? That's me. That's me. You were right when you said that I'd always be a little boy to you. But could you see that little boy when they'd talk on TV about all the men dying? That little boy went and fell in love with someone, Grandma. He fell in love with a wonderful man you never met. A man who's gone now. Lost. You've lost people but so have I, and, for once, I need someone to comfort me. That little boy was me and those dying men were me and this is me and I need you now. Don't leave me. I can't lose one more. I can't lose you, too."

Selma's skinny hand finally rested free of Wayne's grip and slapped back into its resting position on her lap. Wayne's tears were replaced by slow, deep breaths as he looked at his grandmother. "Can't someone help us? Can't *anyone* help us?"

Selma looked at the walls of the room again, trying to recognize them. They were, as before, a deep eggplant color with an orangish trim. "Pretty," she thought. The strangeness of the room became apparent, though, when she looked up toward the far-distant opening. It was as if she were at the bottom of a well or in a chimney looking up. Far above, she could see the white dot of sun past the tree roots and other protrusions that stuck out into the tunnel.

There was no sense of time here. Selma looked at her watch—the hands were still immobile and holding at 4:23. She may have been here for days but doubted it because the light never changed from above and she had no urge to eat, drink, or go to the bathroom. Still there was the sense that time was rushing past, flooding down this deep hole, that time was pouring around her on its way to a deeper chamber. Again, she got up from the straight-backed chair to walk around the small room. She felt too big here. Her long legs had always made tight spaces difficult for her, and here she had to push the chair back against the opposite wall so that she could stand up fully. What seemed to be three feet away when sitting was immediately in front of her as soon as she stood up.

Looking closely at them, Selma could see that the walls were more detailed than she had imagined. They had a swirling paisley design printed in black over the deep purple. In addition, there were cracks behind the wallpaper, seams or joints that ran up and down the wall. Selma took her thumbnail and traced one of the seams—gently at first, and then forcefully enough to cut through the paper. She continued to peel back the paper at about eye level, blowing through the crack to clear away plaster dust. She thought that she could see daylight, dim and unfocused, beyond. It was only now that she realized her glasses were gone. Standing back for a moment, she looked at her hand, at the chair. She could see perfectly. The room seemed larger, almost spacious now. Selma walked quickly around the perimeter of the room, her legs swinging wide, until she was almost running.

She returned again to the spot on the wall that she had been working on. It was easy to find, and she was embarrassed, for a moment, to see that she had made a much larger hole than she had intended. What she had meant to be a tiny slice in the wallpaper had become large enough for her to reach her entire hand into, which she now did. Her fingers explored deeper and deeper, to the extent of her elbow. Another surface met her fingers, a cool glassy surface. Pulling her arm out she peered into the hole again. A gray-brown light filtered through what appeared to be a tiny window, like a porthole in a ship. By returning her hand to the glass and rubbing it, she cleared away some of the dirt and could see a very bright light beyond. Selma pushed hard against the glass. Pushed with all her might. Without warning, her body flew forward against the wall as the glass gave way under the pressure. Her body remained inside, but she could feel air moving on her hand and the warmth of sun on the skin. She hardly cared when, pulling her arm back inside, she saw the blood spurting out of the large vein on top of her hand. Selma just plucked out the shard of broken glass and wiped the ripped flesh on her pant leg.

Putting her face to the hole in the wall, Selma could see clearly out onto a wide lawn gracefully planted with large walnut trees and lilac bushes in full bloom. It reminded her of a large version of her own backyard. It could have been minutes or hours before she saw the man step from behind the walnut tree and look at her. The man had on dark glasses and had very short black hair. A few moments later, he reached up slowly and took off the glasses. His eyes seemed very close to her. These eyes, she knew immediately, were Wayne's eyes. She screamed out his name again and again, but he still stood, leaning against the tree without recognition or expression. Her voice became shriller as she gasped for breath and shouted his name again. Drawing back from the wall, panting, she thrust her arm back through the hole and flailed her wrist back and forth. She waved as hard as she could, trying to attract his attention. A short, hard grunt came from Selma's throat as she felt someone grab hold of her hand on the other side of the wall and give a strong pull. Her head slammed against the wall with the next jerk on her disembodied hand. She felt her arm becoming longer and longer, elastic. The pressure on her hand was painfully intense, pulling and kneading her fingers, pinching the flesh of her palm and, intermittently, yanking her arm deeper. The last tug started to rip a deep muscle in her shoulder, and she could hear a piercing scream issue forth from her throat.

Selma flew backward as the grip on her arm was released without warning. Falling over the chair, she waited for the hard ground to meet her bones, waited for the cracking sound of ribs or hips. Instead, she found herself settling easily into the waiting arms of a man. The room had grown even larger, and the two of them lay comfortably at the far end of what now appeared to be more a hall than a room. Trembling and coughing a bit, she looked into the face of her rescuer. She thought of him as a rescuer, rather than a threat.

His face registered immediately as Greek. She knew because she remembered these features from the Greeks she had worked for so many years ago. The thick eyebrows framed densely lashed brown eyes and a gently curved nose. The arms that held her were very hairy and strong. She stroked the arm absentmindedly, lying there on this man. He was, perhaps, the most beautiful man she had ever seen.

Selma straightened her legs and, looking at them, saw how long and fit they looked. She looked at her flat stomach and small breasts. She brought her soft white hand up to her long red hair, pushing it back from her face. She lay naked on the hard stomach of this man, resting her face now on the sleek hair of his chest. Without strangeness or shame, she shifted even closer to him, feeling the pulse of his blood through his erect cock, which rubbed slowly against her thigh.

"Who are you?" Selma asked, after kissing him lightly.

"I came to help you," the man said and then brought his tongue into her mouth, exploring gently.

"Are we dead?" Selma sighed.

"Just me. Your mind s dead, and your body will be, too. But not quite yet. You have to wait here, but I'll stay with you. Soon you'll be nothing."

"I called to Wayne just now. I could see him. Is he dead, too?" Selma asked.

"No, he's alive. But the living can help the dead if they love strongly enough, and he loves both of us that much."

"Will I see him, again? Will I see Wayne?"

"No. You won't see anyone. It's the end, finally, and everything is gone."

"What is there?"

"Nothing. And it's glorious."

"What's your name?"

"Jack."

"There's not another life?"

"There's nothing, Selma. Nothing. Beautiful."

Wayne had wandered numbly back out onto the grounds when the lunch bell had rung. They had taken Selma away like a sack, like a bag, something to be carried. "That wasn't her," Wayne said now, leaning his head against the tree. Sitting on the bench again, he noticed that he still carried the stupid, pitiful bag that he had thought so reassuring earlier. He took the book out and looked at the curling lines drawn on the pink and green cover. Wayne laid the book carefully on the bench, deciding to abandon it, not wanting it near him. He leaned back and let his eyes wander over the building again. There was only one sign of life. "Poor nut!" he thought, watching the bony hand stuck through the bars of a window into the sun and waving wildly.

IV.

"Pussy, Pussy, Pussy, Pussy," she sang softly, now that she had finally gotten the kids in bed. She stood, swiveling her hips and running her hands up and down her thighs in front of the closet, wondering what to wear for Wayne's visit. Those new tight jeans—that's for sure. Maybe that ruffled pink blouse. "No, too frilly," she decided, pursing her lips and moving back to look at herself in the full-length mirror. Her arms were thin enough, almost skinny. Her stomach wasn't too bad, she decided, giving herself the benefit of the doubt. If those fucking legs would just slim down, though. She turned her back to the mirror and, in slow motion, glanced back over her shoulder. Sexy, really sexy. She was getting hot now and walked back over to the closet to get a pair of high heels. This really got her going. She loved the way her ass looked in heels as she bent over at the waist, looking through her legs back at the mirror. "Show me that box, you foxy babe," she said to her reflection and began to rub herself slowly. She flexed the muscles in her legs and worked her finger slowly inside herself. "Ride that pony, sweetheart." There was something about this position that got her nuts, and she wished she had thought to bring her vibrator over with her, but wasn't about to give up this view to get it. "Show me those pretty pink walls," she groaned as a few more rubs to her clit took her over the edge. This was the weird part for her, after she'd come, the frenzy was over and she would find herself in this embarrassing position, her legs straining not to collapse. "Worth it, though," she thought, as one more ripple of pleasure went up her spine.

Standing up, she stepped into jeans and her bra, straining to close the zipper on the jeans. Pussy thought she looked pretty good, though, and hoped that Wayne would comment on her dramatic weight loss. She was a queen in her palace in this room, with the door closed. It was all decorated in white. The walls, the bedspread, the carpet. All white and she loved it. "Great tits," she growled, trying to make her voice sound like Rick's. "The Cop," that's what she and Wayne had called him. Rick was gonna give her a good fucking tonight before he went to sleep. Trouble was, he didn't get off till nearly two and could get tired by then. She still liked that dick, even after all these years. That hot, hairy body, too. "Oooh, baby, Momma's gonna be waitin' tonight," she had promised him when he left, and rubbed his crotch until she could feel his dick get hard underneath the uniform. Rick had seemed unimpressed that her old friend was going to visit and certainly hadn't been jealous, "That's the fag, ain't it? Just keep him away from the kids."

Pussy wasn't surprised when she picked up the phone that afternoon halfway through *Oprah* ("Damn it, just when it's getting good!") and it was Wayne. His dad had died, he was bound to come into town for that. She just couldn't go out to a bar, though, like he'd wanted. Maybe she was a little worried about going around with him, now that she had kids and all. People could be damn mean, and they didn't mind taking it out on somebody's kids, either. At first, it had made her guilty, but then she figured he'd get to see her house this way, and the kids too, even though Rick wouldn't like that. Pulling out a black V-neck top, she stopped to think about how someone would see her after almost ten years. "Have I changed a lot?" she wondered, looking again in the mirror. The black top was the right choice; she knew when she saw her tits pushing out and her stomach flat below. So sexy. She decided she'd have this on when Rick got home 'cause how could he resist this? If she just looked in the mirror without thinking, she looked the same. It was when she thought of herself with the kids or Rick that she changed. Then she had to narrow her eyes a little to look like her old self. She hated that. Like the one time she'd been using the vibrator, really getting off, and all of a sudden one of the boys started crying in his bedroom. It made her feel kind of sick to her stomach to see that pink vibrator going in and out, her all moany and sweating, and then hear that voice. Those were the times she knew she'd changed.

"Okay, ready," she said touring through the house for one last check. The door on the kids' room was shut, so they wouldn't wake up. She'd made some Rice

Krispies bars and had a bowl of peanuts on the table. Now, for the music. Pussy realized she had no idea what kind of music to put on. Not that country shit that Rick liked. Maybe Metallica or Guns 'n' Roses. No, she decided, it was better to just leave on MTV and then there'd be a variety. So she sat down with her beer and waited. Pussy wasn't nervous. More just curious. He was a fag, so it wasn't hard to figure out why he left and never visited. But what was it like to go so far away? What goes on in New York City? She tried to think of the cities she'd been to. Sioux City wasn't really a city. Omaha...kind of. Minneapolis was definitely the only real city she'd been to. It had seemed very lonely. That was her strongest impression as she'd watched all those people walking along, not talking to each other. They all seemed so busy. What the hell did they have to do that was so important? If she didn't have kids, hadn't wanted kids, she thought. Then maybe. No, she concluded with another sip of the beer, not for me.

The doorbell rang right at 9:30. He was always on time. She closed her eyes and stuck her chest right out when she opened the door. "Why, Pussy Galore, you're beautiful!" Wayne wrapped his arms around her and thought that she still smelled like Love's Baby Soft, that she was still proud of her big tits and that there was still something to love in her. "But where's the other half of you, honey?"

"Me? What about your hair? You didn't tell me you were in the marines!" Pussy was surprised to find she was a little misty eyed and pulled Wayne into the house.

"Now let's look and see if we even recognize each

other," she said. He really hadn't changed that much. His eyes were kind of pinched looking and that hair was so short; but other than that, she thought he'd stayed the same. He had on jeans and a nice white shirt.

Very respectable, she thought. *I wouldn't even know he was gay.*

"Well, I recognize you." He took her hand. "No matter how thin and glamorous you might get, I'll always recognize you. Let me see your house. You are such a respectable married woman. Oh, my God—you're a mother, too!" he said, looking at the pictures on the refrigerator.

"Can you believe it, Wayne? Come on in to the living room and have a seat. Now, I've got beer, or I can make us a nice Kahlua and cream. I won't stay skinny on either one."

"I'll have a beer, Pussy." Giggling, Pussy ran back to the kitchen while Wayne sat down in the living room. It was a typical kind of room, lots of brown and green. There was a family portrait of Pussy and the Cop, with two happy kids. Wayne was relieved to see that the one constant in life, MTV, was on. *Is there anywhere without MTV?* he wondered.

"Now tell me everything," Pussy whispered as she opened his beer. "Have some peanuts. Oh, sorry about your dad."

"Don't be. I'm not," Wayne said after a sip of beer.

"Now, Wayne. Anyway, I don't want to talk about sad stuff. Just tell me everything that's gone on."

Wayne was hard-pressed to think of what to tell her about his life. "It's not so different from here. You still end up knowing everybody at the grocery store and having a best friend. It's weird how things don't change much."

"But everything changed for me," Pussy said. "I look different. I act different. I feel different."

"How did you lose all that weight? Did you do a lot of exercise?"

"Wayne, I would be happy to loan this to you while you're back," Pussy said, grabbing a videotape from the coffee table. "Jane Fonda has changed my life. I could never exercise. You either, right? Well, I don't know how, but this tape just inspired me. I thought that if Jane could look like that at her age, I could look good at thirty. Of course, I still get hungry, but then I just take a Dexatrim and get through it."

"Oh, I love Dexatrim. It's been too long," Wayne said. "But tell me about your kids. They must keep you real busy."

Pussy's face relaxed, its boniness retreating a bit. Wayne thought her face had become too thin, drained and unhealthy looking. Still, she looked intensely happy at the mention of her kids. "I guess it's corny, Wayne, but what they say is true. It changes your life to have kids. Sure they bug me sometimes, but mostly I just get the biggest kick out of seeing those little faces. They both look like me, you know? Do you wanna see them? If we're real quiet, they won't wake up. They're real good sleepers.

"Sometimes I just sit in their room while they're sleeping and look at their little faces. You ever see a kid sleep? I mean, really watch them for a long time? They do all sorts of things while they're asleep. They talk, they laugh, they sit up. They even cry. I guess they're dreaming about something sad. You'll be watching them, and the tears just start rolling down their little cheeks. I go over to whichever one it is and hold his hand and it passes. I always wonder whether they know I'm there. You know, if in the dream, they can feel somebody holding their hand, it makes them more happy. The youngest one, especially—I just hate to think of him being scared in that dream. So I sit there like an idiot and hold his hand. Silly, huh?"

Pussy and Wayne snuck into the dim room, softly illuminated by a Donald Duck night light on one side and Mickey Mouse standing guard on the facing wall. The smaller boy must have been about two and was still curled up in a crib. The other boy, maybe four, was in the bottom of a bunk bed. Wayne looked at his friend and saw her become something else in this room. She had found something here. She looked strong and proud and almost noble in front of these little blond boys. There were tears in her eyes as she took Wayne's hand. "Aren't they beautiful?"

"They're very beautiful," he whispered back. "I'm very proud of you."

She moved close to his ear to whisper again. "It's not easy, you know. It's hard work. This is like a job." The older of the two boys murmured a bit, disturbed by their voices. Pussy moved over to him and motioned Wayne to follow. They knelt beside the little boy as Pussy stroked his hair. "Mommy's here. It's okay."

The boy's eyes half-opened, filled with an absolute love. That little boy was looking at the most important, most reassuring sight in the world. Pussy said very quietly to the boy, "This is Mommy's oldest friend, Wayne. He's here all the way from New York City."

"I'm sleepy," the boy said, unimpressed.

"Good night, honey. I love you," Pussy said and they crept back out of the room. Wayne felt as if he must be the unluckiest person in the world. Alone. In the face of that boy was an unquestioning love that would never be checked. Wayne realized that he had seen that look before, in the faces of the very sick. Wayne had been the recipient of that kind of love but it was just too hard to see the face right now, it was too hard to think of his lover as a scared little boy in a hospital bed.

Back in the brown and green living room, Pussy smiled at Wayne, "Do you have someone special, Wayne? A friend?"

Wayne paused for a long moment. He was unsure how to proceed, how to figure out if it was worth it. Smiling back, he said, "I had someone for almost as long as you've been married. I lost that person this year. It's hard for me to talk about it. Losing him was about the only thing that could have made me come back here. I don't think I'll stay in Iowa but I didn't know where else to go. I didn't come here because of my father. I just came here because I didn't know what else to do. Anyway…it is kind of hard for me to talk about it. It's been wonderful to see you, though. I am proud of you, Pussy. You have a much more important job than I've ever had. A harder one, too." Wayne felt as if it was all going to collapse, and he couldn't get through tonight.

"I'm sorry, baby. I didn't mean to get you upset." Pussy took his hand. "You'll find somebody again. Now, look at me. You will."

"Thanks, Pussy. I'm sorry I never answered your letters or called you. I guess that's what it's like there. You wanted to know what it's like to live there? Everything else disappears. The city just kind of eats you up. I never thought about Iowa when I went there. It was like walking over some kind of line; everything from before was just wiped out. I didn't see my folks or even talk to them very often. Really, it was just when I came back that I realized that I didn't know what happened to all of you. I just lost touch. What happened to everybody?"

"Like who?"

"Well, like Carl. I thought I'd stop by the Pastime. I hear Carl's the bartender up there."

"He sure is. Every night of the week. Didn't make much of himself," Pussy said disdainfully.

"What about Mr. A?"

"Baby, you don't know? I thought you would've heard that."

"I'm telling you, Pussy, I don't know anything."

"He killed himself. It was only about a year after we all graduated. He didn't turn up at school for a couple of days, so they went to his house to check. The cops went.... Rick went, too. They found Mr. A laying there in his bathtub. Rick said he looked awful, like he'd been there for three or four days at least. He'd just pushed himself under the water and drowned. They found all sorts of stuff in that house, Wayne. It never came out in the paper, but Rick told me there was a lot of weird stuff in that house. Didn't anybody ever tell you about that?

"No, I never heard about it. That's why I left, though. That's what they do to people like me here, Pussy."

"I won't let them hurt you, honey. Good God, my husband's a cop! Nobody's gonna hurt you."

"It's terrible what they do to people here. I really should get going."

"Don't go yet. You just got here."

"I have to. I'll call again before I leave. Sorry to leave so soon. You have to realize that this is kind of a hard time for me. But I am so happy to see you again, happy that things are going so well for you."

With a short hug, he was gone. It was so fast that Pussy didn't even have time to really say good-bye. She felt as if something cold and dangerous had brushed past her and went back in to check on the boys. She sat next to the bunk bed. It was safe here. She knew that this was a safe place that she must guard.

Wilson Packing, Inc.
MEMORANDUM
To: Kill-Floor Trainees
From: Management, Cherokee Operations

The kill floor is divided into separate areas of operation which move the animal from stock holding through to finished product ready for government inspection. This memo serves to briefly orient you to each of these areas before you are assigned a permanent position where you will be given a more detailed training session on your duties.

I. HOLDING—Animals are transferred from trucking to this area for no more than two days. Holding is restricted to no more than two days as providing food and water would be prohibitive cost additions. After two days without nutrition, the fiber of the product begins to break down and the product is subject to rejection by federal authorities.

II. INITIAL KILL—Wilson Packing currently uses three kill methods: electrocution, automated impact, and manual impact. Briefly, the three methods entail the following:

A. Electrocution—Subject animal is urged with an electric prod securely into a metal holding gate. When shut from behind, the forward end of the pen can be gripped tightly onto the subject animal's head, automatically delivering electrical current usually sufficient for kill within five minutes.

B. Automated Impact—A similar holding pen as used in electrocution leads the subject animal's forehead into line with a steel piston. When activated by operator, the steel piston is distended six inches through the subject's cranium. Kill is usually immediate, although extended nervous system activity may occur for up to five minutes.

C. Manual Kill—Because all automated systems occasionally fail, kill operators may sometimes make use of standard ball-tine sledgehammers on the kill floor. A blow is delivered to the forehead area of the subject animal. This technique may also be used to supplement the above-listed techniques if kill is not achieved within fifteen minutes.

III. BASIC DISASSEMBLY TECHNIQUES

A. Disembowelment Area—Located over a steel-grated area and equipped with high-pressure hoses, this area's operations remove non-use organs such as intestines while retaining valuable organs such the as liver and heart. After removal of all organs, valuable and disposable, pressure hoses are used to clean the cavity.

B. Saw Areas—Through the use of specially designed chain-saw equipment, the subject animal is divided into portions. These portions are trimmed with smaller saws and knives to government specifications. (See area supervisor for handout specific to your area.)

IV. CONVEYOR—Belts are loaded with trimmed, disassembled product which run off the kill floor for

USDA inspection, grading and packaging.

A Note on Cleanliness—Remember that your uniforms are laundered free of charge by the company. Home washing machines are sometimes unable to remove large waste deposits on uniforms. Also, remember that all exits are equipped with hoses for cleaning of rubber boots.

The Ministry tape pounded out of the speakers as Wayne turned his mother's car onto Main Street. Muffled grunts and howls, bawling, and painful yelps materialized from behind the layers of speed metal drums and rending guitars. The music carried a sense of imminent violence as blurred, frenzied scenes were described by a newscaster's voice unequivocally droning over the top. These sounds, this music, were atmospherically suited to the mostly empty Main Street and the merciless anonymity of the buildings. The street looked as if the storm troopers had just swept up after the slaughter, had piled the bodies in National Guard trucks, leaving the empty streets to fill again with dissent before another attack. Where were all the kids, Wayne wondered. Friday night. Cruising night. Where were they? Pulling up in front of the Pastime, Wayne began to reconsider his decision to come. It served no purpose other than dredging up the old fears of discovery. A bar in Iowa can be more dangerous than a bar in Manhattan or a bar in Los Angeles. Or so it seemed to Wayne, who remembered rows of tough, drinking galoots looking for a fight. Every weekend some fight would break out in a wretched, broken-down bar—VFW, Shamrock, Al's, Danny's Steak House, Twilight, Vista, Jim's Place, or here at the Pastime.

Wayne turned the rearview mirror down towards himself. He looked carefully for some mark that branded him. "Raise your hand to your face," he told himself, "and see what it is that reveals you. Immediately identifies you as the enemy. There must be a sign well understood to everyone that ignites their hatred." The sign, mark, brand could be seen by everyone but Wayne because if he could see it, he would remove it, he would cover it over. But in the mirror there was nothing more remarkable than a pale white face topped by black hair. No waving tentacles. No oozing sores. No uncontrollable twitches. The tape was screaming, repeating, "Hurts fine! Hurts fine! Hurts fine!" The tape clicked off and began to rewind. In the quiet, Wayne felt the fatigue that had rested heavily on him for months now, wrap even tighter. It was as if an avalanche had engulfed him and, though he was already buried by the dirt and rocks, more earth kept piling on. The heaviness, though, also brought out a violence in him. He almost felt like when he was doing a lot of coke and just didn't care. Finally, one loses fear and takes up an edgy potential for violence and self-destruction. Whipping boy, the fag, the town homo. "What can they do to me that hasn't been done already?" he said to himself as he turned off the car and got out.

The Pastime was one of ten bars in Cherokee and tied with the Shamrock as the least glamorous. A lot of bars for a town this size. All the bars had approximately the same look as the others, a plate glass window adorned with a neon sign, COORS, or LOUNGE. These one-story drinking establishments were covered in orangish-brown tin siding. The Pastime's TV was on to the Sports Channel when Wayne swung the door open. It was bright inside. One expects a bar, out of decency if not concern for decor, to be dark. But the fluorescent lights blazed here, to the point where it was difficult for Wayne to see clearly, having coming in from the dark. There were only a few men at the bar and Wayne could see that one of them, the bartender, was unmistakably Carl.

Carl had made the common, but still remarkable, journey from young stud to middle-aged man. There was little of the golden hair left on his head, although his athletic form was still discernible through the thicker muscles bunched along his arms and his graceful legs. Don't recognize me for a second more, Wayne thought. Let me see you first. He wondered whether the fine mist of hair covering the solid body had thickened, darkened. The erotic pull returned to Wayne's mind as he quickly ran his eyes again over the chest that stretched against a T-shirt and he tried to imagine the hard bulge of fur-covered stomach below. He thought, "Keep in mind that your tongue has touched that body." Then Wayne knew that even to think that here was to reveal himself. His desire to bury his head between this man's legs was like the shriek of an air-raid siren here. Don't think, Wayne corrected himself. Don't even imagine it here.

Carl's eyes registered nothing but his general good nature when he first looked up at Wayne and began to walk toward him. As he neared, though, he stopped and smiled. A charming, natural smile that revealed his former self even now without the shag of hair hanging down in his eyes. "Wayne," he said. And that was enough, Wayne thought. It's enough to see him smile and say my name. Things can seem all right with the world when a man says your name and his face shows appreciation. Or surprise. There was no apprehension in Carl's face as he loped over the few remaining feet toward an old friend.

"Carl, you old drunk. How the hell are you?" Wayne extended his hand without fear and felt Carl's damp flesh encircle his as they shook.

"Not drunk enough. That's how I am. What'll you have to drink? It's on me."

"Vodka on the rocks," Wayne said and his friend winked, pulled out a glass and began filling it with Seagram's vodka.

"Don't want any mix with this? This must be the big-city drink."

"It's the big-city drunk drink."

"What're you doing in town, Wayne? Christ, I haven't seen you or heard from you in ten years!"

"My dad died a while ago, Carl. I came to spend some time with my mom."

"Sorry about that," Carl said as he carefully sat the drink down. "You know, I hadn't heard."

"Don't worry about it. Here's to you," Wayne toasted.

"Well, just a minute then. If we're drinking to me, let me get my glass." Carl clinked his rum and Coke with Wayne's glass.

As he was about to take a sip of his drink, Carl was forced to turn toward the ringing telephone behind the bar. "Hold on there, Wayne. Be right back." Carl ambled to the phone sitting between a bottle of Black Label and a pile of cocktail napkins featuring "And then my wife said..." jokes. "Heeello, Pastime," Carl said. His eyes rolled up in his head as he looked toward a table with three men seated at it. "Yeah, he's here. Glen, it's for you," he said holding out the phone.

Wayne jumped, hearing his father's name. A sheepish, portly guy in an Iowa Hawkeyes T-shirt took the phone from Carl and started to whisper into it. From his table of friends came calls of "She's got ya now, Glen. You're up shit's creek now, buddy."

Carl remained standing across the bar from the recalcitrant husband until the man handed him back the phone to hang up. It was strange, thought Wayne, that Carl had matured to match the type of guy he now found so attractive—middle-aged, unexceptional, giving only hints of a former beauty. The young scruffy blond Wayne had known ten years ago would have left him cold now. This newly formed Carl, however, pushed the right buttons. A middle-aged suburban dad with hairy legs, slightly pouting stomach, and still-heroic arms. Wayne could feel a hard-on taking shape in his pants, not there yet, but ready to go. "So what've you been up to, Carl?"

"Sittin' on my fat ass, watching TV, pouring drinks. I think that about covers the last ten years."

"I thought I'd find you a married man with three brats."

"No, I haven't lost my mind." Carl's face tensed slightly and he lowered his voice. "What about you?"

"Oh, yeah, I got married to an airline stewardess three years ago. Doris. She wanted to come back with me, but she works for Japan Air Lines, and they have her over in Tokyo."

"Really? Well, that's great, Wayne. I'm really happy for you. Any kids?"

"Just one. She'll be two this fall. Ashley's her name. What a little charmer. She looks like Doris more than me, though. Blonde, you know."

"Your mom must love having her around."

"She does, she does. Ashley's with her now up at our

house. They've been playing in the backyard all day long. Jumping in the sprinkler, all that stuff." Wayne started to end the lie: "Actually, Carl..."

"Hey, Carl! How 'bout another down here?" A fat guy with a baseball hat summoned Carl away. The fat guy was glaring at Wayne and made a comment to Carl, jerking his head in Wayne's direction. Carl's face reddened as he leaned toward the guy and whispered something back. The fat guy let out a bark of a laugh and said, louder now, "That's a fuckin' faggot if I ever saw one."

Wayne picked up his glass. It was more of a mug, really, and he had downed more than half of the vodka in his first two drinks from it. The liquor burned in his stomach as he walked slowly down the bar, smiling at the fat man. Carl's voice was louder now, too: "Look, man, I told you he's married. He's got a little kid, too."

"How you doin', fat boy?" Wayne drawled, leaning against the bar.

"How you doin, faggot? You don't remember me, do ya? I never forget a fuckin' faggot like you, though. You can't tell me you're married to no woman."

"Who said anything about a woman? No, I got a *husband* named Doris who knocked me up a couple a years ago. Doris's got this real big cock, you see. I couldn't resist. I told Doris I didn't have no birth control, but she just had to get that dick in me." Wayne stepped back from himself, aware of the voice that was coming out of him. He had heard this voice before and knew that it would run its course. The voice was like his but deeper, ironically, considering what it was saying.

"You sick fuck!" the fat man growled, starting to rear back on the stool.

"That's right. I'm sicker than your worst fuckin' nightmare." Wayne began to tap the glass against the edge of the counter. "I suck dicks through holes in bathroom stalls. I get my ass fucked by blacks, Puerto Ricans, Chinese, Indians, and sometimes even fat, fuckin', white-trash pieces of shit like you." The taps were coming harder as he continued, "Hell, sometimes, I'll just get an urge to stick anything I see up my ass. That's why I hang out all day at the grocery store, fingering the vegetables. Hope you didn't buy any squash in the last week. Yeah, I have a friend who taught me how to take a yam and shove it right in my ass. Trouble is, she likes 'em cooked, and I like the hard ones that feel like a greasy cock." With one last tap, the mug finally shattered with a muted cracking sound. The fat man sat back farther, and Wayne screamed, "I think I'll cut your tongue out so I can choke you with my dick!" Wayne's hand swung in a fast, unexpected arc past the jowly face in front of him. Everything was still except for his hand. This was a painting in front of him, and he had taken a knife to slash its garish surface. A red line appeared on the painting over the area of the fat man's lips and right cheek.

"Jesus Christ, Wayne!" Carl yelled, jumping from behind the bar. "Get out of here! Get out! Hurry, get out of here!"

Carl was hurrying Wayne out the door as the first deep moans began to roll out of the fat man. "Cut me, you sonofabitch! I'll get you." The fat man was trying to come toward them but stumbling in pain, in addition to being held back by the other customers.

"You know where to find me, hog face. I'll be that mouth on the other side of the glory hole. I'll be the one that bites it off and licks my lips."

Wayne and Carl sat outside in the car. "Why'd you have to do that, man?" Carl was both angry and titillated by the incident. Nothing much happened in the bar. Not enough fights, in his opinion.

"I just felt like it, Carl. Finally had enough. It won't be the last time, either. Next time, I'll kill him."

"He's just a fat slob. You shouldn't pay any attention."

"Mr. A didn't pay any attention, Carl. He just took it. Took it until it was too much. They don't realize that I don't care what they do to me. Just so long as I can hurt them, I don't care what happens."

"You're not married, right? That stuff about Doris was just you making fun of me, right?"

"Sorry. None of this seems real. God, I haven't seen you in so long, haven't even thought about coming back here. It's all so weird being here that half of the time I don't realize what I'm doing. I really think someday I might kill somebody. Carl, I actually bought a gun the other day." Carl stiffened a bit next to him. "Don't worry. It's in the city. I left it there because I was afraid to bring it on the plane. But I was walking into *my* building, in *my* neighborhood and these white-trash guys from New Jersey started harassing me. I didn't even think about it. I didn't even get mad, but the next day I bought a gun. It worries me. What would have happened just now if I had that gun in my pocket? I'm capable of killing somebody, Carl. That's not me. I'm somebody else now, not the guy you knew. I don't know what happened to that guy you knew. He got lost, I guess. Now I just think about killing somebody. Somebody must deserve it. I know somebody deserves to die; somebody's got to pay for all this. Did you ever think I could kill somebody, Carl? I swear to you I don't know what's happened to me. Too much and I just lost myself. So what happens if I blow away half of some slob's face with a gun? What good does it do? There's always another slob waiting."

"You'd better slow down for a minute. Don't say shit like that. Especially don't say it now. You've got to stay real cool, or you're gonna get us both in deep shit." Carl pointed his finger at the cop car that had just pulled up beside them. "Just stay in here. This town isn't the place for whatever's going on with you, Wayne. Can you keep it together for a few minutes?" Wayne nodded slowly.

Carl got out of the car and intercepted the cop moving toward the front door of the bar. The cop was fat, too. A hairy, fat guy. "Great," thought Wayne, "another fatty to deal with." Carl was smiling his most charming smile, gesturing widely and laughing. The cop looked back at the car and smiled, too. He walked over, his polyester pants straining.

Wayne rolled down the window as the cop leaned forward, his breath stinking like coffee and cigarettes. "Well, well, Wayne. Looks like my wife didn't keep you busy down at the house for too long. Hope you didn't have any fights down there."

"Jesus, Rick! I didn't recognize you," Wayne said, and offered his slightly bloody hand.

Rick looked at the hand but didn't shake it. "I think your stay here's been about long enough, hasn't it? I'm going to do my wife a favor and go straighten out your friend inside. But I don't intend to do it again. When are you leaving?"

"A few more days."

"That'll be just fine. You have a good trip back to New York. I'll say good-bye to Pussy for you. Save you a call."

It was late now. Not late in other places, but 11:00 was late in Iowa to pull up in somebody's driveway, unexpected. Wayne was not only unexpected but unknown by the new resident of Mr. A's house. It had been painted a sky blue with white trim. In the dark, lit only by the moon and the dim cast of streetlights, it appeared gray. The house itself still looked much the same, though, right down to the porch swing which was inhabited even at this hour. Getting out of the car, Wayne was shaking. Not crying or upset, but shaky, as he always was after violence. The shaking was intensified by the unexpected presence outside of the house, swinging back and forth slowly on the porch.

Wayne had intended only to pull up and look at the house. What more could be done? But a welcoming female voice came from the dark porch, unalarmed and curious, "Hi. Can I help you with something?"

"I'm sorry to disturb you."

"You're not disturbing me," said the voice. "I'm just having some iced tea. So damn hot tonight, and I don't have any air conditioning. Are you looking for somebody?"

"Well, I'm a friend of Mr. A's. I mean, Mr. Anderson."

"Why don't you come on over here?" said the woman. Wayne walked reluctantly up the steps onto the porch. The woman was sitting, her legs curled underneath her, and leaned forward now and then to keep the swing moving. She was a small woman with moderately short, dark hair and was wearing khaki shorts with a white T-shirt. "I'm afraid your friend is dead. He died some years back, and I moved in later."

"I know he's dead. I just found out tonight and felt like I should come by here. I'm sorry to disturb you."

"Like I said, you're not disturbing me. In fact, it's nice to meet someone who knew him. I moved here to teach school, and no one else at the school seemed to know much about him. Supposed to have been a good teacher, though. Did he have any family?"

Wayne leaned against the porch railing, relieved by the even sounds of the woman's voice. "He just had his parents but they died before him."

She sighed. "I figured, because no one ever came for his stuff. I wish I would have known he had a friend, I would have saved it for you. I'm afraid I threw most of it out, except for the furniture."

"That's okay. I don't think I would have wanted it." Wayne could only imagine what this woman had found stuffed in Mr. A's drawers. She seemed unshocked, though, if she had uncovered some extreme items.

"He did leave a black book. Kind of a journal, I guess. I kept that if you want it. Have to admit, I read it. Curiosity got the best of me. Would you like to have it?"

Wayne breathed deeply a few times. Was this some kind of trap or sick joke? But the woman just continued to swing slowly back and forth. "Yeah, I'd like to have it. If you don't mind."

"I don't mind." The woman was very short, he could see as she pulled herself off the edge of the swing. She strode purposefully into the house, letting the screen door slam shut after her. Wherever she had the journal, it wasn't hidden away, because she returned almost immediately and handed him the black leather book. "Here you go. You live here?"

"No, I'm just visiting. I grew up here."

"Okay, enjoy your visit. Stop back if you want to."

"Probably not, but thanks. Thanks very much," Wayne said, meaning it, and walked back to his car.

For Wayne, If He Reads It

Too bright
ripples, on the surface tonight.
Sometimes things are done. Times are finished.
This evening the water is too bright
for me to shade my eyes. Any
longer.
Deep below
lights stab sharply.
It has taken years to filter down,
now reaching even these depths, so I
dive farther still from
discovery.

So far
you can go down.
But only so far. Only so long.
Then your arms grow tired and the need to rest
overwhelms the feeble desire to
continue.

Down here,
I can tell you,
All suffering is the same. All pain is equal.
It's just that for our kind,
our torment is more
colorful.

Throw off
your caustic flesh.
And join me. I will always wait.
I have wanted so many men, had so few,
but held only one I loved as a

child.

You bitch…you left, could leave, wanted to go. Finger pussy gone to big town. Told you to but didn't say wanted you to. Told you to but didn't make you. Leave Bob's Big Boy drifting here in enemy territory, frying on the grill. I don't blame you. I don't curse you. I don't have to. The world does it fine.

The world's your curse, my curse, our curse. Here's my real advice, butt banger. Take that ballstretcher off and put it around your neck. Do it before they can do it to you.

But please don't. Please survive. Somehow.

V.

Early on summer mornings in Iowa, the sun comes from everywhere and nowhere at once. The tangible white orb floats hidden in the sky even while its blinding heat sinks into the receptive earth. Invisible or hiding or diffused through dust thrown up by the tiling of fields, the sun seems all the more potent in its effect. Hurled by a forceful hand, the beacon's torch has far to travel on its flight to Iowa, having already glided millions of miles though space only to find that the journey is not over when it reaches earth. There remain thousands of miles between the obvious sunny spots of beaches and rain forests, and this place, which looks to need no more sun. Everything is dry here. The sun shatters its rays in frustration, finally, dropping light everywhere with the hope that a few flashes will fall where needed and find a dark spot somewhere on the flat plains. If light could illuminate people, the sun would be more welcomed here. But the rays that bronze the skin cannot penetrate to the bottomless complex chambers that hold secrets, deep-seated grudges, souls, love, and the hushed yearning we have to understand our pain. If the grueling hours of sun in Iowa could twist around the sharp curves and dead ends finally to penetrate those grottoes, the earth would explode...with all the too-long-buried awareness, with freedom from the past.

On early-summer mornings in Iowa, there are no dark spots. The trees that line Jeffries Street can't identify or delineate the line sufficiently to cast a shadow. So they stand with their branches extended stiffly, unsure of their purpose. Shade trees, shade trees. The name mocks them. This is not the softly modulated light of Old World gardens that they face. Iowa trees are called upon to protect the grass, the ground, and any animal upon it from a light that severely, angrily, denies shade. Oak. Elm. Willow. Maple. Beech. The names alone, in different climates, could provide lush cover. But not here. Wayne remembered now how summer could build in Iowa. Not a week ago, the Nut Hut trees had been able to break the light as breezes ruffled their leaves. Now the final stage of summer had arrived. For an unrelenting month, the glare would continue from dawn until just before dusk. There existed perhaps a half hour when the day finally gave in to the heat, knowing that, by law, the sun must disappear soon. A giddiness would come over children who had been sitting in flat, cartoon wading pools all day and over old folks who had been huddled in a dim corner of the kitchen with an iced tea and over the teenagers who had lain in bed exploring their bodies with lazy fingers and over the adults who had just come home from work and sat on the porch with impossibly cold beer. Over the course of those thirty minutes, everyone would gradually drift to the porch or the front lawn where the trees would suddenly burst forth with shadow and cool shade. A little girl would shriek, seeing the first fireflies light up under the oak. Grandpa would find something wise to say as he pulled a leaf off the elm and rolled in into a ball. Young couples would walk slowly through the arcade of a weeping willow, letting the long fingers caress each other until they could do it themselves. And sometimes a young man would emerge from the house, just out of the shower with only a loose pair of shorts on, to lie under the maple tree, amazed at the beauty of his strong body.

Dusk is when they should have done this, Wayne knew. It would have made it softer, less ghoulish. But neither one of them had the attribute of patience, and as soon as each had showered, had their coffee, and dressed that morning, they silently agreed to go. Ann had used her usual packing methods to prepare the ashes. The small brown box had been secured with masking tape, then wrapped in a plastic grocery sack, and finally set in a shopping bag. The morning's preparations had been completed in silence, mother and son embarrassed by one another's presence. There had been no rituals between them. There had been no enlightening moments. Yet suddenly there was this. They felt it was unfair somehow that they were alone in this task, without preparation. There should have been a course at the Community Center. Ann, for her part, regretted for the first time in her life not being religious. "That's what religion's for," she realized. Not for going to church, but for teaching you how to get through this. Ann had always preferred to be alone, though. If you went to church, she had always thought, you have to put up with all those old biddies visiting you, and you had to smile at everybody on Sunday when you'd rather be sleeping. In general, Ann had always believed it was more satisfying to be alone. With another person, she couldn't really achieve the simple satisfaction she had in cleaning the house or reading a book or watching television without someone yakking the whole time. To a lesser degree, Wayne agreed. So neither came to this day with a cushion of religion and friends. They had not planned anything, not known even how to talk about it. Until they reached the door, ready to go, there had been no preparation.

"I think we should walk," Wayne had said. While he had showered that morning, Wayne had wished for this to be over, but also had looked forward to it. He thought that it was the first important event he and his mother had been able to share in over ten years. All the other times—graduations, funerals, marriages—they had been separate. "We can walk right down to the fields and go over to the river. It's nice to put the ashes in the water. Then they go more than one place."

Ann hadn't cared to argue. In truth, she would have preferred to drive somewhere rather than walk in the atrocious heat past the neighbors' houses, carrying Glen's ashes with her. But mostly she just wanted it over. Wanted something to end. That's what really bothered Ann these days—that nothing ever ended, but just sloppily kept on going. What she wanted was some marker in time that clearly said: "Your old life is over. Here's the new one."

Wayne wore his uniform of a white shirt and shorts. Ann had dressed the same way she had dressed for years. She was not about to put on a dress and high heels in this heat. Now that they were walking, she was doubly glad not to have dressed up. What she wished she did have were sunglasses, like Wayne. She glanced at her son as they walked along Jeffries Street and he looked secure behind the sunglasses. He looked protected. Ann's untinted glasses felt heavy and slick in the heat. She was sure that she could sense eyes peering out from behind curtains as they passed the damn nosy neighbors. She hadn't actually talked to the neighbors in years, just waved sometimes as she pulled out in the car while they were moving or shoveling snow. When they had first moved into this house, people had tried to socialize with them. Ann put a stop to that. She didn't want to be bothered, and she didn't want friends.
"Do you want me to carry the bag?" Wayne asked.

"No, I'm okay." Ann looked guiltily at each house that they passed. Of course, nobody knew what they were doing, she assured herself. And what if they did? There wasn't anything wrong with it. But they would still look and talk. "Bastards," she thought, and her face turned red.

Building had spread farther in the ten years since Wayne had last walked the blocks that separated his neighborhood from the surrounding farms. Although the fields were only a few minutes' walk from their houses, people who lived in town rarely would drive or walk through the countryside. Rather, they would point their cars inward, toward the grocery store, post office, and Kmart that formed the focus of living. Strangely, living in a country town, they had no interest in the countryside. As they crossed a final intersection, Wayne noticed that two houses had been built on the part of the field closest to the road which had once held only sweet corn. Down farther, though, the field remained the same, and the scraggly path that led through it, down to the river, was still where he remembered it. "Do you know when I was here last?" Wayne asked, smiling.

"I guess it must have been a long time ago," Ann said, relieved that the silence had broken. Having spent so many summers in Canada, where it could snow in June, she found herself still unused to the heat. Standing underneath the big white sky made her feel sweaty and small.

"Ten years ago, I stood in this field one night and kissed a man for the first time. I kissed Carl here one night." He left out that they were both tripping on acid, thinking that might be too much. The whole thing was too much, the wrong time to tell secrets like this, but Wayne found he couldn't hold things back anymore. When something came into his head, Wayne had a hard time not just saying it.

"Carl? Well, I have to say I never suspected," Ann said.

"It didn't go much beyond a kiss...I'm sorry to say." They continued through the field, not planted with crops anymore but just overgrown with weeds, leftover patches of corn and occasional sunflowers. "Does that bother you? Does that shock you?" Wayne looked at Ann, who was sweating steadily, carefully stepping along the path in her tennis shoes.

"It doesn't bother me, it just surprises me. No, I'll tell you the truth. It *does* bother me. It scares me what could have happened to you if people would have found out. You took a big risk."

"That's why I left," Wayne said quietly, leaving it at that. There was no sound of the river; it was too small at this point to make much of a rush. There was a coolness that was more imagined than real coming from the lushly vegetated strip directly in front of them. The furrows in the field evened out, and grass overtook the prickly ancient stalks sticking out from the soil. The sun was too intense to allow the trees to provide much relief. But they formed a roof—a covering that, although penetrated by the sun, had its own protective quality. At the edge of the trees, they could see the water just down a low embankment. The single path turned to many smaller paths, worn down over the years by children coming to poke at the water and cows from the surrounding farms that would come to drink in the summer. The paths looked suspiciously like paths Wayne had followed in other parts of the world—in the Ramble of Central Park, along the Tiber in Rome, and around the walls of Avignon. A large cow stood at the water's edge. Her front feet in the river, the cow would drink for a moment and then lift her head, her tail switching at flies. As they made their way down one of the paths, the animal saw them and let out a lazy, friendly moo. The sound was both startlingly loud and reassuring, making them smile at the animal's big, gawky head. Wayne noticed her eyes, particularly. Animals' eyes can be disconcerting because they reveal a personality supposed to be possessed only by humans. This cow (Bessie the Cow, he labeled her mentally) looked very intently at him with dark brown eyes. Bessie stared at Wayne and slowly closed her eyes. She reopened her eyes, and they were deep, endlessly sad. Once more she closed her eyes and turned away. Flies buzzed thicker here by the water and swarmed particularly thick around Bessie's teats, feasting on a few sores. It must be painful for the cow to drag herself through the weeds down here. Bessie moved a few feet farther downstream, looking as though she wanted privacy.

Ann and Wayne found a massive tree root that jutted out from the bank and then submerged itself in the river. The root was a reminder of the terrifying life that goes on beneath the earth. Creatures wait as a coffin slowly disappears below shovels of earth. Worms and insects are the first battalion, taking the soft flesh. Burrowing animals come next to gnaw patiently at bones. Most frightening, though, is the unthinking procession of plants and fungus that, like this root, would grow around a body, incorporate it, irrevocably reclaiming the physical self. This root spread its thick fingers deep down to encase skeletons dropped from the flesh of humans, birds, frogs, fish, cows, pigs, and every other animal that walked and fell into the earth. Ann used the root as a bench while she undid her careful packing. After all the tape and plastic had been removed and the lid of the box opened, Ann said, "I'm not really sure what to do. Should we say something?"

"I don't think we need to say anything. Unless you want to. Why don't you just sprinkle them slowly into the water?"

Ann leaned over the water, hesitated a moment, and then began to pour. When the expected trail of ash failed to appear, she shook the box harder. With an extremely undignified plop and splash, a brick made of the ashes fell heavily into the water. Briefly glimpsed plummeting downward, the ashes looked like a lump of volcanic rock. "What the hell!" Ann said. "Maybe we shouldn't have let them sit so long."

"Maybe the house is too damp. We should have turned up the dehumidifier," Wayne suggested, horrified by the proceedings.

"Oh, God! He's still down there!" Ann groaned. "He's just sitting down there like a little boulder."

"Get a stick and poke it. Here, use this branch," Wayne said, breaking one from the tree. The brick sat sullenly in a few feet of water, unconcerned with dispersing gracefully.

"I can't believe this!" Ann poked savagely. "I'm complaining to that funeral home. They said it would be like sand or dust. I think he's starting to dissolve."

"Jesus, hurry up! Here comes the cow!" Wayne shrieked. "Get away, Bessie! Shoo, shoo." Bessie was approaching steadily with a hungry grin on her face, having heard the promising sound of a plop in the water. She was chewing her cud appreciatively, thinking of a fat juicy ear of corn. "Bessie, move your fat ass out of here! You're the last thing we need...some killer cow." Wayne rushed the cow, startling it into retreat. "You're not eating my father!"

"Wayne, Wayne, it's okay. He's going away now. He's crumbling." Ann was still poking furiously with her stick and occasionally stirring the water, as if it were a bowl of cake batter. She sat back on the ground now as Wayne rejoined her. "I don't know whether to laugh or throw myself in, too," she said, tears not yet coming to her eyes.

Wayne took her hand as they watched the last few chunks of his father crumble and float off. Soon there was nothing left, no trace. Wayne thought that they might as well have thrown the thing in the garbage. No fish swam symbolically around the spot, ingesting his father back into the food chain. No turtle glided past, carrying the remains to shore on its feet. There was no indication that something had occurred. They sat quietly for many minutes. Finally Ann asked, "What are you thinking?"

"About what I'm feeling."

"What are you feeling?"

"Nothing."

"Nothing?"

"Nothing. Nothing for him. Lots for you."

"You loved your father, didn't you?"

"No. Not for a long time. I love you, though. I've tried to hate him, but mostly I just feel nothing for him. A stranger to me. I stopped loving him when Jack got sick and I called to tell you two. You cried. You asked what you could do. Do you know what he said? He said, 'Oh. Merl Johnson got killed the other day in a car wreck.' What the hell was that supposed to mean? What did some drunk getting killed in a car wreck have to do with my lover dying? And I knew what he was really thinking. I know what he wanted to say: 'Serves you right for being a homo.' After that, I never thought of him, and when he died, I didn't cry for him, but for you."

"Honey, he just didn't know what to say."

"That's why I don't love him anymore. He didn't know what to say. I'm sick of these men who don't know what to say. It's not so hard to say, 'I love you,' or 'Let me know if I can help.' You don't have to be a genius to say that. I loved him so much when I was a kid. I remember how much when I look at pictures of me sitting with him after my bath and he would be reading to me. Now he's just another dead stranger."

"And what about me?"

"I love you and I want you with me. I can't stay here,

but I want you to come with me. What does this place have for you now, anyway?"

"Please stay here."

"No. I have to make you understand what this place is for me. This is the place where there is absolutely no possibility for me to live my life. You may not believe it, but they would kill me here. Or I'd kill them. You were right when you said I took a chance kissing Carl in that field. We were two teenagers doing something that every teenager in town was doing. But because we were boys, they would have killed us if they saw. If a car full of men would have been driving by and seen us, do you know what they would have done? They would have gotten out with baseball bats and their fists and anything else they could have found and hit us. Hit us harder than they would hit an animal. The only difference today is that I would hit them back. Today I'd let them hit me once, and then, lying in the dirt, I'd put my hand in my pocket, take out a gun, and shoot each one of them. I wouldn't shoot to kill, at first. No, first I would shoot each one of them in their legs or arms so that they'd suffer. Then I'd lie down on top of each one of them and stick my tongue in their mouths. I'd make out with them, and while they were rolling around in pain with my tongue in their mouths, I'd put the gun up to their heads and pull the trigger so I could see their faces explode right in front of me. Does that sound like your son? That's what this place did to me."

"For God's sake, stop it! It's making me sick!"

"It's ugly. That's what I'm trying to make you understand. Staying here is an ugly thing. Being born here was an ugly thing. Being hated your whole life is an ugly thing. There are maybe three places in this country where I can live. Don't think it's easy there, either.

But it's easier. Easier than here. So please don't make me stay here. Come with me."

"Please stay."

"No. Please come with me."

"No. Not now. Not yet. Maybe someday." Ann smiled and the tears started finally. Not for Wayne, but for Ann. She leaned on her son's shoulder and sobbed, feeling the sun begin to burn the back of her neck. She cried not from loss, but from fear. Now that she was alone and free, she was afraid.

"How could she hurt herself with a tiny, flexible, silver bracelet?" Wayne demanded, his voice inching up in volume and pitch. His hand went instinctively to his waist, striking a pose both queeny and authoritative.

"She could swallow it. She could scratch herself or another patient. She could put in her nostril." The wicked nurse at the ward door was having none of Wayne's sentimentalism. The nurse had a battery of forms in front of her, official-looking documents, and a name tag—all of which countered Wayne's hands-on-hips pose.

"Look, I didn't even have to ask you about it. I could just have given it to her."

"Sir, then we would have just had to take it off her and put it with her other personal items." The nurse made a mark on an one of the documents, as if she were scoring the exchange.

"What's your name?" Wayne asked in a lower, sweeter voice.

"Nurse Hatcher."

"Hatchet?"

"Hatcher."

"Are you a lesbian, Nurse Ratchet?" Wayne pursed

his lips and leaned over the desk. " 'Cause I'm a gay man and I thought maybe we could do the secret handshake, maybe bend the rules a little."

The nurse's face turned a very deep shade of red, and she tapped her shoe agitatedly against the table leg. "Sir, should I call the guard, or would you like to see the patient? It's your choice."

"All right, Nurse Ratchet, you win. You rule absolute over the wacky ward. I hope you enjoy the next ten years sitting at your little desk here in the stairway."

"You can be sure that I will," Nurse Hatcher said as she hit the buzzer to admit Wayne to the ward.

"By the way, I know some great dyke bars in New York, if you ever want to visit. Just ask my grandmother for the address."

The windows were closed today in the ward as currents of air conditioning blew recklessly down the halls attempting to battle the heat that raged outside the thick stone walls. The air seemed to be coming from every direction, lifting the edges of tablecloths on all sides and touching first one side of Wayne's face, then the other, as he walked toward the dayroom. The hum of air conditioning went well with—and added to—the frozen mood here. There was a conspicuous absence of sound, and Wayne thought that music would help. Soft classical music couldn't agitate them too much. Of course, maybe there was no need to reach out at some point. In another hospital, Wayne thought, she might be revived, rather than stored like an animal carcass awaiting the taxidermist. But revived for what? Revived to sit alone in her house, no husband, no son, and a grandson thousands of miles away. Revived for Ann to care for after briefly being cut free from all the ties that held her in this town. There was a time to die.

Not for the young in their twenties, but maybe for the depressed and lonely who had stumbled on for nearly a century. Yet these old souls refused to give in. Their bodies persisted in spite of all the terrible yearnings to leave. "If only I could've taken a bit of that strength," Wayne wished, "and dropped it into his mouth. Or if I could have just lifted him up, out of his young body, and laid him safely in a rattling old frame that refused to break, a sloppy safe home to have him with me for a few more years."

Selma was positioned in the same place as before. The only discernible difference was that one hand rested on her chest, rather than at her side. It was a posture of slight fear or shock. He wondered if the hand had crept slowly into this new position or jerked upward suddenly in the middle of the night. Every muscle in her body looked contorted, and Wayne wanted to run his hands lightly over her, tell her to lie comfortably for a while.

"I'm not going to cry this time, Grandma. All cried out." He took the hand that remained at her side. Despite its tense appearance, the hand didn't resist as he turned it over and trailed the silver bracelet over the wrist and palm. Her hand flexed slightly as he tickled it. "I wanted to give you this but Nurse Hatchet said no. I wanted to give you something, like you gave me something. I lost your ring. But you know that, I told you last time. Maybe I'll wear this and think that it's from you." He put the bracelet around his own wrist and fastened the frail clasp. "Now I have a bracelet, but you don't."

Wayne looked around at the tables and the floor. Unopened magazines sat on the tables along with sheets of paper and crayons. The other old women sitting in the room paid no attention to him, nor to their surroundings. They all faced the window that was covered by a sheer white curtain, waving slightly in the manufactured breeze. The sunlight poured through the window to illuminate the curtain, altering its original function as a block against brightness, making it a screen. The white glow of the rectangle held their eyes. And the women were an audience, transfixed to the screen and waiting. Waiting for the picture to begin. Waiting for the lights to dim. Waiting. Looking down next to the sofa, Wayne saw a length of fuzzy orange yarn, discarded from a knitting project. He picked up the yarn and looped it loosely around Selma's outstretched wrist, tying it in a bow. "Now you have one, too. We don't need presents or jewelry to remember each other, though. You know I'll always remember you and love you. You can feel that, I know. I'm going now. You can go, too. Don't stay here, Grandma. There's nothing left here for either one of us. I love you. I love you."

Ann was waiting in the car with the suitcases. She had offered to come in with him, but Wayne had preferred to be alone. So now she was waiting in the car, and Wayne opened the door to a blast of cool air and Patsy Cline. The grounds lay around them like an estate, so green and manicured that nothing bad could be imagined. Harm was not considered in this setting. As always on these lawns, the birds sang in muffled tones, and the constant breeze, having been given an exemption from the summer's stifling heat, tousled impossibly green leaves that offered themselves and reached out with the promise of shelter. Here they were allowed to bask in their names. A Canadian Pine. A

White Birch. A Copper Beech. A Dutch Elm. An Oak. Wayne breathed in the air and tried to hold it inside of him, tried to transfer its essence onto his lungs. Exhaling with a sigh, he lowered himself into the car and shut the door.

"How'd it go?" Ann asked from behind the sunglasses she had bought earlier that day.

"It went fine. I said good-bye." Wayne thought that he had never seen his mother look so good as in the slightly butch black T-shirt and sunglasses. "That's a good look for you, Mom. Let's go. I have to catch the plane."

Selma was awakened from her long sleep by Jack standing up. She was once again shocked at the animal beauty of his nude body. His body didn't have separate parts, but flowed in perfect proportion from his sloping nose to the firm rise of his chest and stomach pointing down to the slick hair that grew thickly around his groin and continued down to the firm base of his feet. It was all one. "It's time to go, Selma," he said, pulling her up easily by her hand. He held her hand in his for a moment, trailing his fingers lightly over her palm and wrist. It felt like a breeze to her.

Selma looked at the walls slowly falling away and the sun streaming in. As the space became larger and brighter, it also became dimmer and unfocused. She realized that she could no longer see, no longer feel her body.

"Are you coming with me?" she said without a mouth.

"I'm already gone," Jack's voice said as it left.

"Nothing," Selma thought one last time before she, too, was gone. "Beautiful nothing."

About the Author

Patrick Moore is a writer living in Los Angeles. Moore was born in Iowa in 1962 and subsequently moved to Canada with his family. Moore's first novel, *This Every Night,* was published by Amethyst Press in 1991 and was described by *Interview* magazine as "the brave, low literature of the bottom." Moore worked extensively in the New York performance-art scene of the late 1980s. Patrick Moore is also the founding director of the Estate Project for Artists with AIDS. The Estate Project is the first national effort to assist artists with HIV/AIDS in preserving their work and planning their estates. Moore is currently at work on a screenplay.

JOHN PRESTON

Tales from the Dark Lord II **$4.95/176-4**
The second volume of acclaimed eroticist John Preston's masterful short stories. Also includes an interview with the author, and an explicit screenplay written for pornstar Scott O'Hara. An explosive collection from one of erotic publishing's most fertile imaginations.

Tales from the Dark Lord **$5.95/323-6**
A new collection of twelve stunning works from the man *Lambda Book Report* called "the Dark Lord of gay erotica." The relentless ritual of lust and surrender is explored in all its manifestations in this heart-stopping triumph of authority and vision from the Dark Lord!

The Arena **$4.95/3083-0**
There is a place on the edge of fantasy where every desire is indulged with abandon. Men go there to unleash beasts, to let demons roam free, to abolish all limits. At the center of each tale are the men who serve there, who offer themselves for the consummation of any passion, whose own bottomless urges compel their endless subservience.

The Heir•The King **$4.95/3048-2**
The ground-breaking novel *The Heir*, written in the lyric voice of the ancient myths, tells the story of a world where slaves and masters create a new sexual society. This edition also includes a completely original work, *The King*, the story of a soldier who discovers his monarch's most secret desires. Available only from Badboy.

Mr. Benson **$4.95/3041-5**
A classic erotic novel from a time when there was no limit to what a man could dream of doing.... Jamie is an aimless young man lucky enough to encounter Mr. Benson. He is soon led down the path of erotic enlightenment, learning to accept cruelty as love, anguish as affection, and this man as his master. From an opulent penthouse to the infamous Mineshaft, Jamie's incredible adventures never fail to excite—especially when the going gets rough! First serialized in *Drummer*, ***Mr. Benson*** became an immediate classic that inspired many imitators. Preston's knockout novel returns to claim the territory it mapped out years ago. The first runaway success in gay SM literature, ***Mr. Benson*** is sure to inspire further generations.

THE MISSION OF ALEX KANE

Sweet Dreams **$4.95/3062-8**
It's the triumphant return of gay action hero Alex Kane! This classic series has been revised and updated especially for Badboy, and includes loads of raw action. In ***Sweet Dreams***, Alex travels to Boston where he takes on a street gang that stalks gay teenagers. Mighty Alex Kane wreaks a fierce and terrible vengeance on those who prey on gay people everywhere!

Golden Years **$4.95/3069-5**
When evil threatens the plans of a group of older gay men, Kane's got the muscle to take it head on. Along the way, he wins the support—and very specialized attentions—of a cowboy plucked right out of the Old West. But Kane and the Cowboy have a surprise waiting for them....

Deadly Lies **$4.95/3076-8**
Politics is a dirty business and the dirt becomes deadly when a political smear campaign targets gay men. Who better to clean things up than Alex Kane! Alex comes to protect the dreams, and lives, of gay men imperiled by lies.

Stolen Moments **$4.95/3098-9**
Houston's evolving gay community is victimized by a malicious newspaper editor who is more than willing to sacrifice gays on the altar of circulation. He never counted on Alex Kane, fearless defender of gay dreams and desires.

Secret Danger **$4.95/111-X**
Homophobia: a pernicious social ill hardly confined by America's borders. Alex Kane and the faithful Danny are called to a small European country, where a group of gay tourists is being held hostage by ruthless terrorists. Luckily, the Mission of Alex Kane stands as firm foreign policy.

Lethal Silence **$4.95/125-X**
The Mission of Alex Kane thunders to a conclusion. Chicago becomes the scene of the right-wing's most noxious plan—facilitated by unholy political alliances. Alex and Danny head to the Windy City to take up battle with the mercenaries who would squash gay men underfoot.

JAY SHAFFER

Shooters **$5.95/284-1**
A new set of stories from the author of the best-selling erotic collections ***Wet Dreams*** and ***Full Service***. No mere catalog of random acts, ***Shooters*** tells the stories of a variety of stunning men and the ways they connect in sexual and non-sexual ways. A virtuoso storyteller, Shaffer always gets his man.

Animal Handlers **$4.95/264-7**
Another volume from a master of scorching fiction. In Shaffer's world, each and every man finally succumbs to the animal urges deep inside. And if there's any creature that promises a wild time, it's a beast who's been caged for far too long.

Full Service **$4.95/150-0**
A baker's dirty dozen from the author of ***Wet Dreams.*** Wild men build up steam until they finally let loose. No-nonsense guys bear down hard on each other as they work their way toward release in this finely detailed assortment of masculine fantasies.

D.V. SADERO

Revolt of the Naked **$4.95/261-2**
In a distant galaxy, there are two classes of humans: Freemen and Nakeds. Freemen are full citizens in this system, which allows for the buying and selling of Nakeds at whim. Nakeds live only to serve their Masters, and obey every sexual order with haste and devotion. Until the day of revolution—when an army of sex toys rises in anger....

In the Alley **$4.95/144-6**
Twenty cut-to-the-chase yarns inspired by the all-American male. Hardworking men—from cops to carpenters—bring their own special skills and impressive tools to the most satisfying job of all: capturing and breaking the male sexual beast. Hot, incisive and way over the top!

SUTTER POWELL

Executive Privileges **$6.50/383-X**
Wild, witty explorations of male lust from the widely published eroticist. No matter how serious or sexy a predicament his characters find themselves in, Powell conveys the sheer exuberance of their encounters with a warm humor rarely seen in contemporary gay erotica.

GARY BOWEN

Man Hungry **$5.95/374-0**

By the author of ***Diary of a Vampire.*** A riveting collection of stories from one of gay erotica's new stars. Dipping into a variety of genres, Bowen crafts tales of lust unlike anything being published today. Men of every type imaginable—and then some—work up a sweat for readers whose lusts know no bounds.

KYLE STONE

Fire & Ice **$5.95/297-3**

Another collection of stories from Kyle Stone—author of the infamous adventures of PB 500, and the cyber-spunk primer Fantasy Board. Randy, powerful, and just plain bad, Stone's characters always promise one thing: enough hot action to burn away your desire for anyone else....

Hot Bauds **$5.95/285-X**

The author of ***Fantasy Board*** and ***The Initiation of PB 500*** combed cyberspace for the hottest fantasies of the world's horniest hackers. From bulletin boards called Studs, The Mine Shaft, Back Door and the like, Stone has assembled the first collection of the raunchy erotica so many gay men cruise the Information Superhighway for. Plug in—and get ready to download....

Fantasy Board **$4.95/212-4**

The author of the scalding sci-fi adventures of PB 500 explores the more foreseeable future—through the intertwined lives (and private parts) of a collection of randy computer hackers. On the Lambda Gate BBS, every hot and horny male is in search of a little virtual satisfaction—and will surely find just what he's looking for.

The Citadel **$4.95/198-5**

The thundering sequel to ***The Initiation of PB 500.*** Having proven himself worthy of his stunning master, Micah—now known only as '500'—will face new challenges and hardships after his entry into the forbidding Citadel. Only his master knows what awaits—and whether Micah will again distinguish himself as the perfect instrument of pleasure....

Rituals **$4.95/168-3**

Via a computer bulletin board, a young man finds himself drawn into a series of sexual rites that transform him into the willing slave of a mysterious stranger. Gradually, all vestiges of his former life are thrown off, and he learns to live for his Master's touch.... A high-tech fable of good old-fashioned sexual surrender

The Initiation PB 500 **$4.95/141-1**

An insteller accident strands a young stud on an alien planet. He is a stranger on their planet, unschooled in their language, and ignorant of their customs. But this man, Micah—now known only by his number—will soon be trained in every last detail of erotic personal service. And, once nurtured and transformed into the perfect physical specimen, he must begin proving himself worthy of the master who has chosen him.... A scalding sci-fi epic, continued in ***The Citadel.***

ROBERT BAHR

Sex Show **$4.95/225-6**

Luscious dancing boys. Brazen, explicit acts. Unending stimulation. Take a seat, and get very comfortable, because the curtain's going up on a show no discriminating appetite can afford to miss. And the award for Best Performer is up to you....

"BIG" BILL JACKSON

Eighth Wonder **$4.95/200-0**

From the bright lights and back rooms of New York to the open fields and sweaty bods of a small Southern town, "Big" Bill always manages to cause a scene, and the more actors he can involve, the better! Like the man's name says, he's got more than enough for everyone, and turns nobody down....

JASON FURY

The Rope Above, the Bed Below **$4.95/269-8**

The irresistible Jason Fury returns—and if you thought his earlier adventures were hot, this volume will blow you away! Once again, our built, blond hero finds himself in the oddest—and most compromising—positions imaginable.

Eric's Body **$4.95/151-9**

Meet Jason Fury—blond, blue-eyed and up for anything. Perennial favorites in the gay press, Fury's sexiest tales are collected in book form for the first time. Ranging from the bittersweet to the surreal, these stories follow the irresistible Jason through sexual adventures unlike any you have ever read....

JOHN ROWBERRY

Lewd Conduct **$4.95/3091-1**

Flesh-and-blood men vie for power, pleasure and surrender in each of these feverish stories, and no one walks away from his steamy encounter unsated. Rowberry's men are unafraid to push the limits of civilized behavior in search of the elusive and empowering conquest.

LARS EIGHNER

Whispered in the Dark **$5.95/286-8**

Lars Eighner continues to produce gay fiction whose quality rivals the best in the genre. ***Whispered in the Dark*** continues to demonstrate Eighner's unique combination of strengths: poetic descriptive power, an unfailing ear for dialogue, and a finely tuned feeling for the nuances of male passion. ***Whispered in the Dark*** reasserts Eighner's claim to mastery of the gay erotica genre.

American Prelude **$4.95/170-5**

Praised by *The New York Times*, Eighner is widely recognized as one of our best, most exciting gay writers. What the *Times* won't admit, however, is that he is also one of gay erotica's true masters—and ***American Prelude*** shows why. Wonderfully written, blisteringly hot tales of all-American lust.

B.M.O.C. **$4.95/3077-6**

In a college town known as "the Athens of the Southwest," studs of every stripe are up all night—studying, naturally. In *B.M.O.C.*, Lars Eighner includes the very best of his short stories, sure to appeal to the collegian in every man. Relive university life the way it was *supposed* to be, with a cast of handsome honor students majoring in Human Homosexuality.

CALDWELL/EIGHNER

QSFx2 **$5.95/278-7**

One volume of the wickedest, wildest, other-worldliest yarns from two master storytellers—Clay Caldwell and Lars Eighner. Both eroticists take a trip to the furthest reaches of the sexual imagination, sending back ten stories proving that as much as things change, one thing will always remain the same....

J R

French Quarter Nights **$5.95/337-6**

A randy roundup of this author's most popular tales. *French Quarter Nights* is filled with sensual snapshots of the many places where men get down and dirty—from the steamy French Quarter to the steam room at the old Everard baths. In the finest tradition of gay erotic writing, these *Nights* are the type you'll wish went on forever.

AARON TRAVIS

In the Blood **$5.95/283-3**

Written when Travis had just begun to explore the true power of the erotic imagination, these stories laid the groundwork for later masterpieces. Among the many rewarding rarities included in this volume: "In the Blood"—a heart-pounding descent into sexual vampirism, written with the furious erotic power that has distinguished Travis' work from the beginning.

The Flesh Fables **$4.95/243-4**

One of Travis' best collections, finally rereleased. *The Flesh Fables* includes "Blue Light," his most famous story, as well as other masterpieces that established him as the erotic writer to watch. And watch carefully, because Travis always buries a surprise somewhere beneath his scorching detail....

Slaves of the Empire **$4.95/3054-7**

The return of an undisputed classic from this master of the erotic genre.

"*Slaves of the Empire* is a wonderful mythic tale. Set against the backdrop of the exotic and powerful Roman Empire, this wonderfully written novel explores the timeless questions of light and dark in male sexuality. Travis has shown himself expert in manipulating the most primal themes and images. The locale may be the ancient world, but these are the slaves and masters of our time...."

—John Preston

Big Shots **$5.95/448-8**

Two fierce tales in one electrifying volume. In ***Beirut,*** Travis tells the story of ultimate military power and erotic subjugation; ***Kip***, Travis' hypersexed and sinister take on *film noir*, appears in unexpurgated form for the first time—including the final, overwhelming chapter. Unforgettable acts and relentless passions dominate these chronicles of unimaginable lust—as seen from the points of view of raging, powerful men, and the bottomless submissives who mindlessly yield to their desires. One of the rawest titles we've ever published.

Exposed **$4.95/126-8**

A volume of shorter Travis tales, each providing a unique glimpse of the horny gay male in his natural environment! Cops, college jocks, ancient Romans—even Sherlock Holmes and his loyal Watson—cruise these pages, fresh from the throbbing pen of one of our hottest authors.

Beast of Burden **$4.95/105-5**

Five ferocious tales from a master of lascivious prose. Innocents surrender to the brutal sexual mastery of their superiors, as taboos are shattered and replaced with the unwritten rules of masculine conquest. Intense, extreme—and totally Travis.

CLAY CALDWELL

Ask Ol' Buddy **$5.95/346-5**

One of the most popular novels of this legendary gay eroticist. Set in the underground SM world, Caldwell takes you on a journey of discovery—where men initiate one another into the secrets of the rawest sexual realm of all. And when each stud's initiation is complete, he takes his places among the masters—eager to take part in the training of another hungry soul...

Service, Stud **$5.95/336-8**

From the author of the sexy sci-fi epic ***All-Stud***, comes another look at the gay future. The setting is the Los Angeles of a distant future. Here the all-male populace is divided between the served and the servants—an arrangement guaranteeing the erotic satisfaction of all involved. Until one young stud challenges authority, and the sexual rules it so rigidly enforces....

Stud Shorts **$5.95/320-1**

"If anything, Caldwell's charm is more powerful, his nostalgia more poignant, the horniness he captures more sweetly, achingly acute than ever." —Aaron Travis

A new collection of this legendary writer's latest sex-fiction. With his customary candor, Caldwell tells all about cops, cadets, truckers, farmboys (and many more) in these dirty jewels.

Tailpipe Trucker **$5.95/296-5**

With ***Tailpipe Trucker***, Clay Caldwell set the cornerstone of "trucker porn"—a story revolving around the age-old fantasy of horny men on the road. In prose as free and unvarnished as a cross-country highway, Caldwell tells the truth about Trag and Curly—two men hot for the feeling of sweaty manflesh.

Queers Like Us **$4.95/262-0**

"This is Caldwell at his most charming." —Aaron Travis

For years the name Clay Caldwell has been synonymous with the hottest, most finely crafted gay tales available. ***Queers Like Us*** is one of his best: the story of a randy mailman's trek through a landscape of willing, available studs.

All-Stud **$4.95/104-7**

An incredible, erotic trip into the gay future. This classic, sex-soaked tale takes place under the watchful eye of Number Ten: an omniscient figure who has decreed unabashed promiscuity as the law of his all-male land. Men exist to serve men, and all surrender to state-sanctioned fleshly indulgence.

HODDY ALLEN

Al **$5.95/302-3**

Al is a remarkable young man. With his long brown hair, bright green eyes and eagerness to please, many would consider him the perfect submissive. Many would like to mark him as their own—but it is at that point that Al stops. One day Al relates the entire astounding tale of his life....

KEY LINCOLN

Submission Holds **$4.95/266-3**

A bright young talent unleashes his first collection of gay erotica. From tough to tender, the men between these covers stop at nothing to get what they want. These sweat-soaked tales show just how bad boys can really get....

TOM BACCHUS

Rahm **$5.95/315-5**

A volume spanning the many ages of hardcore queer lust—from Creation to the modern day. The imagination of Tom Bacchus brings to life an extraordinary assortment of characters, from the Father of Us All to the cowpoke next door, the early gay literati to rude, queercore mosh rats. No one is better than Bacchus at staking out sexual territory with a swagger and a sly grin.

Bone **$4.95/177-2**

Queer musings from the pen of one of today's hottest young talents. A fresh outlook on fleshly indulgence yields more than a few pleasant surprises. Horny Tom Bacchus maps out the tricking ground of a new generation.

VINCE GILMAN

The Slave Prince **$4.95/199-3**

A runaway royal learns the true meaning of power when he comes under the hand of Korat—a man well-versed in the many ways of subjugating a young man to his relentless sexual appetite.

BOB VICKERY

Skin Deep **$4.95/265-5**

Talk about "something for everyone!" ***Skin Deep*** contains so many varied beauties no one will go away unsatisfied. No tantalizing morsel of manflesh is overlooked—or left unexplored! Beauty may be only skin deep, but a handful of beautiful skin is a tempting proposition.

EDITED BY DAVID LAURENTS

Wanderlust: Homoerotic Tales of Travel **$5.95/395-3**

A volume dedicated to the special pleasures of faraway places. Gay men have always had a special interest in travel—and not only for the scenic vistas. ***Wanderlust*** celebrates the freedom of the open road, and the allure of men who stray from the beaten path....

The Badboy Book of Erotic Poetry **$5.95/382-1**

Over fifty of gay literature's biggest talents are here represented by their hottest verse. Erotic poetry has long been the problem child of the literary world—highly creative and provocative, but somehow too frank to be "literature." Both learned and stimulating, ***The Badboy Book of Erotic Poetry*** restores eros to its rightful place of honor in contemporary gay writing.

JAMES MEDLEY

Huck and Billy **$4.95/245-0**

Young love is always the sweetest, always the most sorrowful. Young lust, on the other hand, knows no bounds—and is often the hottest of one's life! Huck and Billy explore the desires that course through their young male bodies, determined to plumb the lusty depths of passion. Sweet and hot. Very hot.

LARRY TOWNSEND

Leather Ad: S **$5.95/407-0**

The second half of Larry Townsend's acclaimed tale of lust through the personals. This time around, the story's told from a Top's perspective. A simple ad generates responses ranging from the eccentric to the exceptional, and one man finds himself in the enviable position of putting these studly applicants through their paces.....

Leather Ad: M **$5.95/380-5**

The first of leather icon Larry Townsend's two-part exploration of one stud's discovery of SM sexuality. John's curious about what goes on between the leatherclad men he's seen and fantasized about. After receiving little encouragement from friends, he takes out a personal ad—and starts a journey of self-discovery that will leave no part of his life unchanged....

Beware the God Who Smiles **$5.95/321-X**

Two lusty young Americans are transported to ancient Egypt—where they are embroiled in regional warfare and taken as slaves by marauding barbarians. The key to escape from this brutal bondage lies in their own rampant libidos, and urges as old as time itself.

The Construction Worker **$5.95/298-1**
A young, hung construction worker is sent to a building project in Central America, where he finds that man-to-man sex is the accepted norm. The young stud quickly fits right in—until he senses that beneath the constant sexual shenanigans there moves an almost supernatural force. The only thing lying between him and the truth is a string of male bodies—an obstacle he's more than happy to work at overcoming.

2069 Trilogy (This one-volume collection only **$6.95**) **244-2**
For the first time, Larry Townsend's early science-fiction trilogy appears in one massive volume! Set in a future world, the ***2069 Trilogy*** includes the tight plotting and shameless male sexual pleasure that established him as one of gay erotica's first masters. This special one-volume edition available only from Badboy.

Mind Master **$4.95/209-4**
Who better to explore the territory of erotic dominance and submission than an author who helped define the genre—and knows that ultimate mastery always transcends the physical.

The Long Leather Cord **$4.95/201-9**
Chuck's stepfather is an enigma: never lacking in money or clandestine male visitors with whom he enacts intense sexual rituals. As Chuck comes to terms with his own savage desires, he begins to unravel mystery behind his stepfather's secret life.

Man Sword **$4.95/188-8**
The *tres gai* tale of France's King Henri III. Unimaginably spoiled by his mother—the infamous Catherine de Medici—Henri is groomed from a young age to assume the throne of France. Along the way, he encounters enough sexual schemers and randy politicos to alter one's picture of history forever!

The Faustus Contract **$4.95/167-5**
Two attractive young men desperately need $1000. Will do anything. Travel OK. Danger OK. Call anytime... Two cocky young hustlers get more than they bargained for in this story of lust and its discontents.

The Gay Adventures of Captain Goose **$4.95/169-1**
The hot and tender young Jerome Gander is sentenced to serve aboard the *H.M.S. Faerigold*—a ship manned by the most hardened, unrepentant criminals. In no time, Gander becomes well-versed in the ways of men at sea, and the *Faerigold* becomes the most notorious ship of its day.

Chains **$4.95/158-6**
Picking up street punks has always been risky, but in Larry Townsend's classic ***Chains***, it sets off a string of events that must be read to be believed. One of Townsend's most remarkable works.

Kiss of Leather **$4.95/161-6**
A look at the acts and attitudes of an earlier generation of gay leathermen, ***Kiss of Leather*** is full to bursting with the gritty, raw action that has distinguished Townsend's work for years. Pain and pleasure mix in this tightly-plotted tale.

Run No More **$4.95/152-7**
The continuation of Larry Townsend's legendary ***Run, Little Leather Boy***. This volume follows the further adventures of Townsend's leatherclad narrator as he travels every sexual byway available to the S/M male.

Run, Little Leather Boy **$4.95/143-8**
The classic story of one young man's sexual awakening. A chronic underachiever, Wayne seems to be going nowhere fast. When his father puts him to work for a living, Wayne soon finds himself bored with the everyday—and increasingly drawn to the masculine intensity of a dark sexual underground....

The Scorpius Equation **$4.95/119-5**

Set in the far future, ***The Scorpius Equation*** is the story of a man caught between the demands of two galactic empires. Our randy hero must match wits—and more—with the incredible forces that rule his world.

The Sexual Adventures of Sherlock Holmes **$4.95/3097-0**

Holmes' most satisfying adventures, from the unexpurgated memoirs of the faithful Mr. Watson. "A Study in Scarlet" is transformed to expose Mrs. Hudson as a man in drag, the Diogenes Club as an S/M arena, and clues only the redoubtable—and very horny—Sherlock Holmes could piece together. A baffling tale of sex and mystery.

FLEDERMAUS

Flederfiction: Stories of Men and Torture **$5.95/355-4**

Fifteen blistering paeans to men and their suffering. Fledermaus unleashes his most thrilling tales of punishment in this special volume designed with Badboy readers in mind. No less an authority than Larry Townsend introduces this volume of Fledermaus' best work.

DONALD VINING

Cabin Fever and Other Stories **$5.95/338-4**

Eighteen blistering stories in celebration of the most intimate of male bonding. From Native Americans to Buckingham Palace sentries, suburban husbands to kickass bikers—time after time, Donald Vining's men succumb to nature, and reaffirm both love and lust in modern gay life.

Praise for Donald Vining:

"Realistic but upbeat, blunt but graceful, serious but witty...demonstrates the wisdom experience combined with insight and optimism can create."

—*Bay Area Reporter*

DEREK ADAMS

The Mark of the Wolf **$5.95/361-9**

What was happening to me? I didn't understand. I turned to look at the man who stared back at me from the mirror. The familiar outlines of my face seemed coarser, more sinister. An animal? The past comes back to haunt one well-off stud, whose unslakable thirsts lead him into the arms of many men—and the midst of a perilous mystery.

My Double Life **$5.95/314-7**

Every man leads a double life, dividing his hours between the mundanities of the day and the outrageous pursuits of the night. The creator of sexy P.I. Miles Diamond shines a little light on the wicked things men do when no one's looking.

Boy Toy **$4.95/260-4**

Poor Brendan Callan finds himself the guinea pig of a crazed geneticist. The result: Brendan becomes irresistibly alluring—a talent designed for endless pleasure, but coveted by others for the most unsavory means....

Heat Wave **$4.95/159-4**

"His body was draped in baggy clothes, but there was hardly any doubt that they covered anything less than perfection.... His slacks were cinched tight around a narrow waist, and the rise of flesh pushing against the thin fabric promised a firm, melon-shaped ass...."

Miles Diamond and the Demon of Death **$4.95/251-5**

Derek Adams' gay gumshoe returns for further adventures. Miles always find himself in the stickiest situations—with any stud whose path he crosses! His adventures with "The Demon of Death" promise another carnal carnival.

The Adventures of Miles Diamond **$4.95/118-7**

"The Case of the Missing Twin" promises to be a most rewarding case, packed as it is with randy studs. Miles sets about uncovering all as he tracks down the elusive and delectable Daniel Travis....

KELVIN BELIELE

If the Shoe Fits **$4.95/223-X**

An essential and winning volume of tales exploring a world where randy boys can't help but do what comes naturally—as often as possible! Sweaty male bodies grapple in pleasure, proving the old adage: if the shoe fits, one might as well slip right in....

VICTOR TERRY

SM/SD **$6.50/406-2**

A set of hard riding tales from Victor Terry. Set around a South Dakota town called Prairie, these tales offer compelling evidence that the real rough stuff can still be found where men roam free of the restraints of "polite" society—and take what they want despite all rules. Another tour through the masculine libido, by the author of ***WHiPs***.

WHiPs **$4.95/254-X**

Cruising for a hot man? You'd better be, because one way or another, these WHiPs—officers of the Wyoming Highway Patrol—are gonna pull you over for a little impromptu interrogation....

MAX EXANDER

Deeds of the Night: Tales of Eros and Passion **$5.95/348-1**

MAXimum porn! Exander's a writer who's seen it all—and is more than happy to describe every inch of it in pulsating detail. A whirlwind tour of the unrestrained hypermasculine libido.

Leathersex **$4.95/210-8**

Another volume of hard-hitting tales from merciless Max Exander. This time he focuses on the leatherclad lust that draws together only the most willing and talented of tops and bottoms—for an all-out orgy of limitless surrender and control....

Mansex **$4.95/160-8**

"Tex was all his name implied: tall, lanky but muscular, with reddish-blond hair and a handsome, chiseled face that was somewhat leathered. Mark was the classic leatherman: a huge, dark stud in chaps, with a big black moustache, hairy chest and enormous muscles. Exactly the kind of men Todd liked—strong, hunky, masculine, ready to take control...." Rough sex for rugged men.

TOM CAFFREY

Tales From the Men's Room **$5.95/364-3**

Another collection of keenly observed, passionate tales. From shameless cops on the beat to shy studs on stage, Caffrey explores male lust at its most elemental and arousing. And if there's a lesson to be learned, it's that the Men's Room is less a place than a state of mind—one that every man finds himself in, day after day....

Hitting Home **$4.95/222-1**

One of our newest Badboys weighs in with a scorching collection of stories. Titillating and compelling, the stories in ***Hitting Home*** make a strong case for there being only one thing on a man's mind.

TORSTEN BARRING

Prisoners of Torquemada **$5.95/252-3**

The infamously unsparing Torsten Barring weighs in with another volume sure to push you over the edge. How cruel is the "therapy" practiced at Casa Torquemada? Barring is just the writer to evoke such steamy sexual malevolence.

Shadowman **$4.95/178-0**

From spoiled Southern aristocrats to randy youths sowing wild oats at the local picture show, Barring's imagination works overtime in these vignettes of homolust—past, present and future.

Peter Thornwell **$4.95/149-7**

Follow the exploits of Peter Thornwell as he goes from misspent youth to scandalous stardom, all thanks to an insatiable libido and love for the lash. Peter and his sex-crazed sidekicks find themselves pursued by merciless men from all walks of life in this torrid take on Horatio Alger.

The Switch **$4.95/3061-X**

Sometimes a man needs a good whipping, and *The Switch* certainly makes a case! Laced with images of men "in too-tight Levi's, with the faces of angels... and the bodies of devils." Packed with hot studs and unrelenting passions.

BERT McKENZIE

Fringe Benefits **$5.95/354-6**

From the pen of a widely published short story writer comes a volume of highly immodest tales. Not afraid of getting down and dirty, McKenzie produces some of today's most visceral sextales. Learn the real benefits of working long and hard....

SONNY FORD

Reunion in Florence **$4.95/3070-9**

Captured by Turks, Adrian and Tristan will do anything to save their heads. When Tristan is threatened by a Sultan's jealousy, Adrian begins his quest for the only man alive who can replace Tristan as the object of the Sultan's lust.The two soon learn to rely on their wild sexual imaginations.

ROGER HARMAN

First Person **$4.95/179-9**

A highly personal collection. Each story takes the form of a confessional—told by men who've got plenty to confess! From the "first time ever" to firsts of different kinds, *First Person* tells truths too hot to be purely fiction.

CHRISTOPHER MORGAN

The Sportsmen **$5.95/385-6**

A collection of super-hot stories dedicated to that most popular of boys next door—the all-American athlete. Here are enough tales of carnal grand slams, sexy interceptions and highly personal bests to satisfy the hungers of the most ardent sports fan. Editor Christopher Morgan has gathered those writers who know just the type of guys that make up every red-blooded male's starting line-up....

Muscle Bound **$4.95/3028-8**

In the New York City bodybuilding scene, country boy Tommy joins forces with sexy Will Rodriguez in a battle of wits and biceps at the hottest gym in town, where the weak are bound and crushed by iron-pumping gods.

SEAN MARTIN

Scrapbook **$4.95/224-8**

Imagine a book filled with only the best, most vivid remembrances...a book brimming with every hot, sexy encounter its pages can hold... Now you need only open up *Scrapbook* to know that such a volume really exists....

CARO SOLES & STAN TAL

Bizarre Dreams **$4.95/187-X**

An anthology of stirring voices dedicated to exploring the dark side of human fantasy. *Bizarre Dreams* brings together the most talented practitioners of "dark fantasy," the most forbidden sexual realm of all.

J . A . GUERRA

Badboy Fantasies **$4.95/3049-0**

When love eludes them—lust will do! Thrill-seeking men caught up in vivid dreams and dark mysteries—these are the brief encounters you'll pant and gasp over in *Badboy Fantasies.*

Slow Burn **$4.95/3042-3**

Welcome to the Body Shoppe, where men's lives cross in the pursuit of muscle. Torsos get lean and hard, pecs widen, and stomachs ripple in these sexy stories of the power and perils of physical perfection.

DAVE KINNICK

Sorry I Asked **$4.95/3090-3**

Unexpurgated interviews with gay porn's rank and file. Dave Kinnick, longtime video reviewer for *Advocate Men,* gets personal with the men behind (and under) the "stars," and reveals the dirt and details of the porn business.

MICHAEL LOWENTHAL, ED.

The Badboy Erotic Library Volume I **$4.95/190-X**

A Secret Life, Imre, Sins of the Cities of the Plain, Teleny and *more*—the hottest sections of these perennial favorites come together for the first time.

The Badboy Erotic Library Volume II **$4.95/211-6**

This time, selections are taken from *Mike and Me* and *Muscle Bound, Men at Work, Badboy Fantasies,* and *Slowburn.*

ERIC BOYD

Mike and Me **$5.95/419-4**

Mike joined the gym squad to bulk up on muscle. Little did he know he'd be turning on every sexy muscle jock in Minnesota! Hard bodies collide in a series of workouts designed to generate a whole lot more than rips and cuts.

Mike and the Marines **$5.95/347-3**

Mike and Me was one of Badboy's earliest hits, and now readers can revel in another sexy extravaganza. This time, Mike takes on America's most elite corps of studs—running into more than a few good men!

ANONYMOUS

A Secret Life **$4.95/3017-2**

Meet Master Charles: only eighteen, and *quite* innocent, until his arrival at the Sir Percival's Royal Academy, where the daily lessons are supplemented with a crash course in pure, sweet sexual heat!

Sins of the Cities of the Plain **$5.95/322-8**

Indulge yourself in the scorching memoirs of young man-about-town Jack Saul. With his shocking dalliances with the lords and "ladies" of British high society, Jack's positively *sinful* escapades grow wilder with every chapter!

Imre **$4.95/3019-9**

What dark secrets, what fiery passions lay hidden behind strikingly beautiful Lieutenant Imre's emerald eyes? An extraordinary lost classic of fantasy, obsession, gay erotic desire, and romance in a tiny town on the eve of WWI.

Teleny **$4.95/3020-2**

Often attributed to Oscar Wilde. A young stud seeks only a succession of forbidden pleasures, but instead finds love and tragedy when he becomes embroiled in a mysterious cult devoted to fulfilling only the very darkest of fantasies.

PAT CALIFIA

The Sexpert **$4.95/3034-2**

The sophisticated gay man knows that he can turn to one authority for answers to virtually any question on the subjects of intimacy and sexual performance. Straight from the pages of *Advocate Men* comes The Sexpert, responding to real-life sexual concerns with uncanny wisdom and a razor wit.

HARD CANDY

WALTER HOLLAND

The March **$6.95/429-1**

A moving testament to the power of friendship during even the worst of times. Beginning on a hot summer night in 1980, ***The March*** revolves around a circle of young gay men, and the many others their lives touch. Over time, each character changes in unexpected ways; lives and loves come together and fall apart, as society itself is horribly altered by the onslaught of AIDS.

PATRICK MOORE

Iowa **$6.95/423-2**

"Make it new!" Gertrude Stein said, and that's what Patrick Moore has done: he's taken the classic story of the Midwest American boyhood that Hemingway, Sinclair Lewis and Sherwood Anderson made classic; and he's done it fresh and shiny and relevant to our time. ***Iowa*** is full of terrific characters etched in acid-sharp prose, soaked through with just enough ambivalence to make it thoroughly romantic. —Felice Picano

The new novel from the author of the bestselling debut *This Every Night.*

RED JORDAN AROBATEAU

Dirty Pictures **$5.95/345-7**

"More than a writer of raw, steamy, no-holds-barred sex stories—she's also a deep-thinking dyke philosopher with a style all her own..."

—Carol Queen

Another red-hot tale from lesbian sensation Red Jordan. ***Dirty Pictures*** tells the story of a lonely butch tending bar—and the femme she finally calls her own. With the same precision that made ***Lucy and Mickey*** a breakout debut, Arobateau tells a love story that's the flip-side of "lesbian chic."

Lucy and Mickey **$6.95/311-2**

"Both deeply philosophical and powerfully erotic. Most of all this novel is about Mickey, a pugnacious butch who trades her powerlessness on the streets for prowess between the sheets. *Lucy and Mickey* is...a necessary reminder to all who blissfully—some may say ignorantly—ride the wave of lesbian chic into the mainstream." —Heather Findlay, *Girlfriends*

LARS EIGHNER

Gay Cosmos **$6.95/236-1**

A thought-provoking volume from widely-acclaimed author Lars Eighner. Eighner has distinguished himself as one of America's most accomplished new voices. ***Gay Cosmos*** argues passionately for acceptance of homosexuality by society.

JAMES COLTON

Todd **$6.95/312-0**

With ***Todd***, Colton took on the complexities of American race relations, becoming one of the first writers to explore interracial love between two men. Set in 1971, Colton's novel examines the relationship of Todd and Felix, and the ways in which it is threatened by not only the era's politics, but the timeless stumbling block called The Former Lover.

The Outward Side **$6.95/304-X**

The return of a classic tale. Marc Lingard, a handsome, respected young minister, finds himself at a crossroads. The homophobic persecution of a local resident unearths Marc's long-repressed memories of a youthful love affair, and he is irrepressibly drawn to his forbidden urges.

STAN LEVENTHAL

"Generosity, evenness, fairness to the reader, sensitivity—these are qualities that most contemporary writers take for granted or overrule with stylistics. In Leventhal's writing they not only stand out, they're positively addictive." —Dennis Cooper

Barbie in Bondage **$6.95/415-1**

Widely regarded as one of the most refreshing, clear-eyed interpreters of big city gay male life, Leventhal here provides a series of explorations of love and desire between men. For the discerning reader, ***Barbie in Bondage*** is a fitting tribute to the late author's unique talents.

Skydiving on Christopher Street **$6.95/287-6**

Aside from a hateful job, a hateful apartment, a hateful world and an increasingly hateful lover, life seems, well, all right for the protagonist of Stan Leventhal's latest novel. Having already lost most of his friends to AIDS, how could things get any worse? But things soon do, and he's forced to endure much more before finding a new strength.

FELICE PICANO

The Lure **$6.95/398-8**

"Picano does for New York gay life what Arthur Hailey did for airports and hotels. He plays out the novel's secrets brilliantly, one deliberate card at a time... The subject matter, plus the authenticity of Picano's research are, combined, explosive. Felice Picano is one hell of a writer."

—Stephen King

Noel Cummings is about to change—irrevocably. After witnessing a brutal murder, Noel is recruited by the police—to assist as a lure for the killer-at-large. Undercover, Noel moves deeper and deeper into the freneticism of Manhattan's gay highlife—where he gradually becomes aware of the darker forces at work in his once-placid life. In addition to the mystery behind his mission, Noel begins to recognize undeniable changes: in his relationships with the men around him, in himself...

Men Who Loved Me **$6.95/274-4**

In 1966, at the tender-but-bored age of twenty-two, Felice Picano abandoned New York, determined to find true love in Europe. Almost immediately, he encounters Djanko—an exquisite prodigal who sweeps Felice off his feet with the endless string of extravagant parties, glamorous clubs and glittering premieres that made up Rome's *dolce vita*. When the older (slightly) and wiser (vastly) Picano returns to New York at last, he plunges into the city's thriving gay community—experiencing the frenzy and heartbreak that came to define Greenwich Village society in the 1970s. Lush and warm, ***Men Who Loved Me*** is a matchless portrait of an unforgettable decade.

"Zesty...spiked with adventure and romance....a distinguished and humorous portrait of a vanished age." ***—Publishers Weekly***

"A stunner...captures the free-wheeling spirit of an era."

—The Advocate

"Rich, engaging, engrossing... a ravishingly exotic romance."

—New York Native

Ambi*dextrous* **$6.95/275-2**

"Deftly evokes those placid Eisenhower years of bicycles, boners, and book reports. Makes us remember what it feels like to be a child..."

—The Advocate

"Compelling and engrossing... will conjure up memories of everyone's adolescence, straight or gay." ***—Out!***

The touching and funny memories of childhood—as only Felice Picano could tell them. Ambi***dextrous*** tells the story of Picano's youth in the suburbs of New York during the '50's. Beginning at age eleven, Picano's "memoir in the form of a novel" tells all: home life, school face-offs, the ingenuous sophistications of his first sexual steps. In three years' time, he's had his first gay fling—and is on his way to becoming the writer about whom the *L.A. Herald Examiner* said "[he] can run the length of experience from the lyrical to the lewd without missing a beat."

WILLIAM TALSMAN

The Gaudy Image **$6.95/263-9**

Unavailable for years, William Talsman's remarkable pre-Stonewall gay novel returns. Filled with insight into gay life of an earlier period, ***The Gaudy Image*** stands poised to take its place alongside *Better Angel*, *Quatrefoil* and *The City and the Pillar* as not only an invaluable piece of the community's literary history, but a fascinating, highly-entertaining reading experience.

"To read *The Gaudy Image* now is not simply to enjoy a great novel or an artifact of gay history, it is to see first-hand the very issues of identity and positionality with which gay men and gay culture were struggling in the decades before Stonewall. For what Talsman is dealing with...is the very question of how we conceive ourselves gay."

—from the introduction by Michael Bronski

RICHARD KASAK BOOKS

MICHAEL FORD, EDITOR

HAPPILY EVER AFTER: Erotic Fairy Tales for Men

A hefty volume of bedtime stories Mother Goose never thought to write down. Adapting some of childhood's most beloved tales for the adult gay reader, the contributors to ***Happily Ever After*** dig up the subtext of these hitherto "innocent" diversions—adding some surprises of their own along the way. Bad boys such as Bruce Benderson, Michael Lassell, Lev Raphael, Samuel R. Delany, Guy Baldwin, Joseph Bean take you down the less-traveled roads of familiar—but still enchanted—forests. **$12.95/450-X**

SHAR REDNOUR, EDITOR

VIRGIN TERRITORY

An anthology of writing by women about their first-time erotic experiences with other women. From the longings and ecstasies of awakening dykes to the sometimes awkward pleasures of sexual experimentation on the edge, each of these true stories reveals a different, radical perspective on one of the most traditional subjects around: virginity.

"[*Virgin Territory*] is all true stories, consequently the curious about and/or connoisseurs of lesbian erotic adventures get a potent shot of exactly what they want—the real thing." **—Carol A. Queen**

$12.95/457-7

HEATHER FINDLAY, EDITOR

A MOVEMENT OF EROS: 25 Years of Lesbian Erotica

One of the most scintillating overviews of lesbian erotic writing ever published. Dyke firebrand Heather Findlay has assembled a roster of stellar talents, each represented by their best, most provocative work. Tracing the course of the genre from its pre-Stonewall roots to its current renaissance, Findlay examines such diverse talents as Jewelle Gomez, Chrystos, Pat Califia and Linda Smukler, always placing them within the context of the lesbian community and politics. A singularly diverse and vibrant collection, *A Movement of Eros* examines the traditions and innovations of lesbian sexual writing, claiming a special place for the erotic in the continuing advance toward empowerment and liberation. **$12.95/421-6**

MICHAEL BRONSKI, EDITOR

FLASHPOINT: Gay Male Sexual Writing

A collection of the most compelling, provocative testaments to gay eros. Longtime cultural critic Michael Bronski *(Culture Clash: The Making of Gay and Lesbian Sensibility)* presents over twenty of the genre's best writers, exploring areas such as Enlightenment, Violence, True Life Adventures, Transformations and more. Sure to be one of the most talked about and influential volumes ever dedicated to the exploration of gay sex and sexuality. **$12.95/424-0**

MICHAEL PERKINS, EDITOR

COMING UP: The World's Best Erotic Writing

Author and critic Michael Perkins *(The Secret Record: Modern Erotic Literature, Evil Companions)* has scoured the field of erotic writing to produce this anthology sure to challenge the limits of even the most seasoned reader. Using the same sharp eye and transgressive instinct that have established him as America's leading commentator on sexually explicit fiction, Perkins here presents the cream of the current crop: a trend-setting, boundary-crashing bunch including such talents as Carol Queen, Samuel R. Delany, Maxim Jakubowski, and Lucy Taylor among many others. **$12.95/370-8**

CECILIA TAN, EDITOR

SM VISIONS: The Best of Circlet Press

Fabulous books! There's nothing else like them.

—Susie Bright, *Best American Erotica* and *Herotica 3*

A volume of the very best speculative erotica available today. Circlet Press, the first publishing house to devote itself exclusively to the erotic science fiction and fantasy genre, is now represented by the best of its very best: *SM Visions*. Compiled by Circlet founder Cecilia Tan, and including such writers as Gary Bowen, Lauren P. Burka and Mason Powell, *SM Visions* is sure to be one of the most thrilling and eye-opening rides through the erotic imagination ever published. **$10.95/339-2**

FELICE PICANO

DRYLAND'S END

Set five thousand years in the future, *Dryland's End* takes place in a fabulous techno-empire ruled by powerful women. Military rivalries, religious fanaticism and economic competition threaten to destroy the empire from within—just as a fierce rebellion also threatens human existence throughout the galaxy. The long-awaited science fiction debut of Felice Picano—the widely-praised author of *Like People in History*, and the classics *Men Who Loved Me*, *Ambidextrous* and *The Lure*. **$12.95/279-5**

MICHAEL ROWE

WRITING BELOW THE BELT: Conversations with Erotic Authors

A revealing, complex look at loneliness, curiosity, and pleasure.

—Village Voice

Award-winning journalist Michael Rowe interviewed the best and brightest erotic writers—both those well-known for their work in the field and those just starting out—and presents the collected wisdom in *Writing Below the Belt*. Rowe speaks frankly with cult favorites such as Pat Califia, crossover success stories like John Preston, and up-and-comers Michael Lowenthal and Will Leber. The personal, the political and the just plain prurient collide and complement one another in fascinating ways in this candid, compelling volume. **$19.95/363-5**

RANDY TUROFF, EDITOR

LESBIAN WORDS: State of the Art

This is a terrific book that should be on every thinking lesbian's bookshelf.

—Nisa Donnelly

Lesbian Words collects one of the widest assortments of lesbian nonfiction writing in one revealing volume. Dorothy Allison, Jewelle Gomez, Judy Grahn, Eileen Myles, Robin Podolsky and many others are represented by some of their best work, looking at not only the current fashionability the media has brought to the lesbian "image," but important considerations of the lesbian past via historical inquiry and personal recollections. A fascinating, provocative volume, ***Lesbian Words*** is a virtual primer to contemporary trends in lesbian thought. **$10.95/340-6**

EURYDICE

f/32

f/32 has been called "the most controversial and dangerous novel ever written by a woman." With the story of Ela (whose name is a pseudonym for orgasm), Eurydice won the National Fiction competition sponsored by Fiction Collective Two and Illinois State University. A funny, disturbing quest for unity, ***f/32*** prompted Frederic Tuten to proclaim that "almost any page... redeems us from the anemic writing and banalities we have endured in the past decade of bloodless fiction." **$10.95/350-3**

LARRY TOWNSEND

ASK LARRY

Twelve years of Masterful advice from Larry Townsend, the leatherman's long-time confidant and adviser. Starting just before the onslaught of AIDS, Townsend wrote the "Leather Notebook" column for *Drummer* magazine. Now, with ***Ask Larry***, readers can avail themselves of Townsend's collected wisdom and contemporary commentary—a careful consideration of the way life has changed in the AIDS era, and the specific ways in which the disease has altered perceptions of once-simple problems. **$12.95/289-2**

WILLIAM CARNEY

THE REAL THING

"Carney gives us a good look at the mores and lifestyle of the first generation of gay leathermen. A chilling mystery/romance novel as well." —Pat Califia

With a new Introduction by Michael Bronski. William Carney's ***The Real Thing*** has long served as a touchstone in any consideration of gay "edge fiction." First published in 1968, this uncompromising story of New York leathermen received instant acclaim—and in the years since, has become a rare and highly-prized volume to those lucky enough to acquire a copy. Finally, ***The Real Thing*** returns from exile.... **$10.95/280-9**

LOOKING FOR MR. PRESTON

Edited by Laura Antoniou, ***Looking for Mr. Preston*** includes work by Lars Eighner, Michael Bronski, Felice Picano, Joan Nestle, Larry Townsend, and others who contributed interviews, essays and personal reminiscences of John Preston—a man whose career spanned the industry from the early pages of the *Advocate* to national bestseller lists. Preston was the author of over twenty books, including *Franny, the Queen of Provincetown*, and *Mr. Benson*. He also edited the noted *Flesh and the Word* erotic anthologies, *Hometowns*, and *A Member of the Family*. More importantly, Preston became an inspiration, friend and occasionally a mentor to many of today's gay and lesbian authors and editors. Ten percent of the proceeds from sale of the book will go to the AIDS Project of Southern Maine, for whom Preston had served as President of the Board. **$23.95/288-4**

MICHAEL LASSELL

THE HARD WAY

Lassell is a master of the necessary word. In an age of tepid and whining verse, his bawdy and bittersweet songs are like a plunge in cold champagne.

—Paul Monette

Lassell is regarded as one of the most distinctive and accomplished talents of his generation. As much a chronicle of post-Stonewall gay life as a compendium of a remarkable writer's work, ***The Hard Way*** is sure to appeal to anyone interested in the state of contemporary writing. **$12.95/231-0**

CARO SOLES, EDITOR

MELTDOWN!

An Anthology of Erotic Science Fiction and Dark Fantasy for Gay Men

Caro Soles has put together one of the most explosive collections of gay erotic writing ever published. A hot-seller, this volume rides the newest wave of gay erotic publishing—where no limits are recognized.... **$12.95/203-5**

JOHN PRESTON

MY LIFE AS \ PORNOGRAPHER

...essential and enlightening...Hi: sex-positive stand on safer-sex education as the only truly effective AIDS-prevention strategy will certainly not win him any conservative converts, but AIDS activists will be shouting their assent....*[My Life as a Pornographer] *is a bridge from the sexually liberated 1970s to the more cautious 1990s, and Preston has walked much of that way as a standard-bearer to the cause for equal rights....

—Library Journal

$12.95/135-7

HUSTLING:

A Gentleman's Guide to the Fine Art of Homosexual Prostitution

...valuable insights to many aspects of the world of gay male prostitution. Throughout the book, Preston uses materials gathered from interviews and letters from former and active hustlers, as well as insights gleaned from his own experience as a hustler.... Preston does fulfill his desire to entertain as well as educate.

—Lambda Book Report

...fun and highly literary. what more could you expect from such an accomplished activist, author and editor?

—Drummer

$12.95/137-3

RUSS KICK

OUTPOSTS: A Catalog of Rare and Disturbing Alternative Information

Russ Kick has tracked down the real McCoy and compiled over five hundred reviews of work penned by political extremists, conspiracy theorists, hallucinogenic pathfinders, sexual explorers, religious iconoclasts and social malcontents. Better yet, each review is followed by ordering information for the many readers sure to want these publications for themselves. No one with a "need to know" can afford to miss this ultra-alternative resource. **$18.95/0202-8**

SAMUEL R. DELANY

THE MAD MAN

Reads like a pornographic reflection of Peter Ackroyd's Chatterton *or A.S. Byatt's* Possession.... *The pornographic element... becomes more than simple shock or titillation, though, as Delany develops an insightful dichotomy between [his protagonist]'s two worlds: the one of cerebral philosophy and dry academia, the other of heedless, 'impersonal' obsessive sexual extremism. When these worlds finally collide...the novel achieves a surprisingly satisfying resolution....*

—Publishers Weekly

$23.95/193-4/hardcover

THE MOTION OF LIGHT IN WATER

The first unexpurgated American edition of award-winning author Samuel R. Delany's autobiography covers the early years of one of science fiction's most important voices. Delany paints a compelling picture of New York's East Village in the early '60s—when Bob Dylan took second billing to a certain guitar-toting science fiction writer, W. H. Auden stopped by for dinner, and a walk on the Brooklyn Bridge changed the course of a literary genre. **$12.95/133-0**

ROBERT PATRICK

TEMPLE SLAVE

You must read this book. —Quentin Crisp

The birth of Off-off Broadway and the modern gay movement, via the wit of legendary playwright Robert Patrick. **$12.95/191-8**

PAT CALIFIA

SENSUOUS MAGIC

Clear, succinct and engaging even for the reader for whom S/M isn't the sexual behavior of choice.... Califia is the Dr. Ruth of the alternative sexuality set....

—Lambda Book Report

Renowned erotic pioneer Pat Califia provides this honest, unpretentious peek behind the mask of dominant/submissive sexuality—an adventurous adult world of pleasure too often obscured by ignorance and fear. Califia demystifies "the scene" for the novice, explaining the terminology and technique behind many misunderstood sexual practices. The adventurous (or just plain curious) lover won't want to miss this ultimate "how to" volume. **$12.95/458-5**

LARS EIGHNER

ELEMENTS OF AROUSAL

Lars Eighner develops a guideline for success with one of publishing's best kept secrets: the novice-friendly field of gay erotica. Eighner paints a picture of a diverse array of outlets for a writer's work. Because, writing is what *Elements of Arousal* is about: a writer's craft, which brought Eighner fame with not only the steamy *Bayou Boy*, but the illuminating *Travels with Lizbeth*. **$12.95/230-2**